BELLE AND THE BEAST

FAIRELLE BOOK SIX

REBEKAH R. GANIERE

FALLEN ANGEL PRESS

ISBN: 978-1-63300-043-8
ISBN: 978-1-63300-045-2

Cover art by Rebekah R. Ganiere
www.vwzdesigns.com

DEDICATION

For all the strong women in my life that teach me to be brave.

NEWSLETTER

To claim your Two **FREE** Books and find out more about
Rebekah R. Ganiere and her other Upcoming Releases
You can Go Here:
www.RebekahGaniere.com/Newsletter

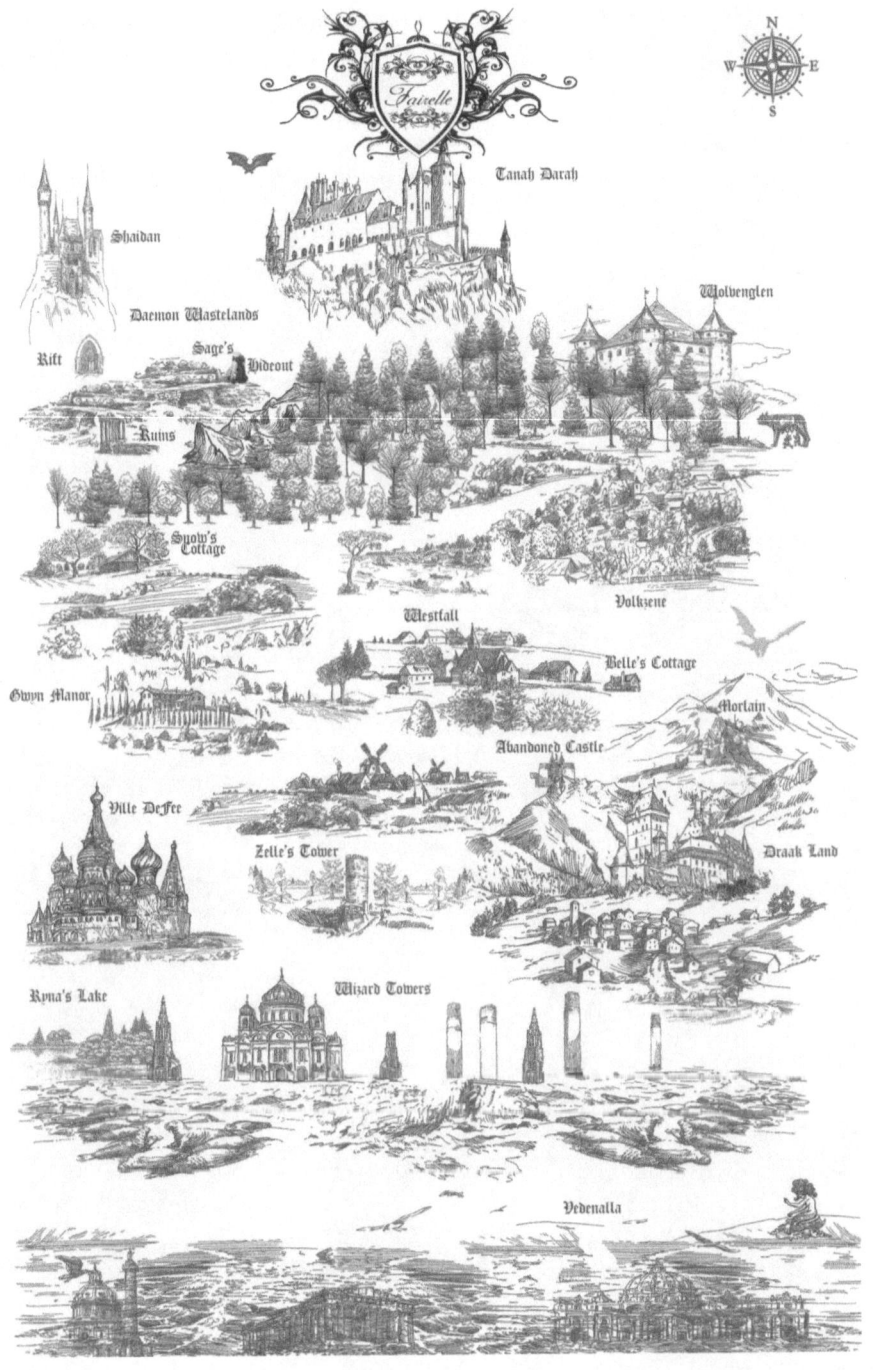

Fairelle

Tanah Darah

Shaidan

Daemon Wastelands

Wolvenglen

Rift

Sage's Hideout

Ruins

Snow's Cottage

Volkzene

Westfall

Belle's Cottage

Gwyn Manor

Mortain

Abandoned Castle

Ville DeFee

Draak Land

Zelle's Tower

Ryna's Lake

Wizard Towers

Vedenalla

PROLOGUE

PEREUM, FAIRELLE YEAR 200

In the year 200, in the city of Pereum, the heart of Fairelle, King Isodor lay on his deathbed. With all of Fairelle united under his banner, his four sons vied for the crown. One by one the brothers called forth a djinn named Xereus from Shaidan, the daemon realm, to grant a single wish. But Xereus tricked the brothers, twisting their wishes.

The eldest wished to forever be bloodthirsty in battle, and was thus transformed into a Vampire. The second wished for the unending loyalty of his men, and was turned into a Werewolf. The third asked for the ability to manipulate the elements of Fairelle; he became physically weak but mighty in magick, a Fae. And the last asked to rule the sea. A Nereid.

When the king died, each brother took a piece of Fairelle for himself and waged war for control of the rest. Xereus, having been called forth so many times, tore a rift between his daemonic plane and Fairelle, allowing thousands of daemons to pour into Pereum.

Years upon years of bloody warring went by with all races fighting for control and eventually the daemons gained dominion of the heart of Fairelle. Realizing that all lands would soon fall into the daemons' control, the High Elders of the Fae and the Mages from the south, combined their magicks to seal the rift. The daemons were banished back to their own plane, but Pereum was wiped off the map in the process, leaving only charred waste behind forever known as The Daemon Wastelands.

Upon the day of the rift closing, a Mage soothsayer prophesied of the healing of Fairelle. Over the next thousand years the races continued to war against each other, waiting for the day when the ancient prophesies would begin.

Eight prophesies, a thousand years old, to unite the lands and heal Fairelle. The fifth is ready to be restored. The Dragons have been waiting to return.

CHAPTER ONE

SOUTHERN WESTFALL FOREST, FAIRELLE - NEW YEAR, 1213 A.D. (AFTER DAEMONS)

B elle's limbs shook, but she forced her face to remain impassive so as not to upset Chloe.

"Mama, my head hurts," her little girl moaned.

Belle grabbed a cloth and dipped it in a bowl of warm water before crossing to where Chloe sat at the kitchen table.

Chloe rubbed her forehead with her chubby little pink hand. The bracelet Klaus had bought her years prior hung from her wrist like a cheap buy-off. It took everything inside Belle not to rip it from her daughter's skin and fling it into the fire.

"Hey, Sugarpie." Belle shoved the corners of her mouth into a smile, cracking the split in her lip and making it ooze again. She ignored her own, and blotted the blood from Chloe's nose. "I know it hurts. Just let me get your nose cleaned up and then I'll get you some medicine."

The desire to kill Klaus had never run so deep. Over the

past year he'd become more abusive. Belle had been fighting to save up enough money to take Chloe and run, but it didn't matter anymore. She was ready to stomp down her pride and beg for help if needed.

Chloe raised her hand and cupped Belle's cheek. "Your eye is purple."

Belle swallowed down a sob. She'd tried to shield Chloe from Klaus' temper, but ever since he'd learned of Chloe's...*ability*, it had been harder to protect her from just about any facet of her father's personality.

Belle finished wiping the blood from Chloe's nose and then stripped her daughter's shirt off. "Let's get you into your sleeping gown and stockings."

Belle crossed to Chloe's small bedroom and pulled her nightclothes from the little trunk at the end of her wooden bed.

Klaus' use of Chloe's ability to enhance his criminal behavior was a new low, even for him.

She grabbed a bottle of extract from her medicine shelf and headed back to find Chloe staring into the fire.

"Here Sugarpie, let's get you into your night clothes."

Chloe continued to look into the fire; her eyes blank, bright blue and glassy. "Going on a trip into the woods. Somewhere new."

"What?" Belle slid Chloe's gown over her head. "No sweetie. We're going to go stay with Uncle Jamen and Auntie Scarlet, Uncle Flint and Auntie Zelle for a while."

Chloe shook her head. "We're going to make a new friend. You'll like him. You'll like him a lot. He's going to like you, too."

A chill ran over Belle's shoulders as she stared at her daughter for a moment, then opened the vial of opia. "Sip this."

Chloe drank the medicine without a hitch, her eyes still on the dying fire. Since Klaus had been using Chloe's ability, her headaches had become more frequent. Belle needed to be careful with the opia. Using it too frequently would end badly; but couldn't stand seeing her little girl in pain.

Chloe yawned. Belle took off her daughter's breeches and pulled up her stockings. Then, Belle picked up her little girl and carried her to bed. She wrapped the already sleeping Chloe in a thick blanket and kissed her on the head.

Panic threatened to overtake her as Belle raced to her own room and closed the door before crumbling to the floor.

How many years had she tried to make it work? The lies, the infidelities, the robberies. She'd put up with it because her father had been the same type of man. But in the past year since Klaus' friend Craigen had died, things had gotten worse. She didn't know what had happened, he wouldn't say, but he'd become more and more paranoid. He'd moved them to a cabin far outside of Westfall and no longer allowed her to go into town. She'd tried to focus on a way to get out for months. But making gadgets and clocks and small things that moved and then hiding them from him so he couldn't see, had gotten harder and harder as the months had passed. When he'd brought home the two extra horses the week before she knew her time was close at hand.

But she couldn't wait any longer. Her black eye and split

lip were testament to that. Not to mention Chloe… Belle either left now, or she'd die in that cabin.

Belle sucked in a ragged breath and swiped at her tears, making her bruises ache. No matter how little she had in life, she still had her dignity and there was no way in hell she'd let Chloe grow up thinking it was all right for a man to shove her around.

Belle pushed to her feet, her mind made up. She needed to pack and get out before Klaus returned. She didn't have much time.

Belle lifted the groggy Chloe onto their horse, then pulled herself into the saddle. She shoved her blunderbuss into a strap on her bags and positioned her satchel of tools behind her. She didn't have time to pack the gadgets she'd wanted to sell in Westfall, but it didn't matter anymore. All that mattered was getting herself and Chloe to safety.

She laid Chloe's cheek against her chest, then wrapped the leather straps she'd fashioned around Chloe's back and buckled them to her belt. Chloe snuggled closer before Belle covered them both with her cloak.

"Are we going to the forest now?" Chloe slurred.

Belle kissed her daughter's golden curls. "No Sweetums, we're going to Uncle Jamen's, remember?"

Belle nudged the horse, and they trotted away from the small cabin, out of the woods. She fought the urge to turn back; to look, one last time, at the place she'd called home for nigh on a year and praise the gods that she would never have to look at it again, but she didn't. Instead, she kicked her horse again and headed for the road leading to Westfall.

THE MOON SHONE DOWN ON THE BARREN ROAD. IT WAS A good twenty miles to Gwyn Manor, yet the longer she rode on the open thoroughfare, the worse the pit in her stomach grew.

She glanced left and right but found nothing more than fields and trees for company. The night breeze pinched her cheeks and made her eyes water. The clunking sound of her belongings shifted with each quick step the horse took. A half hour passed, Chloe's breathing evened out, and a light snore resonated against Belle's breast.

Five years old. Still a babe, yet Chloe had seen, heard, and endured things no child should have. Hunger and cold. Fighting and drunkenness. All of them at Klaus' hand. None of them worse than using their daughter.

Chloe had been special from the moment she came into the world. She'd made not a peep when born. She'd simply looked up into Belle's face with those wide, blue eyes and stared. By the time Chloe had reached the age of one, she'd begun exhibiting strange behavior. She'd run to Belle's leg and hide her face moments before someone knocked on the door. One blustery night, she'd screamed out mere seconds before a tree limb came crashing through the window, landing where Belle had been sleeping.

And once she'd learned to talk, she said odd things. She knew things, things she should not know.

Belle had tried to hide the oddities from Klaus, but he'd

figured it out. And that's when the real nightmare had started.

He'd come home once again penniless and with a new scheme. Pulling Chloe into his lap by the fire, he'd told her a story. Within minutes, the story had turned to questions. And the questions had turned to demands. This time, Chloe's eyes rolled back into her head, and her nose began bleeding. That's when Belle had attacked.

Pulling Chloe from him, she and Klaus had fought. He'd caught her in the eye, but she'd brandished a knife and told him to leave. She'd thought, for a minute, that she might have to stab him. But finally, he'd grabbed his coat and shoved off.

She'd put up with the torment and terror herself. But she'd be damned if she'd let him ruin their daughter.

Hoofbeats pulled Belle from her memories. She reigned in her mount and listened. Several horses closed in at a fast clip. She glanced around, but there was nowhere to hide.

Her heartbeat kicked up and she urged her horse down the roadside embankment. It wouldn't hide them, but at least they'd be out of the way.

She waited as the horses drew closer. One horse. Two horses. Three. She pulled the hood of her cloak up and dropped her face from sight. She trotted forward and prayed the horsemen wouldn't notice her as they passed. Her hand rested on her blunderbuss.

Seconds clicked by, and her heart thumped louder with each pounding step as the hoofbeats drew closer. She could just make out their outlines growing larger. She kept moving forward, pulling Chloe in tighter against her.

Closer... Closer... They moved at a brisk pace, as if being chased. Less than twenty yards away now, they had to have seen her; but their horses didn't slow. She kept her head down and her fingers tight on the wooden hilt of her blunderbuss.

Keep moving. Just keep going.

They were less than ten yards... Her fingers twitched. *Five.* Her legs pressed into her horse's ribs, ready to spur him forward. *Two.* Her entire body tensed.

They passed by.

Relief washed over her. *Thank the gods.*

She waited a moment before looking over her shoulder. One of the men slowed and turned back.

"Belle!"

She kicked her horse. *Klaus.*

DAX STIRRED HIS GLUEY OATS, AND THEN SHOVELED SOME into his mouth without tasting a bite.

It'd been close to six months since Cinder had told him to stay in the abandoned castle and find his past. But he had yet to figure out what she meant for him to do there. Every waking moment had been spent tearing through the rooms. Looking through chests and drawers and cabinets. Reading books and parchments and maps — and still he was no closer to finding out who he was than he had been with the werewolves, the vampires, or even his time with Flint.

Evidence suggested that the castle had been deserted for months, maybe more than a year. The long-term food supply was plentiful, but a thick layer of dust covered everything. Much the same as when he'd gone with Sage to his hideout in the Wastelands. He feared that any answers he searched for had been taken with Morgana, when she'd fled.

Morgana.

Every day new memories built on the last, and he found, with each one he acquired of the place, the less he wished to know.

Morgana had kidnapped him. She had tortured him, and humiliated him. Everything short of raping him. It was inconceivable to him that she was Zelle's mother. Zelle was everything she wasn't; kind, loving, and the perfect match for Flint. But Morgana… All those horrible moments tied in her bed, the whippings and more, now plagued him. What he still could not remember though was who he'd been before that.

Dax dropped his spoon into the silver bowl and hung his head, clearing the panic that swept over him and dug its talons into his ribcage. He pushed his chair from the cold stone table and walked across the kitchen, rinsing his bowl in the washbasin and set it to dry.

Out the open window, the moon hung above the trees in the clear sky. He took a deep breath. Being in the woods had left him lonely and even more desperate to find out who he was. But somehow, it also felt familiar.

Alabrax swooped down and peered in the window. It was a good thing they'd left Ville DeFee when they had, in the past months he'd tripled in size. There was no way Cinder would have been able to hide and feed Alabrax much longer. But out in the woods, Alabrax fended mostly for himself.

The dragon squawked, and Dax nodded. "I'm coming."

His nightly walks through the woods with the dragon did them both good. It offered Alabrax companionship and gave Dax an hour or so to clear a wasted day's search from his head.

He made for the back door of the kitchen. Though the castle appeared to be a ruin on the outside, and dust covered most everything inside, the castle itself was in good shape. The ruination was a façade meant to keep people out. The furniture was rich and all manner of finery adorned the walls as well as the shelves and tables. If a thief managed to get beyond the traps and spells, they'd become rich beyond imagining. But of the forty-seven traps he'd found outside, it was unlikely anyone without an intimate knowledge of the place would get within twenty feet of any door.

He walked outside and greeted Alabrax with a scratch to the chin. Alabrax purred like a kitten. Then, his head popped up and his ears flattened to his skull. His gaze whipped toward the front of the castle and he hissed.

Dax's gut clenched. Someone drew near.

Alabrax grumbled and Dax raced around the side of the castle, sidestepping the spell trap he'd fallen into the week before. Alabrax flew to an upper tier of one of the turrets, staring into the woods.

"What is it?" he called.

Alabrax hissed again, and Dax sniffed the air. The breeze swept several scents his way. Men, three of them, and two females. He hesitated. He could go back inside and wait them out, see if they made it to the castle, or if they headed a different direction. No one had come this close in a month.

A scream rang out and a chill raced up his arms. His inner bear growled. *Dammit.* Hiding wasn't in either of their natures.

He whistled for Alabrax and tore into the woods. His night vision allowed him to see clear as noonday. Following the scents of the newcomers, he prowled closer to the group. He stopped and listened, as another cry rang out. Smaller. Weaker. *A child.*

"Alabrax. Find them," Dax commanded.

The dragon roared and charged ahead.

"Stop! Let mommy go," yelled a small voice.

"Grab Chloe," a familiar voice ordered.

Dax sniffed again and caught a scent he'd never forget—*Klaus.*

"Don't you touch her you son of a—" A blast sounded and a zip of pain ripped through Dax's shoulder. Dax roared as fire burned through his chest and down his arm.

He fell against the nearest tree and grabbed his arm. A small hole marred his shirt and his shoulder. Blood oozed from the wound. Just like what had happened to Sage.

Rage rippled through Dax, and he fought off his bear's desire to shift.

No. This time, Klaus was all his.

Dax let the pain spur him on as he lumbered forward, arriving as three men accosted a woman and child. One of them grabbed for the little girl, and she screamed again.

The woman punched the man in the face, doubling him over. "Run, Chloe!"

The little girl turned and raced straight at Dax. She brushed against him and grabbed onto his pant leg. Startled, Dax looked down at her.

"Don't let her get away," Klaus yelled.

A thin, unshaven man ran in their direction and Dax picked up the girl with his good arm and spun out of the way, holding her close.

"Come here, Chloe," the man called as he passed. "I don't want to hurt you. I just want to bring you to daddy."

"You bitch. You think you can take my daughter and leave me?" Klaus demanded. "You're nothing, Belle. Nothing." The sound of skin smacking skin split the air.

He waited until Chloe's assailant got further away, calling her name, and then he whistled. Alabrax swooped down and followed the man. A moment later the man screamed, and then went silent.

"Help Mama," the little girl whispered. "Please."

Dax looked down at the angelic, tear-stained face. He had to do something.

He set the little girl down and crouched until they were eye to eye. "Stay here."

The little girl nodded.

"Don't move until I come for you."

She nodded again. "Thank you, Dax."

Dax took a deep breath and held his injured arm close to his stomach. He raced to where the two men had the woman pinned down and he rushed them. Tackling the first man to the ground he roared and smashed him in the face. Startled, Klaus let go of the woman and backed up.

She wasted no time. Hopping to her feet, she kicked him in the groin. He fell to his knees and she closed in behind him, whipped a knife from her boot and held it to his throat.

"Don't you ever come near me or Chloe again or so help me, Klaus, I'll kill you."

"Then kill me you stupid whore, because I'll never let you leave with her."

The woman pressed her knife deeper into Klaus' throat, and Dax punched the guy on the ground one more time before getting to his feet. His vision blurred slightly, and his head grew light. He blinked several times, trying to keep upright.

"Hang on," he said.

The woman's wild eyes scanned the area and lit on him. "Stay away from me."

His bear roared to be let out. But as much as Dax wanted to see Klaus dead, he couldn't let this woman kill the ruffian. Killing him, in the vicinity of her child, would break her in ways she couldn't comprehend.

"You don't want to kill him," Dax said. "Trust me. Killing isn't as easy as you think."

"You don't know what this piece of *shite* has done," she said.

"On the contrary," said Dax. "I know more than you think."

Klaus looked Dax up and down. "Who the hell are you?"

"Shut up!" She jammed the knife deeper into this throat.

"Your daughter is safe," said Dax. "I won't let them take her. Just, put the knife down, and let him go. Then I'll get you both to safety."

The woman shifted from foot to foot, her eyes wide with fear and anger. The pain in his shoulder intensified, and his chest burned like dragon fire — it took all of Dax's strength to keep upright.

If she made a move, he doubted he'd be able to stop her, and honestly, she was right about Klaus. He'd have ripped Klaus' throat out himself, for what he'd done to Zelle and Flint, if he had the strength right now.

Minutes passed, and then she bent to Klaus' ear. "I should kill you for what you've done to both of us and leave you to rot in this forest. But I won't. For, as much as I hate you, I could never do that to Chloe." She withdrew her blade from his neck, and in a quick movement, sliced open his right cheek from nose to ear.

Klaus swore and grabbed his face.

"If you ever come near us again, I will kill you. Chloe or no Chloe." She let go of Klaus's head and pushed him to the ground.

Klaus struggled to his feet and looked between them, blood seeping through his fingers.

"This isn't the end, Belle. Chloe's my daughter. You cannot keep her from me."

Dax strode to Belle's side and whistled, Alabrax roared and headed their direction. "You come back and see us any time," he said.

Alabrax landed on the branch above Dax and a stream of icy fire burst overhead as the dragon hissed.

Klaus slipped and fell to the ground in panic. Then he jumped to his feet and kicked his friend.

"Fagan, get up." Klaus pointed at Dax. "I remember you now, bear," he spat. "I'll be back. And next time, I'll have an army with me."

Dax nodded. "You get right on that."

Fagan got to his feet, and together the men hobbled out of sight. Dax waited, in case there was any chance they might turn around and follow him to the castle.

A breeze made the leaves rustle in the wind and the scent of juniper blend whipped around him. The seconds ticked by and the men's footsteps died away.

"I think they're gone," he said.

Belle turned to him, her eyes wide. "Chloe? Where's my daughter."

Dax pointed to the trees and Belle tore into them.

"Chloe?" she called.

The little girl didn't emerge.

"Chloe," she called more frantically.

Dax trudged over to where he'd hidden Chloe. His labored breathing came out gurgled and heavy as he leaned against the tree Chloe crouched by.

"She's here."

Belle pushed past him and grabbed the little girl, stifling a sob.

"Why didn't you answer me?" she demanded.

Chloe looked up at Dax. "He told me not to come out until he came back."

Belle pulled the little girl in close and cried into her hair.

"I told you we'd meet a friend in the woods," Chloe whispered.

Belle laughed and brushed the tears from her eyes. "Yes, you did." She looked up at Dax.

The trees spun in and out of view. He needed to lie down.

"I have a place," he said. "You'll be safe there."

Belle stared at him with a wary expression. "I thank you for your help, but I need to find my horse and my things."

Chloe pointed to Dax's shoulder. "Mama you hit him."

Belle stood and touched his wound, making him grit his teeth.

"We should get that tended to first," she said.

He nodded. "It'll heal. I just need to rest." He had to get moving before he fell on his face.

Alabrax warbled and nudged Dax with his nose.

"I'm all right boy… We just need… to get home."

"My things," Belle called.

Alabrax dropped to the ground and Dax leaned heavily on the dragon's leathery shoulder. They started for the castle, going at a slower pace than Dax liked.

"We'll get them tomorrow."

His chest felt like a boulder lay on it. Dax coughed, and blood splattered the ground. He ripped his tunic open and surveyed the small pellets marring his skin.

"Well that's not good," he mused.

BELLE CARRIED CHLOE, HOLDING HER CLOSE AND THANKING the gods they'd made it out of Klaus' grasp for the moment. She tried to stave off the shakes from their encounter. She needed to be strong for Chloe. And for herself.

She meant what she'd said. She'd kill Klaus if he came near them again. And he'd meant what he said when he told her he'd kill her for taking Chloe. Belle knew him well enough to know when he meant it.

The night air ruffled Chloe's soft curls. Belle inhaled and hung on to her daughter tighter. Her eyes stayed planted on the broad shoulders of the man who'd helped them. At the moment, he seemed friendly enough, but Belle wasn't taking any chances. She knew who a man appeared to be, and who he really was, could be very different.

Chloe had told her they'd meet a friend in the woods, but that didn't mean this was the man.

The man stumbled and his dragon whined.

"He needs help, Mama," said Chloe.

She was probably right. And it was Belle's fault he'd been shot. She'd been aiming for Fagan, but Klaus had grabbed the gun at the last second and the pellets had gone wild. But... She swallowed hard. He had a dragon. A real dragon he leaned on for support. The animal seemed tame, but they weren't known for their gentle temperaments. What they *were* known for, was being extremely territorial. Then again it had obeyed her white knight with a single command.

She had to take her chances, she decided, or they may not even make it to wherever he was taking them and then they would all freeze to death in the woods.

Belle set Chloe on the ground and strode to the large man. She hefted his arm over her shoulders and took some of his weight. Alabrax tilted his head her direction, but didn't move from his post.

He grunted, his glassy, but kind, hazel eyes stared at her from under thick lush lashes and a heavyset brow.

"It's not much further." His breathing sounded like it took three times as much energy as it should.

"Good," she replied. "Because I don't think you're going to make it more than another ten minutes before you pass out."

He chuckled. "I'm tougher than I look."

They stepped forward, with the dragon on one side, and her on the other.

"I'm sure you're tough as a centaur. Just not at this moment." She crunched over branches and leaves being sure to plant her feet, so they didn't slip.

"You'd... be surprised," he wheezed.

She gritted her teeth as the minutes passed excruciatingly slow with his weight bearing down on her. Her back ached from the strain, right down to her hips. When they finally reached a small clearing surrounding a castle, she stopped and took a deep breath. Even in the dark she could make out the crumbling and dilapidated nature of the place.

Her gaze traversed the gnarled vines that seemed to be holding the place together.

"Are you sure it's secure?" she asked.

Dax nodded.

She led him toward the front door, but he pulled to a halt.

"Not that way… If you hit the portal, I'll have to go to the basement to let you out… and I don't have the energy to walk all the way down there tonight."

He steered her to the side of the structure.

Portal? What kind of castle was it?

"We won't all fit around the traps." He straightened from the dragon and scratched its head. "Go."

Belle backed up as the dragon nudged against Dax, then eyed her.

"I'll be fine. Go," Dax said.

Belle grabbed Chloe as the dragon grumbled, then lifted to the sky.

Dax turned to her. "Step where I step."

He stepped deliberate and slow. Belle followed close behind.

Keeping Chloe safe was paramount. In the morning she would find her horse, her gun, her bags, and head to the Gwyns. When she told them what Klaus had been doing, they'd help. Snow and her brothers had made it clear that she and Chloe were family no matter what.

They rounded the castle to a back door and entered a large kitchen. Her entire hut could have fit inside the one room. Dax stumbled to a large, ornate stone slab table and fell atop it.

Belle stared at the man before her. Almost as wide as the table itself, he took up more than his share. She'd seen large men before. Hell, Flint Gwyn was huge, but this man… his very presence felt bigger than the kitchen. A bead of sweat trickled from his sandy blond hairline, down his chiseled scruffy cheek. His clothes were clean and well made. He came from money. Or at least, he stole from people with money.

Damn. He'd helped her. At the bare minimum she could clean the wound she'd caused.

She set Chloe on the floor. "Let's get some water and a rag."

Chloe nodded and ran to the washbasin.

Belle stripped off her gloves and strode to the table. She looked over his handsome face, then parted his ripped and blood-soaked tunic. A smattering of blond hair covered his chest, and her fingers twitched to touch it.

It'd been close to a year since she'd let Klaus touch her, but that didn't mean she needed to drool all over a white knight whose name she didn't even know.

"Here, Mama." Chloe held out a bowl with a rag in it.

Belle forced a smile on her face. "Thank you, sweetie."

"Are we going to help Dax now?" Chloe climbed up on a chair and slipped her tiny hand into Dax's large one.

The sight made Belle's gut clench. "How do you know his name?"

Belle moved around the table to get closer to the wound. She plunged the rag into the water and dripped it over the holes, which seemed to already be healing over the shots.

"He's special," Chloe replied.

Belle dabbed at the wounds and cleaned them as best she could. She needed to get the projectiles out. She blew out a breath. This wasn't going to be fun for either of them. She grabbed the knife from her boot and cleaned it in the water before placing the tip against one of the small holes.

Dax grabbed her wrist so fast she hadn't even seen him

move. Her mind screamed at her to defend herself, and her heart thundered.

His hazel eyes searched her face and then his grip softened, and he rubbed her wrist with the pad of his large thumb.

"Thank you for helping me."

She nodded and a piece of the wall she'd built around herself stripped away. She gave him a weak smile. "It's the least I could do. All things considered, it's I who owe you a debt of gratitude."

"Still. I thank you."

She tucked his hand back onto his chest. "This isn't going to feel good. Do you need ale?"

He shook his head and coughed, spitting out blood.

Shite. It was worse than she thought.

Dax's eyelids drooped. She dipped the rag into the water basin and wiped the damp curls from his forehead.

Chloe beamed up at Belle. "We're going to have fun here."

Belle pulled away. Oh no, they were not getting attached to this man. "We're only staying the night."

Chloe giggled. "No, we aren't."

A chill ran up Belle's spine. "I need you to try to do me a favor, all right sweetie? I need you to stop telling me what is going to happen."

"Because it upsets you." Chloe rubbed Dax's hand.

Yes. "No... because it upsets other people. And because it's dangerous," she whispered unsure of what Dax might hear.

Belle's throat dried and she swallowed before placing the

blade over the first hole again, which appeared impossibly smaller already.

"Others won't understand that you're just a little girl, and they might hurt you to get what they want."

Chloe nodded. "Like Daddy."

Belle couldn't respond. She dug into the hole and a small projectile popped out. She grabbed it and dropped it into the water basin. She flicked her eyes at Dax, but he hadn't so much as flinched.

"I'll not tell, Mama. But it's all right. Dax wouldn't hurt us."

Belle looked down at the unconscious, handsome man. She ached to believe Chloe. But she wouldn't take chances with her daughter's safety.

She dipped the tip into the next tiny hole and retrieved the small piece of metal.

Never again would she allow a man to hurt her the way Klaus had. She refused to allow a man to rule her life— or her heart— ever again.

CHAPTER TWO

WESTERN FAIRELLE FOREST, FAIRELLE - EARLY WINTER, 1213 A.D. (AFTER DAEMONS)

Dax groaned awake, his back aching from the hard table. He grabbed his chest as he sat up, pulling away a barely wet rag to reveal a dozen healed wounds. He rolled his shoulder and cracked his neck.

Glancing around the kitchen he tried to remember how he'd gotten there. The woman, Belle. He spotted her on the floor on top of a makeshift bed made from a few sacks and her cloak, her daughter cradled tight against her.

She'd helped him.

He stood and stretched, letting the chill of the air caress his skin. The fire burned as embers. Soon it would be freezing in the room. He wanted to go to his room and crawl under the covers for a week... but he couldn't leave Belle and Chloe to freeze on the floor.

He walked to the pile of wood in the corner and lifted two large logs and several smaller sticks. He set them in front of the substantial cooking pit and poked at the embers making them glow. He piled the small sticks on top and blew on them until they caught. He waited for the flames to rise before placing one of the large logs on.

He stood and moved to the corner, being careful not to wake Belle or Chloe. He stripped off his torn and bloodied tunic and pulled on a spare one from where it hung by the fire. He tossed the ruined one in the fire. Watching the cloth burn, Dax prodded his tender shoulder again. The dawn light peeked through the window and he walked to look out. The ground had been blanketed in thick snow that still fell in giant sheets to the ground.

He looked over his shoulder at the mother and daughter. Belle and Chloe wouldn't be going anywhere soon. Not that it bothered him, but he got the feeling Belle wouldn't like it.

She'd been brave the night before protecting her little girl. Brave as Red and Snow. And she'd been wary of him, rightly so. He grabbed a cup of water, drained the glass, and then poured another and drained it as well.

He stared at Belle. Her high cheekbones were touched by a peachy glow in the firelight. Curled protectively around her child, with her hair fanned out behind her. His gut clenched, and he set his cup on the counter at the sight. Family. The one thing he wanted most for himself. And the one thing always kept from him. Connection, true connection with other people. He had friendship with the Gwyns, as well as with Sage and Adrian; even kinship, but he'd never felt the connection that they experienced with their own family members.

Belle's eye flew open as if she'd never been asleep. She

pulled Chloe in tighter and he noticed the knife in her hand for the first time.

"Don't you think if I was going to hurt you, I would have done it while you were asleep? I understand why you are protective of your child, but I promise you, I'm only trying to help."

She stared at him.

"Would you like something to eat? I can make some porridge."

She shook her head. "As soon as Chloe wakes we need to be on our way."

He crossed his arms over his chest, wincing at the twinge of pain. "Due to the snow that would be impossible," he nodded at the window.

Concern creased her features and she looked to the window.

"There's at least two feet out there already and even I can't find my way out of here with that much snow."

"What about your dragon? He could show us."

Dax snorted. "He could but likely he is in the highest tower nestled down until it clears. As friendly as we are with each other, I doubt even I could get him to go out in this storm."

She closed her eyes and licked her lips. "Then what am I to do? I need to get out of here."

"Where were you going?"

"Somewhere safe."

"What's safer than this? You're in a castle no one can find, in woods that no one would dare venture into if they were in their right mind. There are traps all about this place even if someone did find it, and a dragon—"

"A sleeping dragon."

"As well as me. Trust me, there is no safer place for you and Chloe right now."

"But I need to get to Gwyn manor—"

"Erik and Flint's?"

"You know them?"

He shook his head. He should have connected those dots sooner. Klaus. Belle. "You're *that* Belle. I should have realized."

Her face scrunched up like she'd bitten into a lemon. "What do you mean *that* Belle?"

He held up his hand. "I didn't mean it like that. I heard of you when Flint and I got back from our journey. You're Snow's oldest friend."

"Yes…" Her eyes held skepticism.

"I'm Kondak. Dax. I'm a friend of both the Gwyns and Snow's husband—"

"The vampire."

"Sage. I lived with him before I went with Flint when he… took some time away."

She stared at him for a minute and then her expression softened. "You're the one who lost your memories. Erik and Jamen told me about you when we stayed with them last Yuletide."

He nodded.

"Is that why you're here? Is this where you're from?"

"Not exactly."

Chloe stirred. "Mama."

Belle bent in and kissed her on the head. "Sleep darling. It's not quite light yet."

Dax walked over and pulled a blanket from the sideboard and covered Chloe with it.

She peered up at him with sleepy eyes. "Hi, Dax."

He smiled and backed away. Belle tucked the blanket around Chloe then got up from the bed and sheathed her knife.

"Let me take a look at your wounds." She stepped toward him.

Dax backed up a pace. "It's fine. Thank you."

She gave him an incredulous look. "I need to see if I got them all. They could get infected." She strode forward again until she'd backed Dax into the washbasin. "I'm not going to hurt you."

"I'm fine. I don't need you to look."

She reached for his tunic and he grabbed her hand.

"Truly, it's fine. Thank you."

She stood so close that he could smell the scents of metal and leather on her. He held her hand for a moment before letting it drop. Her large brown eyes rounded with fear.

"I apologize," he said. "I didn't mean to scare you."

"You didn't."

His gut clenched tight at her lie. She owned a wild fierceness that not many women possessed. But her eyes held years of sadness and pain. His gaze ran over her pouty rosy lips. He clenched his jaw as he noticed for the first time a large bruise that puffed the skin under her eye, as well as the scab on her lip. He moved to touch her, but she backed away.

Anger rippled over his skin and his bear growled.

"Did Klaus do that?"

Belle licked her lip and her eyes steeled. "He'll never do it again."

Good girl. "Damn right he won't."

The corner of her mouth upturned almost into a smile. "I never did get to thank you properly for helping Chloe and myself."

"I only did what any man would."

She snorted. "I beg to differ. Did you not see the men with Klaus?"

"I did what any *real* man would do."

"How do you know Klaus? He said he recognized you."

"He tried to kidnap Flint's wife Zelle, and kill both Flint and myself."

She blew out a breath and nodded.

"You don't seem surprised."

"Nothing about him surprises me anymore. Not after what he's done. Things I never thought him capable of, especially to—" She stopped and looked over his shoulder and out the window. "How long do you think we're stuck here?"

He glanced out at the dawning light. The snow still fell in a steady stream. "A week, possibly more."

She shook her head. "But my things. My horse."

"I'm sure Klaus took your horse. And as for your things, they'll still be there when we can get to them. They may be a bit wet and stiff, but they'll be there."

She looked down at her clothes. "These are all I have. And Chloe only has her night clothes."

Dax looked over her mahogany colored leather corset, linen tunic and black breeches. "All things considered those clothes are as practical as any."

"Yes, but I don't care to keep wearing them night and day."

Dax nodded. "Well, then you're in luck. The castle is full of dresses."

KLAUS TWIRLED THE MUG OF ALE IN A CIRCLE, STARING AT IT. He couldn't believe Belle had really left him. And with that stupid werebear. Anger bubbled like poison inside him. After all he'd done for her, how could she? Take Chloe and run.

He might not have been the best of fiancés to her, but he was better than a good number. It was her fault he'd been forced to use Chloe's ability to make money. If Belle hadn't demanded so much from him...

He picked up his mug, drained it and signaled the bar wench for another.

"What do we do now?" asked Fagan.

Klaus stared at his mug. "About what?"

"About Mick."

Klaus shrugged. "He's dead. We're here. And all the better for it. Now we only have to split the purse two ways."

Fagan stared at Klaus until he lifted his gaze. "Something you want to say to me?"

Fagan continued to stare for another minute before

leaning in close. "I want to know what the hell you're gonna do about Belle and the man from the woods."

What was he going to do about Belle? Did Fagan think he hadn't been trying to decide that for the last twelve hours?

He'd taken the horse and with the snow falling like thick cotton, he doubted they'd be traveling anywhere anytime soon. She'd been headed for Jamen's, he knew that much. Stupid Gwyns. She always ran to them for help. And if she'd reached there with that black eye... No one, not even Jamen, would have been able to save him from the wrath of Erik and Flint. Jamen's brothers had never approved of their friendship growing up. And with what had happened with Flint and his wife the previous year. Klaus would never be able to go back to Westfall.

No, he needed a game plan to get Belle back, or to keep her quiet.

A smile crept across his face.

"Finally come up with a plan?" Fagan asked.

"As a matter of fact, yes. I promised Belle and that stupid bear that when I came back I'd bring an army with me, and that's what I intend on doing."

Fagan snorted and sat back in his seat. "And where are you going to get an army?"

Klaus gulped down his new mug of ale and slammed the tankard on the solid wooden table. "From a daemon."

CHAPTER THREE

Dax carried the still sleeping Chloe down the hallway. In his arms the child felt as frail and helpless as a spring doe. Behind him, Belle followed with a large candle lighting the way.

He crept up the winding stairs and across the drafty hallway to the first door on the second floor. Belle pushed it open and he stepped into the dusty yet beautiful room with a large comfortable bed in the center.

"We can't stay in here," Belle whispered. "It's too nice."

Dax looked down at her and snickered. "It's the least opulent room in this place."

She glanced around and then nodded. Belle walked to the bed, set the candle on the nightstand and then pulled down the covers.

Dax laid Chloe on it as Belle covered her with the blankets. She brushed back Chloe's hair from her forehead and kissed her.

Picking up the candle, she followed him to a wardrobe in the corner. He pulled open the creaky doors revealing a dozen beautiful gowns.

"You expect me to wear those?"

Dax looked her up and down. Her curvy and strong body was lush in all the right places. He coughed and looked away as his arousal kicked up. "I have some pants but they'll be too big."

She stared at the dresses like they were foreign objects.

Dax chuckled.

"What?" Her gaze hardened.

"You remind me of Redlynn. She too didn't know what to do with such fancy dresses either."

Belle pulled out a beautiful golden-toned dress to look at it, but then threw it back. "These are impractical. They're too long. The bodice is too... revealing, and the sleeves are way too flowy. How will I get anything done in them?"

Dax walked to a small desk, rolled back the lid and pointed inside to the scissors, needles and thread.

"Make something else out of them."

"I can't just cut up someone else's property."

"These dresses haven't been used in years. If someone had wanted them, they would have taken them long ago."

Chloe stirred. Dax looked over at her and then motioned Belle to follow him. They walked into the hallway and Dax closed the door.

"You do what makes you comfortable. I simply offered a solution to the problem you posed."

An argument twitched Belle's lips, but to his surprise her shoulders slumped.

"You've been more than kind."

"I sleep at the end of the hallway. If you need me, I'll be there. In a few hours, we'll know better what the weather has brought us."

Belle nodded. "Again, I thank you. I've not met many men besides the Gwyns who would do what you have done."

"Then you need to start keeping better company." Again, his gaze lit on the bruise that marred her face and his fists clenched tight.

Dax excused himself and walked down the hall, forcing himself not to look back at her. He had no inclination toward having any kind of relationship, not while he still had no idea who he was; but having her and Chloe in the castle made it seem not so large and barren. As if their very presences had breathed life into the place. Even from all the way down the hall, he felt their light seeping into the cold stone. Especially Chloe's.

And heavens knew after some of the things he'd seen in the castle, it could use some light.

BELLE WALKED BACK TO THE WARDROBE AND PULLED OUT the yellow gown again. More beautiful and expensive than anything she'd ever owned, she placed it back inside. She'd rather go naked than cut that one up.

Instead, she found a light blue gown, long enough to turn into a simple dress for herself and a small jumper for Chloe. A pang of guilt rushed through her. She'd sworn she'd never steal. Not even as a girl when her father had gambled away all their money and there'd been no food in the house. Her pride had filled her belly when nothing else could.

She looked in the wardrobe again and waited for it to give her permission to take the dress, but it didn't.

She closed the door and walked to the desk. Grabbing the scissors and pins, she laid the dress on the floor and began to cut.

By the time Chloe awoke Belle finished up the final touches on her jumper.

"Morning, Mama."

Belle looked up at Chloe and smiled. "I made you something."

Belle held up the jumper and Chloe slid from her bed, her eyes wide with delight. "It's beautiful."

"We need to get you washed up and then you can put it on."

Chloe nodded.

Together they headed down the hallway to the stairs, and then onward to the kitchen. Belle located a large metal clothing scrub tub and pulled it near the fire as Chloe skipped off into another room.

Belle put water on the fire to heat and searched for a clean rag. She remembered the outside of the castle looking like a crumbling ruin, but inside appeared quite different. Though it had been neglected, the castle was far from crumbling to dust.

Chloe bounded back into the kitchen. "Mama, you have to come see!"

Belle chuckled. "What have you found?"

Chloe pulled Belle into the other room and Belle's mouth fell open. She'd never seen a cold cellar stocked with so much food. Dried meats and cheeses, grains and dried fruits, and all sorts of root vegetables she'd been inept at growing herself.

"There's enough food here to feed an army."

"Can we make tarts?" asked Chloe. "And bread? And meat pie? And—"

Belle chuckled. "Slow down. How about if we wash you up and then decide what to make first."

"All right. But my vote is for tarts first."

BELLE SCRUBBED CHLOE IN THE BASIN AND THEN RAN A RAG over herself before getting into her dress and slipping Chloe into her jumper. Belle fought the urge to run her fingers over the soft fabric. She located an apron crumpled on the pantry floor and slipped it over her dress, and then set to work on making the tarts.

Chloe helped pick out the fruit and together they soaked them in brandy before placing them in the dough.

As Belle took the tray and placed it over the fire, Chloe said, "We're never going to live with daddy again."

Belle looked over to see Chloe twirling her bracelet on her wrist. Belle's gut clenched tight. Her words were more statement than question.

Belle slid the tray on top of a baking shelf. "No. We

aren't." She waited for a reaction, but Chloe didn't give one. "Are you sad about that?"

"Daddy isn't who he used to be. He doesn't love us anymore."

Chloe's flat tone wrenched Belle's heart. To be so young and to already see what it had taken Belle years to see, was too much to bear.

"You know what? Why don't you run upstairs and see if Dax wants to join us for food."

Chloe smiled and nodded before skipping off.

"He's in the last room," Belle called.

"I know."

Belle smiled and split her scabbed lip. She put her fist to it and closed her eyes. She blew out a long, low breath and fought back the urge to cry again. She refused to give him one more moment to torment them. They were safe for now, that was all that mattered. But they couldn't stay in the castle forever. Klaus would be back.

DAX JOLTED AWAKE, TRYING TO GET HIS BEARINGS. Something touched his hand and his head whipped around.

Chloe.

He blinked several times.

"You were having a bad dream."

Dax stared down at the small angelic girl and blinked twice. "I think so."

"Mama said I shouldn't tell people what I see, but I know you won't hurt me."

"And what do you see?" he asked.

She cocked her head to the side ever so slightly. "A bad lady put a wall in your mind so you can't see your home."

His heartbeat quickened. "Can you see it?"

She nodded. "But I like you being here with us."

"Do you know where my home is, Chloe?" He held his breath, praying that the small child in front of him might be some gift of the gods sent to help him home. A ridiculous notion but he'd been searching for so long that, at that moment, he'd take any help he could get.

She skipped to the door. "Mama and I made tarts. You should come eat some."

She headed out the door as he called after her, but she didn't return. Dax stared at the door for a moment. He'd seen a lot in the past five years traveling Fairelle, but he'd never met anyone like her before. A child that could see things no one else could. Dax wondered what Stil would think of her.

His heart thundered as the name crossed his mind. *Stil*... He didn't know a Stil. So why had he thought the name? He wracked his brain for a memory. Something to grab on to and make sense of but... there was nothing. Had Cinder mentioned a Stil? He was certain she had. Maybe that's where he'd gotten the name.

He threw his hand over his face and fought the urge to scream. What if he never remembered who he was? Or never made it back to his people? Why couldn't he give up his search and just make a life for himself? Settle down. Be happy... The image of the beautiful girl with the sharp bright blue eyes flashed into his mind again. She was why he didn't give up. Why he kept searching. Because somewhere deep inside, he knew, she would never give up searching for him.

DAX WENT INTO THE KITCHEN AND BELLE LOOKED UP AT him. She'd cut one of the dresses to fit her. Too nice to be considered common, but no longer a dancing gown, it suited her.

"Uh... Chloe said that you'd made food."

"The tarts are finished and then we'll make some meat pies and bread."

His stomach growled. All he'd had the energy to prepare for months was plain oatburn with a drizzle of jam.

He headed for the table, but Belle stepped in front of him.

"If you want to eat, you have to let me look at your wounds first." The determination in her eyes told him that he wasn't going to get away from her again. Not if he wanted the fruit tarts that smelled so delicious, he could eat the entire tray by himself. His bear growled and paced at the sight of the food.

"If I had an infection do you think I'd be on my feet? More likely I'd have a fever and wouldn't be able to move."

She planted her hands on her hourglass waist, accentuating it.

"Even so, if you don't let me look, you don't eat. I don't want to be responsible for you dying after Chloe and I leave because you didn't let me check."

Dax glanced at Chloe, who had cherries smeared on her face. She smiled at him and nodded.

Dammit. "Flint told me you were stubborn."

"Did he also tell you I always get my way in the end?" She flashed him a brilliant smile and batted her eyelashes, lighting up her face.

Dax scratched his chin. "I think he failed to mention that."

Her smile fell. "Well I do. So, come on. Show me."

Dax licked his lips. He didn't want to scare Chloe.

"All right. But not in front of the child."

Belle snorted. "Chloe has seen wounds before."

His bear grumbled, and Dax crossed his arms over his chest. "Not in front of the child."

"All right." She turned to Chloe. "You keep eating sweetie. We'll be back in a minute."

Chloe waved and shoved the rest of her tart in her mouth.

Dax headed across the kitchen and through the cold cellar to a door on the other side. He pulled it open and stepped into the large dining hall. Several long tables lined the room, and Dax walked to the closest one and sat on it. He unbuttoned the top of his tunic as Belle strode forward with a rag, bowl and bandages.

"Don't be startled," he said.

"You think I haven't seen a man's chest before? I saw yours just last night."

"That's not what I mean."

She set the bowl and supplies down next to him and stepped forward. Dax stared at her for a minute and then pulled his tunic open. Belle blinked several times and then her head cocked to the side, the same way Chloe did.

She pushed his tunic aside and looked at his entire chest. A confused expression crossed her face.

"Is this a jest?" Her soft fingers pushed aside the fabric again. "But... you had wounds all over you."

"I heal fast."

"I shot you last night. This isn't possible." She pushed the tunic off him and ran her fingers over his skin, making him twitch. "But—"

Before he could move she rounded him looked at his back, and gasped.

Dax jumped from the table.

"Like I said, I heal fast." His gut twisted at the expression of knowing and pity in her eyes.

Only the wolves had ever seen his scars. If Flint had seen them in their travels together, he'd never said anything. But then, Flint too wasn't a stranger to scars.

Dax had tried to count them once, but they crisscrossed the surface of his skin, so tightly packed, that he had a hard time telling one from another.

"Where... where did you get all those?" she whispered.

"I don't know who caused them," Dax lied. "But I got them here."

Belle shook her head. "I'm sorry. I am so sorry."

"It's nothing," he replied. "We all have scars. I just wear most of mine on my skin."

A moment passed between them and Dax picked up the rag and dipped it in the small bowl of water. He crept toward Belle and wiped a spot of blood from her chin from where her lip wept once more.

In the light, he caught the extent of her facial injuries. He raised his hand and waited until she nodded consent and then he tipped her head sideways to look at her eye. In the corner of the white part, blood ran into her vision. He prodded the skin around her eye socket and she winced but didn't cry out. At least the bones weren't broken.

He patted the area with the rag.

"What are you?" Belle's eyes connected with his and they stared at each other for a long minute.

Dax wanted to tell her, but he wasn't sure if she could take the shock, or if it would send her running out into the blizzard to die with Chloe.

He dropped the rag back into the bowl. "One of a kind."

Her brows knit together and she opened her mouth to say something.

"Mama, can I feed the dragon?" Chloe called.

Dax chuckled.

"I don't think he likes tarts," Belle replied.

"I could ask him."

Belle looked at him again. "I should go because she *will* try to ask."

Dax nodded. "I understand."

She brushed the hair back over her eye, hiding the bruise, and picked up her supplies.

As Dax watched her go, a memory surfaced; *a woman in a long red dress walked away from him.*

"If you don't marry me. You don't marry at all."

The lash hit his back again and he bit down on his cheek, refusing to give her the satisfaction of hearing him cry out.

"Keep going," she said. "Until he sees things my way."

The memory faded and Dax stumbled forward, resting his hands on the table. He blew out a harsh breath as the memory of the pain coursed through him. *Morgana.* What had she wanted him for? And what did it have to do with him losing his memories?

CHAPTER FOUR

After they'd stuffed themselves on fruit tarts, Dax helped clean the plates and then walked to the sideboard and pulled out his journal. He unwrapped the leather strap and opened it scanning the pages.

"What's that?" asked Chloe.

Dax looked over at her. "It's my journal."

"What do you write in it?"

"Chloe, that's private," Belle admonished.

"It's all right." He turned the book and showed Chloe the page.

Her bright blue eyes looked over the words. "What does it say?"

"It tells all the rooms I've been through in the castle, here," he pointed. "And it tells how many times, here. And this tells me if I found anything new."

Chloe stared at it in thoughtful silence. "You're looking

for the thing you lost."

Anger rippled through him. "I'm looking for the thing that was stolen."

"By the bad lady."

"All right," Belle interjected. "Chloe, I think that's enough for now. Dax has things he needs to do, why don't you run along and see how thick the snow is?"

Chloe smiled. "I'll go get my boots and cape."

Belle gave a tight smile and Chloe jogged out of the room. The tension in her shoulders and fear in her eyes told Dax everything he needed to know.

"She has a gift," he said.

Belle licked her bottom lip. "You say gift, I say curse."

"How can it be a curse? Her very presence soothes people and her words give hope and comfort."

"Not for her. So far, she's known only pain from telling people what she sees or knows. Her own father—" Belle stopped and pressed her hand to her mouth. When she pulled it away her lip wept again. She looked down at her hand. "My toth, will the thing never stop?" She pressed her apron into the cut.

"I have a salve that might help with that."

"You make salves?"

He shrugged. "I learned a bit from Queen Redlynn and Princess Cinder. It's a fernblend salve."

"How is it that you know so many royal women?"

Dax chuckled. Did he catch a hint of jealousy in her voice? "I've traveled along the northern and western borders of Fairelle and I've seen many kingdoms."

"And you just happen to become friends with the royalty?"

"I tend to have friends who marry them. Sage and Snow. Adrian and Redlynn. Cinder is a friend of the Gwyns. She's the one who led me here."

She nodded. "So where is this fernblend salve?"

"In a room in the basement. I found the space a few months back. It's full of alchemical supplies as well as herbs."

Chloe ran back in. "I found my things."

Belle walked to her little girl and fastened Chloe's cloak around her neck. "You can go just outside the door and no further."

"There's a garden to the left. It's frozen, but safe. As far as I can tell there are no traps in there," Dax said.

"As far as you know?"

"Well, there could always be traps, but I've walked the garden many times and never found one."

Belle looked between them, conflicted.

"I'll be safe, Mama."

"The garden. No further."

Chloe nodded and ran out the door.

Belle looked after her. "I should go with her. If she gets lost or hurt—"

"You can't baby her forever."

"But she is a baby."

Dax sighed. "That's not what I meant. I just mean, you protect her because she's seen and been through terrible things. You both have. But here you can take a breath. We're safe. You, are safe."

Belle stared at him for a moment.

A desire to wrap her in his arms and comfort her burned through him. Even his inner bear sat up and looked at her. *Nope. Not going there.*

Dax jumped to his feet. "I should go get—"

"Yes, thank you."

He strode from the room and through the cold cellar to the dining hall. His boots clunked on the stone floor as he headed toward a door in the back. He allowed the sound to pound through his head, clearing his thoughts.

Falling for Belle wasn't an option. Belle and Chloe didn't deserve to be mixed up in his messy life. They had enough to deal with without him trying to drag them under with his problems. And his problems were bigger than even Dax wanted to admit.

He walked into a small solar behind the dining room and over to a painting in the corner. He pulled it back, revealing a passageway. Taking the steps two at a time, he hurried down barely noticing the ever-glowing lanterns on the walls. He'd spent weeks trying to take one apart and figure out how it worked, but to no avail. In the end he'd decided that some magick was better left undiscovered.

Everything in the room was made of stone or glass. The shelves, the workbench, jars and bottles. He walked to the workbench and stared at it. In all of his life he hadn't paid so much attention to things so small, but now, in a castle where it seemed every lock, every stone, every jar held an answer that he couldn't see, his frustrations mounted.

So many times in the past months he'd thought of leaving. Walking across every inch of Fairelle until he discovered the truth, until his memories returned, or he just gave up. But Cinder had told him that the castle held the answers he'd been searching for. That this was where he needed to be. Only his faith in her words kept him on his course.

He grabbed an empty bottle and hurled it across the room. Why couldn't he just give up? Why couldn't he just move on? A face popped into his head. A beautiful girl of no more than eighteen. Hair like sunlight. Eyes hazel like his. And an infectious smile that could light up any room. She was kind and fun and strong of heart.

The picture faded but the feeling of sadness and loss remained. He loved her, whomever she was. He loved her the way he loved Zelle. The way he loved Cinder. As a sister.

She was the reason he kept fighting, kept searching, kept moving forward. He had to find her. Because aside from caring for her, when he saw her face a terrible sense of dread also overcame him.

"Dax?" Belle's voice floated down from somewhere up above.

He grabbed the small jar of salve and headed for the stairs. He'd help Belle and Chloe as much as he was able, but he couldn't let them distract him from his mission. He had to find the girl from his dreams. The girl with the sunlit hair. She would know his identity.

BELLE WALKED AROUND THE LARGE DINING HALL AND RAN her fingers over the hardwood. The room stood larger than the Gwyns' hall by half, with its exposed beam vaulted ceiling close to three stories high, and over a hundred feet long. Yet the entire castle didn't look larger than a manor house from the outside.

"I found it." Dax entered through a room behind the head table.

"There must be a powerful magick protecting this castle," she said. "It looks not half this size from the outside."

Dax nodded and stopped in front of her. "There are many things I've found that point to a powerful magick user."

He unscrewed the lid to the ointment and dipped his finger inside.

"How long have you been here?"

He set the tin on the table and sat next to it, so they were eye to eye. She stepped forward until their bodies almost touched.

"About six months."

He lightly touched his finger to her lower lip. It slid along the outer corner and down below. The sensation sent tingles skittering over her skin. She stared into his hazel eyes as he concentrated, trying not to pay attention to the heat of his body as it permeated her dress. To the way his body loomed around hers like a human blanket. To the gentleness of his touch as his rough fingertip pulled at her skin. A gentleness that Klaus had never possessed. Even in the beginning. Claiming, wanting, needing; those where Klaus' emotions with her, but never gentleness.

"Where—" She cleared her throat. "Where were you before this?"

His gaze met hers. "I could put some on your eye as well if you'd like."

"All right."

Again, he dipped his large fingers into the jar. He looked up at her and then slipped his hand around her waist, pulling her closer. She stepped between his powerful thighs and he tipped her chin up.

Her heartbeat kicked up and her skin flushed with warmth and she fidgeted trying to figure out where to rest her hands. Finally, she clasped her fingers together in front of her.

It'd been so long since she'd felt the bare skin of another person. Klaus had been her one and only, but she'd often wondered what it would be like to lie with another man. She pondered what Dax would be like in bed. Would he be greedy and selfish like Klaus, or would he be generous and attentive to what she wanted? She knew inside that he would be nothing like Klaus. Nothing about him resembled Klaus. Not his body, not his personality, nothing.

Heat flushed her cheeks and she looked away, fighting the urge to move out of Dax's grip as embarrassment flooded her. How could she look at a man as good and kind as Dax and think he'd want anything more from her than to help her and get her on her way. He didn't need her wanting possible companionship interfering with what he'd been dealing with.

Dax studied her eye for a moment and then dabbed the ointment around it.

"I went to stay with Cinder and the fae before I came here," he said. "Honestly, we found this place on a fluke. If she hadn't been kidnapped and brought here, I'd still be searching Fairelle."

Someone had kidnapped the fae princess? "I'm surprised they let you in the city. I thought the fae didn't like humans."

"They don't usually, but we had a work around."

She chuckled as his finger tickled her skin. "A work around?"

"She gave me a magick cloak to help me blend in."

Belle snorted. "I'm sure a cloak wasn't near enough to make you look like a fae."

The corners of his mouth cocked up in a slight smile revealing a dimple. "It's a very special cloak."

He studied her face for a moment. "I think that should be good. Hopefully the bruising will be gone by tomorrow."

"Thank you," she said. "For everything. I know—"

Alabrax's roar echoed through the hall. Dax raced to the window so fast Belle barely saw him move.

"What is it?" she ran up beside him.

Chloe!

The pair raced through the hall back toward the kitchen. Dax threw the outside door open and disappeared into the snow. Belle raced out behind him, the icy snowflakes whipping her in the face.

"Chloe! Chloe!" Belle caught sight of Dax's tunic as he raced around the back of the castle. She followed and just as she rounded the corner, Dax grabbed her around the waist.

"Chlo—"

"Shhh," Dax's warm body pressed against hers and his arms encircled her. "Wait."

Several feet away, Alabrax stood, head bowed, allowing Chloe to pet him. He purred like a kitten at the touch of her hand.

"Yes, I know," Chloe said. "I don't like the cold either. But don't worry, we're gonna go soon and it'll be warmer there."

Alabrax warbled.

"Yes, you'll like it. You'll fit right in."

A scream crept up Belle's throat and she clutched onto Dax. "Go get her. Please?"

"He won't hurt her," Dax replied.

"You can't know that."

He looked deep into her eyes. "Yes, I can." Dax looked at Chloe again. "Stay here."

Belle nodded and wrapped her arms around herself. Dax walked toward Chloe and Alabrax. Belle had to cover her mouth to keep from crying out.

Alabrax lifted his head as Dax approached. He looked at Chloe and then lumbered over to Dax. Dax scratched Alabrax's chin.

"Have you eaten?" he asked the dragon.

"I gave him a jam tart. I knew he'd like them," said Chloe.

"Go back to sleep boy, we aren't going anywhere today."

Alabrax yawned and smoke furled out of his nostrils. Then he spread his wings and pushed off of the ground. He rose barely above Dax's head before Dax swooped up Chloe and headed toward Belle. She fought every instinct to run to them until after the dragon had crawled back into his tower and disappeared.

Belle cried out as she pulled Chloe from Dax's arms and hugged her tight. "Chloe, how could you do that? Don't you know you could have been killed?"

"Alabrax wouldn't hurt me. We're friends."

Belle's limbs shook and she fought to hold back tears.

"Come," said Dax. "Let's get inside before we all freeze."

They crunched back through the snow to the kitchen door and set Chloe near the fire. Dax closed the door and joined them, putting his bare feet to the fire.

"Great toth, you have no boots on." Belle ran to the sideboard and whipped open the top drawer. She found an ancient looking tablecloth and ran back to Dax's purple feet. She wrapped the cloth around them. "You could lose your feet being out in the cold like that."

"I'll be fine as soon as they warm up."

"And if they don't? You can't just do things like that."

"Like what? Help people?"

"Yes!"

"Yes?" His eyebrow arched.

"No."

"So, you want me to help people."

"No. I mean— uh..." Belle stopped and took a deep breath. "Thank you for helping us again, but you can't do that at the risk of harm to yourself."

"I don't just stop and think about whether there is a risk to myself before I help someone. I either help, or I don't."

"And how often do you *not* help?"

He gave her a rueful smile. "Not often."

She'd not known many men like him before. Men who would help someone they didn't know, risking their own wellbeing to do it— but she was grateful for him nonetheless.

She turned to Chloe who had curled in a ball and fallen asleep on the floor. Belle sat down with a bump and hung her head.

"Are you all right?" Dax asked.

"I just..." She laughed. "This is not how I saw my life going. On the run with my child from the man that used and abused me for the last seven years. Trapped in a castle in the middle of nowhere with a dragon sleeping in the tower."

"How did you see your life going?"

She looked up at him. A burning desire to tell him rushed through her. She'd never told anyone what she'd really wanted for her life.

"A princess."

Dax chuckled. "I'm sorry?"

"A princess. I thought that someday, I would be swept off my feet by a prince and taken to a faraway castle where we would live happily forever after."

"Well, not to pop your bread dough but I can tell you that being royalty isn't something I'd wish on anyone. It's not all sitting around and eating delicious food. It's entertaining people you don't like in an effort to keep peace. Smiling when you don't feel like it, or don't want to. It's having to make tough decisions and knowing that in doing so, someone could or will die. And worst of all, it's being told what to do and when to do it and how to do it."

"You speak as if you have experience."

His eyes saddened and he stared into the fire. "I wouldn't know if I had. But I saw Cinder go through it. It almost broke her and Rome apart. Luckily, she married a man who knew who she was and fought for her to stay who she was even after they married. And she was able to compromise and see where she needed to bend as well. So it worked."

For all of the pain she'd been through in her life, Belle at least had her memories. The good and the bad, she wouldn't trade them for anything. They'd shaped her into who she'd become.

Dax wiggled his feet. "I think I can feel my toes again."

"You should sit here for another few minutes, just to be sure."

She looked around at the large kitchen. "This room is bigger than my whole hut."

"A space can feel vast or stifling just depending on who you occupy it with."

She gazed into the fire. "The hut had been choking me for months. I just never got the courage to leave before. But I decided I didn't want Chloe to grow up thinking that what Klaus did was normal. To think that she deserved to be treated the same way."

"You didn't deserve it."

She shrugged. "My heart tells me that. But my head tells me that there were times I did."

"No offense but your head is wrong."

A comfortable silence fell between them and they stared at the fire, neither talking. She wondered what he thought about but didn't dare intrude on his reflections. He'd been kind enough to allow them to stay, his life was his business, just as hers was her own.

CHAPTER FIVE

"Dax... Dax... Dax..."

Dax opened his eyes a crack and looked over into Chloe's cherubic face.

"Good morning." She smiled at him as he rolled over and sat up, rubbing sleep from his eyes. He looked to the window where sunlight filtered through the clouds.

"The snow stopped."

Dax nodded. "So it seems."

It'd been three days since Chloe had played outside and met Alabrax, and the snow hadn't let up once. And though the three of them had spent time reading and playing games, he knew Belle grew as anxious to leave as he was to get back to his search, despite enjoying himself.

"There's muffins downstairs if you're hungry."

His stomach growled at the thought. "Thank you. I'll get dressed and be right down."

Chloe nodded. "Can you show me the room today?"

"The room?"

"The hidden one down below. Mama said I'm not supposed to go in there unless you take me."

"You mother is right. There are lots of things in there that could be dangerous for a little girl. When did you go in there?"

"I didn't yet, but I know it's there. I feel it."

A pit grew in Dax's stomach. Belle had made it clear she didn't want anyone to find out about Chloe's abilities, she didn't even like to talk about it herself. But she couldn't keep running from it. Chloe's abilities were not something common- or anything he'd heard of someone having before. He'd read about it, but there hadn't been someone like her in a thousand years.

"Run downstairs and I'll meet you there."

Chloe toddled off his large bed and skipped to the door. Part of him wanted to show her the room and see if she could tell him anything, but Belle wasn't likely to agree once she saw some of the darker magickal items down there.

But an idea took root, intriguing him. Could it be possible that fate had brought Chloe and Belle into his life to help him find what he'd been searching for?

DAX WALKED DOWN THE STAIRS TO THE KITCHEN AND FOUND Chloe sitting at the table eating a muffin and thumbing through a picture book he'd found her. He walked to the counter and poured a glass of water. Out the window at least two feet of snow blanketed everything. The tree branches were weighted down with the load and looked as if they might snap at any moment. Dax drank his water and then walked to the table and sat next to Chloe.

"Do you want to read some today?" he asked.

Chloe nodded. "Can you read me this one?"

She pointed to a poem written on a page of a book decorated with dancing bears.

"Sure."

He shoved a piece of muffin into his mouth and pulled the book between them. Dusting off the crumbs from his fingers, he read the poem once and then lifted her index finger and covered it with his own, following along as he read the words to her again. Every once in a while he would stop and have her sound out a word before continuing on. When he finished, Chloe clapped and laughed.

"I like that one, but I don't think it's true," she said.

"Why is that?"

"Because bears don't dance."

"Maybe they do, who knows?"

Chloe looked up at him. "Do you dance?"

"I can dance, but I'm not very good."

"Like the bears?"

He swallowed hard. "Like the bears."

The clock on the sideboard showed almost eleven. Belle was usually baking by that time.

"Chloe, where's Mama?"

"She went to get her bag."

Dax jumped from his seat. "What?"

"She said to stay here and she would be back soon."

Dax crouched in front of Chloe, his heart racing. "How long ago did she leave?"

"A long time, maybe?"

"Shite." Dax ran to the back door and shoved his feet into his boots before grabbing his cloak. "Stay here," he told Chloe.

Dax opened the door and found Belle's footprints in the snow. He followed them around the side of the castle and sniffed the air. He couldn't smell anything. *Damn.*

He followed her footsteps through the trees and headed in the direction they went. Fear crushed his chest. What if she'd gotten lost? Or hurt? Dammit. He'd said he'd watch after her. He'd told her he wouldn't let anything happen to her or Chloe, but how the hell did he protect her when she wouldn't even listen to reason and stay inside the castle?

A howl sounded from up ahead, then a scream. Dax's bear roared inside his chest to be let out. He tore through the woods as fast as the snow would let him. A blast sounded and then another scream. He rushed through the trees in time to see Belle swinging her large weapon at something. Dax sniffed the air. *Awe, toth!*

Dax sprinted forward, pushing off a rock leaping through the air and landing in front of her.

"Stop!"

Belle's weapon came down and he grabbed it right before it hit him in the face. He stared at her for a moment, terror etching her features. Dazed, Belle backed up a step, breathing heavy.

"It's all right." He moved forward but she backed up again. "Easy."

The sounds of bones breaking and shifting sounded behind him. Belle's eyes widened as she watched. Dax glanced over his shoulder to see Redlynn standing behind him.

"Belle, this is Queen Redlynn. I told you about her."

Belle looked between the two.

"I apologize for frightening you," said Redlynn. "We didn't expect humans to be in these woods."

"It's all right," said Dax. "I wasn't expecting Belle to be out here alone." Dax turned and looked over the wolves. There were five in all. Redlynn stood in front of her father Angus and three other males. "What are you doing this far south of Wolvenglen?"

"Fendrick is missing."

"Missing?"

Redlynn nodded. "We've searched everywhere but cannot find him. Adrian tracked his scent to Westfall, but then it cut off."

"Did his wife Hanna go with him?"

Redlynn shook her head. "Now you see the concern."

"I haven't seen nor smelled him anywhere near here, but I'll be sure to keep an eye out."

"What are you doing so far out here? We thought you were with the fae."

"I was, but my search has led me here."

"Good to know. We need to continue onward. You and I both know what could happen with Fendrick separated from his mate and the pack."

"You are welcome to come and eat and rest where I'm staying. It isn't far."

"Thank you, but we should keep moving. We need to get back to Wolvenglen by light tomorrow and we have a lot of ground to cover."

Dax nodded. "Tell Adrian and the others I said hello."

Redlynn gave a rare smile. "I will."

With the cracking of bones, she shifted into wolf again and trotted to the north. Angus' large russet colored form drew close to Dax.

Dax smiled. "Good to see you're still kicking, old friend."

Angus snorted and followed the rest of the group into the snow-laden trees.

Dax watched them disappear and then turned to Belle. She stared at him with a mixture of fascination and wariness.

"You knew them."

"I lived with them for a while when I first lost my memories."

"And the queen was naked, yet you didn't even look away."

Dax tromped back toward the castle.

"Nakedness is not something shifters think about too much. They shift in front of each other so often that it's not the same as how humans view nakedness. Redlynn's hair is long enough to cover most of her, but modesty is not a virtue shifters propagate."

"And the wolf that approached you? Was that a female as well?"

Dax chuckled. "That's Angus, Redlynn's father. All of the other shifters are male, so far."

"So far?" He turned to see her rubbing her shoulder.

He tromped back to her. "Did one of them hurt you?"

"No. It was my blunderbuss. It sat in the snow too long and the mechanisms froze. It backfired and I took a blow to my shoulder, is all. It's not the first time. It'll be fine."

"I should look at it when we get back."

She rolled her shoulder and moved her bag to the other side. He hadn't noticed it before, but she'd found her things, surprisingly.

"Let me get that for you." He removed the strap from her shoulder, but she hung onto it.

"I can carry my bag, it's not that heavy."

He tugged on it. "I don't mind."

She pulled it back. "Neither do I."

"I've got it," he said.

She pulled it from his grip. "I said I can do it."

Anger flared inside him. "You're in pain and it's no cost to me to carry it."

"I can do things on my own. I'm very capable."

"I never assumed you weren't. I'm simply trying to help."

"Well maybe I don't want your help. Maybe I'm fine doing it on my own."

Dax threw up his hands. "Fine."

"Fine."

He turned and stomped back to the castle. "Fine."

He'd met stubborn women before. Hell, Redlynn was about as stubborn as they came, but Belle took the crown.

She was so hell-bent on proving that she didn't need anyone else that she refused to even let people be nice to her without thinking they had some ulterior motive. He shook his head and continued to tromp forward. Klaus had really messed her up. If Dax ever got his hands on that man again, he didn't want to think of what he'd do.

BELLE'S SHOULDER THROBBED THE ENTIRE WAY BACK TO THE castle. She was being stubborn and she knew it, but she was tired of feeling so helpless. First, Dax had saved her from Klaus, then he'd saved Chloe from the dragon—though both claimed she'd never been in danger—and now he'd saved her from werewolves. Though she was grateful, the thoughts angered her to no end.

All her life with Klaus he'd treated her as if she were weak; a burden. But she wasn't weak, and she needed others to know it. How would she ever make a life for herself and her daughter in this world if she didn't at least garner some respect from men? Fairelle wasn't the kind of place that a woman with a small child had many prospects. She needed to find a place she could go and stand on her own two feet and make a life without having to rely on the handouts of others. Woman seen as desperate tended to attract men who thought they could take advantage. And she'd be damned if she would let a man take advantage of her again.

Yes, that was in complete contrast to what she'd tried to do at first, running off to stay with the Gwyns, but she had planned to go there to regroup; that's all.

They approached the castle and she followed Dax's broad, hunched shoulders as he led the way, the same as she had the first night at the castle nearly a week prior. Belle found it strange how familiar his form had become and how much having him around comforted her.

No! She couldn't fall into that trap again. She'd only just left Klaus. To make it on her own, she had to stand on her own two feet.

Belle used a small tool to undo the barrel of her blunderbuss and check the mechanism inside. She hadn't seen Dax the rest of the day since he'd come to find her in the woods. Guilt gnawed at her gut for how she'd treated him, but she had no words to explain why she'd been so obstinate.

Next to Belle Chloe tinkered with a broken clock Belle had found and dismantled days before. As if sensing the tension, Chloe retreated into her own world like she always had when things were bad between Belle and Klaus.

Belle forced a smile. "What do you think is wrong with the clock?"

Chloe's face scrunched up. "I don't know. Maybe the gooberblat is broken."

Belle chuckled. "The gooberblat, huh?"

"Yeah. Or maybe the spinnywhirl."

"Ahhh. Yes, I'll be sure to look at that next."

"Mama, can I go see Alabrax?"

Fear stabbed Belle. "Not today."

"Can I go find Dax?"

"I think we should give Dax some space."

Chloe put down her tools. "I'm bored."

"Why don't we bake then?"

"I'm tired of baking."

Belle stared at Chloe and her gut twisted. She hated that Chloe wasn't in school. She hated that she had to just sit around with nothing to do.

"How about you go to the library and pick out a book and I'll read to you?"

Chloe hopped down from her chair. "I guess so."

Belle watched Chloe wander out the door and up the stairs to the main floor. Belle set her blunderbuss barrel on the table and stared at the clock that lay in pieces. Chloe would be six in less than a year. Belle wouldn't be able to keep her home much longer. She needed to go learn so she could do better in life than Belle had. But with them unsettled, there was nowhere for Belle to send her. They needed to leave. As much peace as being in the hidden castle had brought Belle, they had to move on. They needed to find a home— and the castle wasn't it.

DAX SCOURED THE TWENTIETH BOOK OF THE DAY, searching, hoping for something that might help him.

He slammed the book shut and then shoved the huge pile of books from the table in a roar.

All around him, rows upon rows upon rows of books still waited for him to open their pages and devourer them. It would take him a lifetime to do it though, and his patience wore thin.

He stared at the table.

"Hi."

He forced a smile at Chloe, who stood in the grand doorway. "Hey there. Are you looking for me?"

"Mama said for me to find a book."

"Well, this is the place to find them."

Chloe walked across the large wooden floor, her bare feet scarcely making a sound. She looked down at the books on the floor.

"Did you not like them?"

"They're good enough as books go, they just don't have the information I'm looking for."

"What are you looking for?"

Dax licked his lips. "It doesn't matter. Come on, I'll help you find a book." He pushed from the table and stood. Chloe slipped her tiny hand into his large one and together they walked to the small shelf in the back of the room that held primary books. He had no clue why the books were even there except to think that at some point, children must have lived in the castle.

"What do you want to read about?"

Chloe's eyes lit up. "I want to read about dragons."

"Dragons? I don't know that your mother would like that."

"But I need to. I need to know more about them."

Dax knit his brows. "Why?"

"Because they are amazing. And Alabrax said that there are more of his kind, sort of."

Dax stopped. "Alabrax said?"

Chloe smiled up at him with childlike innocence. "Yes. When I fed him the tart."

Dax opened his mouth but closed it again when no words formed. He had no idea what to say.

Chloe looked to the corner with the primary bookshelf and ran to it. She thumbed through the books as Dax watched her in silence. Belle hid Chloe for a reason, and he didn't blame her. The girl was unique. Possibly one of a kind.

Chloe pulled a book from the shelf and then another. Something fell out of the book and rolled under the bookshelf. Chloe got down on her hands and knees and peered under the shelf.

"Hey," she said. "There's something back here."

"What?" Dax walked forward and joined her.

"There's a hole in the wall."

Dax scanned the seamless wall. "I don't see anything."

"It's behind."

Dax walked to the shelf and ran his hand over it. Unlike the others that were attached to the wall, this smaller shelf wasn't built in. He slipped his hand behind it and pulled the heavy object to the side. Still he didn't see what Chloe had meant.

"I don't see anything."

Chloe got down on her hands and knees again and pointed. "Look, see?" She slid her fingers up to the wall and they disappeared underneath it.

"What the—"

Dax crouched down on his knees and looked. Sure enough, an inch gap appeared at the bottom. He pressed his hand against it. Cool air rushed to meet his fingers, and a dim light shone through. He stood and ran his fingers up the wall. At first he felt nothing, but then his fingers ran over a slight divot. He followed the divot from the floor all the way up to his head and around to the other side in the shape of a door. A chill swept over his shoulders. A gnawing in his gut told him to not press forward, but another part of him had to know.

"Move out of the way, sweets," he said.

Chloe scampered out of the way.

Dax pushed on the door and it clicked from the inside. A panel popped open and Dax pried his fingers around the edge and pulled open the heavy section. In all his months in the castle he'd never once found the hidden opening.

A splash of crisp, dusty air tinged with the scent of dried blood washed over his face. The gnawing in Dax's gut turned to panic. His mind screamed at him to close the wall back up and walk away.

"Can we see what's in there?" Chloe asked.

Dax peered into the dimly lit stairwell that descended lower into the ground. "I... I don't know that your mama is going to like that too much. Maybe you should stay here and I'll go down first."

"But I found it." Her bottom lip stuck out and the stubborn expression she donned mimicked Belle's exactly.

Dax looked down the descending staircase with the same ever lit lanterns.

"How about you wait here until I get down there, just to make sure there aren't any traps, and then you can join me."

Chloe thought about it for a moment and then nodded. "But I do get to come down."

"Yes. Just let me make sure it's safe first." Dax walked

into the chilled stairwell and an odd sense of foreboding raced through him. A feeling that made his skin goosebump. He wanted to slam the door shut and forget he'd ever seen it, but he couldn't because an even stronger sense pulled him downward like the whisper of a lover calling him near.

Step after step, he drew closer. Dread flooded him, threatening to strangle him from the inside. He rounded a corner and ran his hand over the ice-cold stone, trying to keep a hold of his senses. His legs trembled the lower he descended, and images bombarded him.

Pain as he broke his own wrist to get out of the shackles.

Running up the stairs, naked and freezing.

Slipping on the steps and falling.

Strong arms grabbing him and pulling him to his feet. "Go. Get out and save us." He pitched forward, and the strong male hauled him up the stairs. At the top another male waited with a pair of breeches and a tunic. They yanked the clothes on him and carried him through the library and down the hallway to the front door.

A screech sounded behind them. He turned his head, which felt two times too heavy, to see Morgana running toward them.

"Stop!"

The three men rushed the door. The man with the clothes pulled it open as a spell hit him in the back, crumpling him to the floor.

The door swung inward and the second man shoved Dax through it. "Go!"

He pulled a vial of powder from his pocket and blew it on Dax, yelling,, "Transparo."

Dax flew through the air as a wail sounded from the castle.

Dax opened his eyes and sucked in a shuddered breath. Sweat ran down his neck despite the cold.

"Can I come down now?" Chloe called.

He panted and rubbed his head, his heart thundering like dragon's wings. "Not yet. I'm not all the way down."

"Hurry," she called.

Dax leaned against the wall, his body shaking with the memories. He had to do this. He had to see what lay below.

He shuffled down the stairs toward the basement. He rounded the last corner and closed his eyes as the room came into view. This was why he'd come. What he'd spent months trying to discover. Sucking in a deep breath he walked toward the large stone room. He stepped inside and breathed deep before opening his eyes. Memories flooded him again at the scents of blood, sweat, and magick. His stomach turned, and he fought back the bile that lurched up his throat.

He blinked several times as his head swam. Dax took in every inch of the room. Nothing had changed. He knew the room like he knew every inch of his skin and not a thing had changed from the moment he'd fled from it.

Shackles hung from a corner of the ceiling, blood staining the floor and walls surrounding them.

On the other side of the room stood a large four-poster bed swathed in red silk. More images bombarded him.

Morgana, naked, splayed on the bed. "Don't you want to touch me? I can bring you such pleasure."

Morgana making love to a man her eyes never leaving Dax's.

Morgana.

"STOP!" He grabbed his head. He didn't want to see anymore. He didn't want to remember.

"Dax?"

His head whipped up and Chloe stood in front of him, wide-eyed.

"Chloe, sweetie, you shouldn't be down here." He snatched her up and headed for the stairs. She shouldn't be around this; see these horrible things.

"What's that?" Chloe pointed over his shoulder.

Dax turned despite his best efforts not to. In the corner by the bed stood a large, ornate mirror with a red stone on top.

"My toth!" Dax hurried to the mirror and set Chloe on the floor.

"Is it a mirror?"

Dax stared at it for a moment, his heart galloping. With a mirror he could travel to Tanah Darah. Oh, how he needed to be with friends right then. Without a second thought he pushed the red stone. The surface swam and morphed into view, but unlike the other mirrors where he had to call to where he wanted to see, this one opened up on a lavish, long ballroom. Red carpeting stretched across a white marble floor. Huge paintings hung on every wall, surrounding the mirror he looked out of. Muffled sounds of people walking here and there while talking floated softly through. A feeling of nostalgia struck him deep inside. He knew the room, though he couldn't place it.

Chloe stepped forward and reached for the surface just as the door to the room burst open. Dax grabbed her hand as her fingertips touched the surface and he slammed his fist on the stone closing the portal. He swept her into his arms.

"We need to leave this place."

"But the mirror—"

"It's not a toy, Chloe." Dax stormed from the room and up the stairs. Every painting he'd seen in the room stuck out in vivid detail and thinking of it brought just one word to his mind.

Home.

CHAPTER SIX

The smell of ash and smoke filled Klaus' nostrils as he marched into the large cave, escorted by a sharp spear at the small of his back.

"I'm a friend you know," he said. "You don't need to treat me like this."

"I'll treat you any way I like, until the Queen tells me otherwise."

A jab of the spear to the kidneys made Klaus lurch forward and almost fall to his knees. He cursed under his breath and clenched his fists, ready to fight. He breathed in deeply and got to his feet. The guard would be sorry as soon as he saw Morgana and Klaus told her what the man had done. That alone was worth enduring the humiliation.

The cave opened into an enormous cavern, and if Klaus hadn't walked in through the rock face, he never would've believed that the room resided inside a mountain. Some sort of translucent stone made up the entire top of the cavern, letting light rain down and illuminate the entire space.

The guard pushed him forward, and Klaus walked to the edge of the upper floor and down the steep, wide staircase that descended to the open floor below. The grand hall had been cut into sections. Large tables adorned one side near an enormous fireplace and the opposite end of the room was set up with rows of cots.

Every male in the room stood as Klaus entered, their eyes tracking him down the stairs. Despite his best effort to appear calm, being amongst dozens of dragon shifters was enough to make the strongest of men at least a little uneasy.

"Well, this is a surprise." Morgana strode forward, touching the dragon shifters in turn making them resume what they'd been doing.

"I found him wandering in the woods," said the guard. "He said you'd want to see him."

Morgana's eyes narrowed. "Did he?"

She stopped in front of Klaus. Her long red dress plunged all the way to her belly button. Her long wavy hair twisted into an intricate up-do that exposed her long slender neck. Klaus' arousal kicked at the memories of her naked body wrapped around his time and time again.

"You've been too lax with him, mother." Rasmuss stood from a deep, high-backed chair near the fire. "He thinks he can walk in whenever he wants now."

Morgana grabbed Klaus' face. "Do you? Do you think you own me now, human?"

Fear and anger rolled through Klaus making him clench his fists.

Rasmuss strode to where they stood, his eyes glittering with interest.

"No, I don't," Klaus replied. "I came to you to ask for your help."

Morgana let go of his face and turned in disgust. "Again you ask for my help and yet you offer me nothing in return. Be gone! And if you ever darken my sight again, I'll feed to you my guards for dinner."

The guard grabbed Klaus by the arm and pulled him back toward the stairs. No. He needed her help. He had to get Chloe back.

"It's my daughter! She's been taken by her mother."

"Not my concern," Morgana called.

The guard dragged Klaus further away as the dragon shifters looked on with mild interest.

"Please! I have to get her back."

"Then get her yourself!"

"I can't. She at a hidden castle. There's a dragon and Dax—"

Morgana flew at him so fast Klaus didn't see her move. She flung the guard away and grabbed Klaus' shirt, lifting him off the floor.

"Kondak? Your daughter is with Kondak?" Her wild red eyes flashed and sparkled. "You know where he is?" Her nostrils flared like a snake's.

He was no fool. Morgana held power that no human could possess, but seeing her in that moment gave him the distinct impression that she was not at all of Fairelle.

"There... There's a castle in the woods east of Westfall. It's old and crumbling—"

Morgana let go of Klaus and he dropped to his feet. She turned to Rasmuss, who joined her side.

"He found his way back."

"What if he's found the mirror?" Rasmuss questioned.

"He'll go home and the spell will be broken." Morgana paced, her dress swishing across the obsidian floor. "I can't have that. I need him."

"Give me your guards. I'll go to the castle and get my daughter, and bring Dax to you," Klaus offered.

Morgana waved him off. "You couldn't do anything right if I compelled you to. This is something I must do myself." Morgana looked around the room. "Prepare. We leave at midnight."

A hushed whispered traveled through the room. The dragon shifters looked one to another, stealing glances at Morgana.

"But mother—" Rasmuss began.

Morgana hit the red stone on her amulet and the dragons' collars lit up like Festivus lights. They cried out and dropped to their knees.

"You will do as I say, or you will die! All of you." Her gaze fell on Rasmuss. "Prepare!"

Rasmuss bowed and turned to bark orders at the dragon shifters as Morgana fled from the room down a small hallway, her dress trailing after her.

Klaus looked around to find the dragon shifters staring at him as they went about preparing to leave. Klaus held his head high and looked at each of them in turn. He didn't care what they thought. They were no more than dogs on leashes. Nothing mattered but Chloe.

Getting Chloe, and killing Belle and Dax.

CHAPTER SEVEN

Belle, Dax and Chloe sat in silence eating the meat pie she'd made. Chloe glanced at Dax several times, but he seemed pre-occupied. The guilt inside Belle almost burst to the surface. She couldn't stand the tension between them.

"Chloe, did you find a book to read?"

She looked at Dax. "I picked one out but forgot it in the library."

Dax glanced up before going back to his food. A sense of unease settled on Belle's shoulders. Suddenly, she no longer felt like his preoccupation had anything to do with her.

"Why did you forget it?" asked Belle. "Did something happen?"

Chloe shrugged. "We found a secret room instead."

"A secret room?"

Chloe frowned. "A bad place."

Dax stood abruptly. "Thank you for dinner. If you will excuse me."

He strode to the dish basin and put his plate and fork inside before taking the stairs two at a time out of the kitchen. Belle looked on as he fled the room. A wash of panic swept over her and she grabbed Chloe's hand.

"Where is the secret room?"

"Behind the books."

"Did Dax go in the room with you?"

Chloe nodded. "It made him sad."

"Chloe, you must tell mommy. What happened in the secret room?"

"Bad things. A long time ago."

Belle's hands shook. She didn't want to ask. "What bad stuff?"

"The bad lady. She hurt Dax in there. He didn't want me to see, so he carried me out, but I felt it. She hurt him a lot."

Belle's gaze went to the stairs. "Chloe, sweetie, you finish your dinner and then please scrub the dishes. I'll be back in a few minutes."

Chloe nodded as Belle walked to the stairs and headed to the first floor. She stopped and looked toward the library, but instead she continued up the second flight to the bedrooms. Butterflies fluttered in her stomach, but she walked down the hallway toward Dax's room anyway. The walls seemed to close in on her the closer she got. Dim candlelight peeked out from under the door and she raised her hand to knock, but stopped.

This wasn't her business. *He* wasn't her business. Yet it

was obvious he was hurting and if she could help him... She lowered her hand and rubbed her sweaty palms on her skirt and then raised her hand again and knocked.

Silence emanated from inside. For a moment, she looked down the hallway wondering if he wasn't in there, but then the bed creaked inside, and she knocked again.

"Dax?"

His heavy steps approached the door and he unlocked it before pulling it open enough for her to see his face, lined with pain.

"Did you need something?"

"No. I... uh... I just wanted to apologize for the way I spoke to you this morning, it was uncalled for."

"Apology excepted." He started to close the door, but she stuck out her hand to stop him. Their eyes connected.

"May I come in?" She expected him to say no, but then he opened the door wider.

She entered the large bedroom decorated in dark blues and purples, as he shut the door behind her. A small fireplace burned low with embers in the corner. An enormous bed took up an entire section of the chilly room. She strode to the fire and poked at it before adding a log. Turning she took in the entirety of the large space. Portraits of people long since dead adorned the walls. Beautifully ornate furniture filled the chamber. The wooden floor had been done in a masterfully intricate design. She got the sense that at some point, it had been the master room.

"I didn't mean for Chloe to see that room," he said. "She discovered it and insisted on seeing it. I wasn't going to let her once I realized what it was, but she snuck in and—"

"Was it *the* room. The room where..." She couldn't finish the question.

The pain in his eyes told her everything.

He dropped onto the bed and hung his head. "It was my prison."

"You were imprisoned here?"

"Memories have been coming back to me in bits and pieces, but being down in that room knocked something loose. Memories that I wish I had kept locked away."

She stared at him not wanting to pry. "I'm sorry," she said. "I know what it is to be a prisoner."

He shook his head. "Not like this."

"We're all prisoners—"

He leapt from the bed so fast she didn't see him come. She stepped back as he stripped his tunic off and flung it to the floor.

"Some of us are prisoners. Some of us are toys in other people's sick games." He turned around and the room swam as she took in the full extent of the scars that she'd glimpsed days before. Long thin lines marred every inch of his back. Some deep red, some white and puckered. They crisscrossed like a lattice work.

"Those are just the physical reminders."

She reached out to touch him, but he spun around before she could. A brand upon his shoulder caught her eye. A dragon inside a shield. "Dax, I'm so—"

"Sorry? I am too."

He picked up his tunic, walked back to the bed and sat again. Tears blurred her eyes as she realized how long it must have taken to get that many scars. Months? Years? He was right. She'd been a prisoner to Klaus' torment, but nothing like that. She hadn't been chained and whipped. If she'd really wanted to, she could have left any time.

She followed him to the bed, trying to find words.

He looked up at her and pushed a tear from her cheek.

His gaze saddened and he took in a heavy breath before shaking his head. "I'm sorry I upset you."

Without thinking Belle stepped between his thighs and hugged him tight. He stiffened for a moment, and then wrapped his large arms around her, pulling her close. She rested her cheek on top of his head and closed her eyes. How could someone *do* that to him? Whip him like livestock. Someone as kind and gentle as Dax. What could he possibly have done to garner such hatred?

Minutes passed as they clung to each other, and she relished in the comfort of being near him. Finally, he let go of her and breathed in a deep lungful of air.

"Who did that to you? Why did they do it?"

He sighed. "A woman named Morgana. A daemon. She wanted me to marry her and I refused. So, she thought she could beat me into it. She was wrong, but that didn't stop her from trying."

Belle let out a bark of laughter. "Is there a race you don't know?"

Dax smiled. "Probably not at this point."

"So that room. That's where she kept you?"

"Two men helped me escape and one of them transported me to Wolvenglen with magick. I remember it finally."

She ran her fingers through his soft hair. "I'm glad they saved you."

He touched her lip where it had healed. "I'm glad you saved yourself."

Their gazes locked and the butterflies in Belle's stomach fluttered. His large calloused hand slid across her cheek to her neck. He squeezed it and massaged the muscles with his large palm. Belle shivered as her heartbeat quickened. His gaze went from gentle to something deeper. Needy. Wanting.

She slid her palm up his solid chest. He pulled her face to his gradually and waited. His breath tickled her skin as their lips lingered inches from each other. Anticipation lit through her like black powder.

She sucked in his sweet breath and then he closed the distance between them. Soft and warm, his lips pressed to hers. Her heart and mind collided in a battle of what she needed versus what she should do. Her heart won out, and she kissed him deeper. He tangled both hands in her hair, planting goosebumps from the top of her head to the tips of her toes. She wrapped her arms around him as he parted her lips with his tongue and drew her bottom lip into his mouth.

Need coursed through Belle and all at once she wanted to feel him; every inch. She crawled onto his lap and ran her hands down his back feeling the scars beneath her fingertips. He stiffened for a moment and then his rough hands roamed over her skirt and he gripped her rear.

She cupped his face as he kissed her deeper. Desire she'd

not felt before flowed through her veins like wine delighting her and making her body ache to be touched.

Dax's lips traversed down her throat to the tops of her breasts and placed soft suckling kisses over her skin. Belle moaned, wanting him to go lower. She needed this. Too long she'd been without tender affection. They both had.

Desire pooled deep inside her and she pulled his mouth to hers again. Pushing him back on the bed she pressed her body against his. Her hand moved down his packed abs to the top of his breeches. She needed him. To feel him. To touch him. To have him inside her. She wanted to show him all the tenderness and passion he'd been denied. To help him to feel the loving embrace of a woman who saw him for who and what he was.

"Mama?"

Belle bolted upright and looked at the door. Chloe knocked on the wood and the handle moved as she jiggled it from the other side, but the door stuck.

"Dax, do you know where mama is?"

Dax looked to Belle and she jumped from the bed. She swayed on the spot, trying to get her mind to quit focusing on the thrumming noise her body made and the desire that rapidly turned to frustration.

"I'll be right there, sweets," Belle called. She tried to concentrate. "Go... get your sleeping gown on."

For a moment Belle heard nothing but the pounding of her heart.

"Can Dax read us a story tonight?"

Belle shook her head. "I—"

"Of course," Dax called.

Belle turned to him and he looked between her and the door. A moment passed.

"She's gone," he said.

Belle let out a huge sigh. The last thing she needed was for Chloe to walk in on them like that. Chloe liked Dax, but they hadn't known each other that long. Hell, what had Belle been thinking? She didn't know him, either.

"Belle—"

No. She couldn't be doing this. She had to get Chloe to safety. "I should help Chloe. You don't have to read to her."

"I told her I would."

Belle nodded, trying to form words. Dax watched her as she backed toward the door. She opened her mouth to tell him again he didn't need to.

"I'll get the book she wanted to read in the library."

Belle reached the door and flipped the lock. Her mind tore between wanting to be near him and the fear of what might happen if she got too close.

Afraid that she might run to him once more, she slipped into the hallway without another word and closed the door. Belle stood for a long moment before resting her forehead on the wood. What the hell was she doing? How had she let herself feel for him over the last week? She'd told herself not to get involved. Not to care. Not to fall into the trap again; but it was too late.

As much as she'd tried to close her heart away, it had flooded wide open and ready for the taking – by a man she barely knew.

DAX HEADED DOWN THE STAIRS REPLAYING THE MOMENTS IN his head before he'd kissed Belle, and fighting the new sensations racing through him. He hadn't meant to. It hadn't been planned, but in that moment, he'd needed connection. Connection to another person who in the slightest way knew his pain. Connection to the beautiful, strong creature who'd invaded his solitude. Connection with Belle. The problem was, now that he'd kissed her, and she'd kissed him back, his bear thought they were meant for each other. Never before had his bear noticed a female. But something had happened when Belle kissed him. The scent of her skin, the taste of her mouth, it lingered on him like expensive soap and left his bear wide awake and wanting.

But he wasn't a wolf, he didn't mate for life. And Belle wasn't a bear. Hell, she didn't even know what he was... which was now one of his biggest problems. How did he tell her without her running screaming? And how did he get his bear to back down? His head and gut tied in knots tighter than when he'd remembered the room. Suddenly, his problems were no longer based on his past, but firmly planted in the present.

He entered the library and walked to the back where Chloe had dropped her books. He picked them up and fought the urge to go down and look at the room that had once been his prison. And more than that, to open the portal on the mirror that resided there as well. The one that called to him like a lighthouse beacon. He knew in his gut that the mirror could be the answer to his past, but now that he'd found it, strangely, he wasn't sure he was ready to deal with it.

He stared at the wall for several minutes, then turned away and walked out of the library. He looked at the book Chloe had chosen. A mythical tale of a dragon lost in a new world, and a picture book about a dragon afraid of flying. He stared at the books and shook his head. Belle wasn't going to be happy about Chloe's choices.

He headed up the stairs to Chloe and Belle's room, trying to keep his mind off how Belle's soft lips felt pressed against his. How her curvy body molded into his hands as he'd grabbed her rear. Something he should not have done. And wondering what her body would feel like, pressed under his; naked, slick and soft.

He stopped on the stairs. Dammit, she would think him just a common man after one thing from her. Guilt swept over him at the realization. She'd been through enough, she didn't need him lusting all over her as well. Not when she'd just gotten away from that rat Klaus.

He crept up the rest of the stairs. *Not again.* He wouldn't do anything like that again. Not unless she initiated would he try to pursue something with her. It wasn't fair.

He knocked on their door and Chloe threw it open. "Mama, he found them." She clapped her hands and jumped up on her big bed.

Belle emerged from behind a screen in her sleeping gown, her hair braided down her back. Dax's gaze traveled her body noticing the ripe peaks firm and round underneath her chemise. He cleared his throat and looked away as she slipped under the blanket and pulled Chloe next to her.

Chloe patted the spot on the other side. "You sit here, next to me so I can see the pictures."

Dax smiled. "Yes, ma'am." He arranged himself on the bed and propped his feet up before looking over at Belle. An expression planted on her face that he couldn't read. He wanted to apologize for kissing her, but Chloe pulled the picture book from his hands and pointed to the dragon.

"Look Mama, a dragon."

Belle's gaze shifted to the book and Dax followed it, reading the title.

Chloe held the book as Dax read, stopping him every once in a while to point something out. Soon though, her eyelids drooped and her head fell against Belle's breast.

Dax took the book and closed it.

"Thank you for reading to her," Belle whispered.

He nodded and got up. "My pleasure."

He got up and took a step toward the door.

"Dax."

He turned, and Belle stared at him conflicted.

"I—"

"It's all right," he said. "I understand."

Her brows knit together. "You do?"

"Yes. And I want to apologize. It was wrong of me to kiss you like that and to... man handle you. I didn't mean to be so disrespectful."

"Disrespectful?"

"It won't happen again. I promise. Not unless you want it to."

"Do *you* want it to?"

His bear grumbled in his chest to tell her how he felt. "I've been here a long time and I've been alone for even longer."

"Are you saying you only kissed me because you haven't been with a woman in a long time?"

"No." He wasn't doing it right. Wasn't saying it right. "No, it's not that, it's just... I... don't know how to do this."

"Do what?"

"Whatever it is that we are doing. Or not doing." He held up his hands and took a deep breath. "I am going to go now. I think I have said enough for one night."

"But you haven't said anything," she mused.

"Even worse. Goodnight."

Before he could put his foot in his mouth any further Dax strode from the room and closed the door. He laid his head back on it for a moment and shook his head.

He could swear from the other side he heard Belle chuckle.

CHAPTER EIGHT

"Mama. Mama wake up."

Belle roused to Chloe shaking her. "What's the matter, sweets?"

"People are outside."

Belle looked to the still darkened sky. Something flickered in the distance. She sprung from the bed and ran to the window. Glowing lights moved through the trees.

"Get your clothes on," Belle shouted. "And your boots."

She raced from the room and down the hallway. Dax's door threw open and he stepped out already dressed.

"There are people—"

"I heard them."

Heard them? How could he hear them?

"We should leave, now," she said.

"There's no reason to. They can't get in. They probably don't even know the castle is here."

"In the months you've been here how many people have you seen?"

"You and Chloe, and the wolves."

"And aside from us how many times have you seen an entire group of people? At night? In two feet of snow?"

He stared at her for a moment. "Point taken. You and Chloe gather your things. I'll go see. But stay in the castle. Promise me."

"What if it's Klaus?"

He squeezed her arm. "He's not taking Chloe and he won't hurt you. I promise." She nodded and ran back to her room.

Already dressed Chloe shoved her two books into Belle's bag.

"It's Daddy, isn't it?" she said.

"I don't know, sweets." Belle chucked off her chemise and grabbed her breeches and tunic. "Dax is going to protect us."

"I know," said Chloe. "He always will."

DAX RACED DOWN TO THE KITCHEN AND OUT THE SIDE door. He sniffed the air; they were drawing close. The desire to shift rippled through him, but he fought the urge. He raced down the path to the front of the castle. Lights, over a dozen of them, edged toward the castle. Dax raced toward them, careful to stay as quiet as possible. No voices floated back to him, only the sounds of fabric and weapons moving. When he was within a hundred yards he stopped and climbed the nearest tree. Peering out at the group, his heart froze. Morgana marched behind two dozen of her dragon guards and at her side, walked Klaus. A rumble grew deep in Dax's chest. He fought to keep from shifting as they advanced through the thick wood. He needed to get back to the castle. He needed to get to Belle.

The group marched less than thirty yards away, heading straight for him. Morgana knew where she was headed. There was no chance trying to trick her. The best thing he could do, was run.

An ear-splitting shriek sounded overhead and Dax looked up to find Rasmuss on his dragon directly above.

"Mother, he's in the trees!" Rasmuss yelled.

"Find him!" she shouted. "Capture Kondak and bring him to me!"

The dragon guard stopped moving, but then their collars lit up the night and they raced forward. Dax jumped to the next tree and ran across the branches to the following tree. Above him Rasmuss cast a spell and an arc of blue lightning hit the tree Dax jumped to, splitting the branch and toppling him to the ground. He hit a snow-covered rock with a crack and his mind fogged over. Dazed, his bear refused to hold back any longer. It tore through Dax like a cleaver, ripping his clothing to shreds. Dax roared into the night as the guard advanced upon him. Armed with nets, two guards ran at Dax and threw them toward him. He backed up and jumped out of the way, the nets narrowly missing him.

"Don't harm him!" Morgana shouted. "I want him alive."

The two guards advanced and one of them stopped short. "We're sorry, M'lord. We don't want to do this."

"Run," the second hissed. "Get out of here Thaddeus."

Confused Dax shook his head.

Two more dragon guards advanced and the first guard punched Dax on the snout. "Get out of here before she captures you. Use the mirror. Go! Save us, break the curse."

A name popped into Dax's mind. *Hunter.* The man's name was Hunter.

Hunter raised his fist again and Dax turned and ran back for the castle. Behind him, shouting ensued, as did a cry of pain. Dax raced through the trees while the rustle of Rasmuss' dragon's wings followed him overhead. Another arc of blue lightning shot down and Dax rolled out of the way at the last minute. A tree next to him cracked in two, and fell over.

When the castle sprang in sight Dax sprinted for it, but Rasmuss swooped down in front of him, barring his path.

"Sorry old friend, mother wants a word with you."

Dax roared, and his roar was echoed by Alabrax. Rasmuss turned to see the dragon glide onto the roof of the castle and climb across it.

"My gods!" said Rasmuss. "Where did you come from, little one?"

Dax used Alabrax's distraction to run underneath Rasmuss' dragon and head for the side door of the kitchen. The dragon guard raced after him.

"Grab him!" Rasmuss yelled. "Don't let him get to the mirror!"

Dax roared again and Alabrax answered the call. Over

Dax's shoulder he saw Alabrax swoop down on the dragon guard, knocking several of them to the ground. Two of them cried out as they set off traps and were sucked down through the ground.

"Traps," Rasmuss yelled. "Use the front door."

Dax called Alabrax and the dragon glided to a stop next to him as Dax lumbered into the kitchen. Belle screamed and backed away. Alabrax followed Dax through the door and Dax pushed it shut with his body. Belle grabbed a carving knife from the counter and brandished it.

"No Mama," said Chloe. "It's Dax."

Belle stared at Dax wide-eyed. This wasn't the way he'd wanted her to find out the truth, but it didn't matter anymore. Three of the dragon guard ran at the kitchen door. Chloe raced to it and locked it so they couldn't get in. Alabrax screeched and clawed at the door, wanting to get out.

Dax pushed his inner bear away as his bones cracked and he got to his feet. Belle grabbed Chloe and adverted her eyes as Dax resumed his human form.

"You're a— You're a— a—"

"A werebear. I'm sorry. This wasn't how I intended on telling you."

Banging came from the front door and then yelling which subsided as they set off the portal trap to the basement.

"We have to go." Dax dashed up the stairs.

"Go where?" Belle ran after him.

"Out of this castle." He raced down the hallway to his room and grabbed a pair of breeches from the wardrobe.

The sounds of metal clattering downstairs pulled his attention. Dax pulled on his pants and tunic and then grabbed the book from Zelle's tower and his journal and ran back to the kitchen. Belle shoved her tools and pieces back into her bag as Chloe stood with Alabrax.

"How are we going to get out?" Belle questioned.

"The mirror," said Chloe.

Dax shoved his books in Belle's bag and picked up Chloe. Grabbing Belle's hand, he dragged her down the stairs.

"Dax. How are we going to get out of here?" Belle pleaded.

Morgana's slaves banged on the door to the kitchen as Rasmuss' dragon roared from above.

Dax whistled and Alabrax lumbered up the stairs to meet them on the first floor, just inside the front door. Chanting stopped Dax in his tracks. The door began to glow with an eerie red light and the walls shook as Morgana removed the traps. Alabrax hissed and Dax's bear roared, wanting to be let out to feast on Morgana's organs.

"What the hell is that?" asked Belle, her voice shaky.

They were out of time. Dax raced down the hallway pulling Belle behind him. He kicked open the library door and raced to the back wall. Alabrax screeched as he ran into rows of books knocking over the shelves.

"Come on boy," Dax yelled. "Cinder's store room was tighter than this."

He rounded the last corner and dropped Chloe to her feet. Running to the small shelf he shoved it out of the way. Pressing on the panel he forced it open, and the three of them bounded down the stone stairs. Dax took a deep breath as he entered the torture chamber. He picked up Chloe and crossed to the mirror, forcing himself not to look around and shoving Chloe's face into his chest to keep her from seeing it as well.

"My gods," Belle gasped.

Dax pushed the red stone on the top of the mirror. "Don't look, Belle."

Belle stood stunned, staring at the shackles on the wall. "Is... Is... that?"

Dax crossed to her and cradled her face, pulling her gaze to his. "Focus on me. Don't look at it."

She stared at him, her jaw dropping open. He could see on her face she was putting it all together. Playing in her mind what she thought had been done to him. But even her imagination couldn't begin to see the horrors that had taken place. The shackles and the blood were nothing compared to the devices that Morgana had kept in the wardrobe next to the bed.

"We need to go," he said.

"Go where?"

Dax pulled her to the mirror. The same ballroom shone through.

Belle gasped, "What is that?"

"A magick mirror."

Somewhere up above an explosion rocked the castle. Dust rained down upon them and Chloe screamed. Alabrax whimpered and nudged closer to them.

"This isn't going to feel good," said Dax. "But trust me. I'm going to protect you."

"Chloe? Chloe!" Klaus yelled from the floor above.

"We have to go, now." Dax grabbed Belle by the hand. "Whatever you do, don't let go of me. And don't lose your bag."

She nodded, terror flashing in her eyes.

Dax whistled. "Alabrax. Come on."

The dragon lumbered toward them as footsteps rushed across the library floor. Dax took a deep breath. There was no more time to wait. No time to process. No time to weigh his options. If they stayed, they died, or worse. They didn't.

He jumped into the mirror.

Every particle of his body pushed together and like an enormous hand, the pressure squeezed every inch of him. Belle's mouth opened in a scream, but nothing came out. Chloe clung to his neck enhancing the fact that he couldn't breathe. The room with all the pictures loomed closer. Closer. Closer... And then they were out. The group toppled to the floor and sucked in a huge, collective breath. A moment later, Alabrax flew through the mirror and skidded to a stop half way across the room. Belle flipped to her hands and knees and heaved, but nothing came up. Dax pried Chloe loose and pushed her toward Belle.

"Stay. Here."

Belle heaved again, grabbing onto Chloe.

Alabrax tried to stand but fell back down again. Dax staggered to his feet and hurried to the mirror. Voices echoed from inside it. They were on their way.

Dax punched the red stone on the mirror, but nothing happened. He pushed it again, but it still glowed red.

"Dammit!"

The voices grew louder.

Dax grabbed the stone and pulled on it.

The shouts were almost upon them.

The stone wiggled. He allowed his claws to lengthen and he dug them under the stone and yanked with all of his strength. Faces flashed into view on the mirror. Klaus and several of the dragon guard.

"Come on, dammit!" Dax bellowed. He roared and leaned back using his weight for leverage. With a crack and the stone flew through the air and landed next to Belle. Dax fell to the floor. The edges of the mirror dimmed as the faces grew closer and closer.

Just as he could make out their forms, the mirror darkened until he saw nothing more than his reflection.

He jumped to his feet and punched the mirror, shattering the glass.

The sounds of marching footsteps pounded down the hallway outside the large ballroom.

Dax helped Belle to her feet and whistled for Alabrax. He picked up the red stone and dropped it into Belle's bag just as the doors flung open. An entire armed guard marched into the room, swords drawn and pointed right at them.

They wore green and purple crests depicting a dragon flying. Like everything else, it was familiar, but he couldn't place it all the way.

"What's going on?" Came a female voice from the hallway.

"Go back to bed, Aurora," answered a familiar male voice.

"Darling, are you sure you should go in there?" The mature female voice struck Dax in the heart.

"Of course." A tall man with blond hair and piercing hazel eyes strode forward. He pushed the guard out of the way as he approached.

"Who are you? How did you get in— a dragon." He stopped in the middle of the room.

Behind him, a beautiful woman with long brown hair entered carrying a large candelabra. A third person marched in and stopped by the other two. Dax took in the three of them. They'd aged, but there was no mistaking them. He knew them.

The third was *her*. The girl from his dreams. She stared at him for a moment, then her eyes widened and she smiled. "Thad?"

The beautiful woman gasped.

The girl strode forward and then stopped. Her eyes filled with tears and she rushed the last couple of feet to Dax, throwing her arms around him.

"Thad! You're alive!"

He hugged her tight. "Aurora." *Aurora.* His little sister.

The man and woman rushed forward as well and embraced him.

"My son," the woman cried. "My son is home."

Like a curtain being pushed back to let in the morning light, a veil rolled off Dax's mind. Memories flooded him. His entire childhood, adolescence and adulthood up to five years previous. *Playing in the castle. Teasing his sister Aurora. Jousting with his men, and romping with women. Laughter. Love. Happiness.*

He grabbed onto them tight and the years melted away. "MaMaw. PaPaw."

The group shed tears until the sniffles became too great and turned into laughter. Each one hugged him in turn and lastly, his father.

"My son. I never thought I'd see you again."

"And I you," Dax replied.

"Sound the bells," his father called. "Raise the lanterns. Let the whole kingdom know! Prince Thaddeus has returned to Draakland."

A guard raced from the room shouting down the hallway of Dax's return.

He'd scarily began to process the happenings around him. Home. He'd finally returned home. After so many years of searching and hoping, he'd never actually thought he'd find it, and yet standing in the great hall, it was as if he'd never left to begin with.

His mother took his face in her hands. "My baby boy. I feared I would never see your handsome face again."

Dax placed his hands over hers. "Nor I yours."

The bells rang out across the castle. Loud and shrill they shook the entire building. In the distance, he heard the sound of a familiar horn. The horn of battle that signaled to the kingdom that the men were returning home. Dax smiled at the sound he'd heard a thousand times, hailing the return of him and his men. His men... Hunter. It flooded back. The dragon guard that Morgana used. They were his dragon riders. His men.

Aurora hugged him again and he squeezed her tight. "I missed you, little sister."

"And I you, you big burly bear."

Was that where Morgana had gotten the idea to turn him into a bear? From his sister's nickname? Oh, how surprised she would be to find out he really was a bear. Probably even more surprised than—

Dax glanced over at Belle, who stood apart and stared at him like she was just seeing him for the first time. His heart reached for her and ached to pull her close and tell her that everything was going to be all right. But the expression on her face told him that being hugged by him was the last thing she wanted.

CHAPTER NINE

Belle stared at the scene unable to speak. Dax was prince of Draakland? A numbness blanketed her body and she hugged Chloe closer to her side. Even Alabrax edged closer to them. She couldn't take much more. Klaus was friends with the daemon who had imprisoned and tortured Dax. Dax was a bear and a prince. She didn't know whether to laugh or scream. How small her world had been just weeks prior in their little cabin. It felt like she'd blinked her eyes and suddenly her entire existence had changed. Dragons. Werewolves. Werebears. Princes. Daemons... what else?

After what felt like an unending night, Dax turned to her bearing a smile so bright, he looked like a different person.

"Where are my manners? I'm so sorry. Mother, father, this is Belle and Chloe." He motioned them forward, but Belle stayed planted on the spot.

The king smiled and it was like looking into Dax's face thirty years in the future.

"My dear, it is lovely to meet you." The king swept forward and took Belle's hand in his. "Any loved one of Thaddeus's is one of our own."

The king looked at Chloe and then at Belle again. The gears turned in his head as surely as they did in one of Belle's clocks.

Dax stepped forward. "Belle is my—"

"Friend," Belle finished. "Dax saved us."

Dax gave her a quizzical look.

The queen rushed forward. "Of course he did. That's just like Thaddeus." She knelt in front of Chloe. "Hello dear one. I'm Queen Caralyna."

"I'm Chloe. I'm five but I'm going to be six in nine months."

The queen chuckled. "It's very nice to meet you Chloe." The queen stood once more. "You as well, Belle."

Belle gave a tight smile unsure how to respond. A warble came from Alabrax and Belle turned to find Princess Aurora petting the dragon.

"He likes you," Chloe said. "He thinks you're pretty."

Everyone chuckled and a pit grew in Belle's stomach. She needed to get Chloe out of there.

She lifted Chloe into her arms and whispered, "Remember what I said about telling people things?"

Chloe nodded.

"I don't understand," said the queen, turning back to Dax. "Where have you been? And how did you get here?"

Dax pointed to the broken mirror. "It's a magick mirror.

Connected to a myriad of other mirrors throughout Fairelle."

"A magick mirror?" asked the king. "But... it was a simple gift from Lady Morgana back when—"

"And was how Morgana kidnapped me, as well."

Dax's mother stifled a cry and the king put his arm around her.

"It's a story I will definitely tell you." Dax strode to Belle and placed his hand on the small of her back. "But not tonight. We should find Belle and Chloe a room. It's been a rough and unsettling evening for all of us."

Belle wanted nothing more than to bolt out of the castle and make a run for it. If the daemon Morgana knew where they'd gone, then Klaus knew where they were, too. They were sitting ducks in Draakland.

Chloe yawned. "I'm tired, Mama."

"Yes, of course," replied the queen. "We can have a room readied immediately." She snapped her fingers and two maids appeared out of nowhere. "Ready a room for Lady Belle and Miss Chloe."

The maids nodded and bustled across the large hall.

"Next to mine," Dax called.

The maids turned and looked at the queen.

"Why are you looking to me?" she asked. "My son has spoken."

The maids took off at twice the speed.

In the corner of the ballroom a young man walked out of a flash of light surrounded by a puff of smoke. Belle jumped at the sight, but the others simply turned to the newcomer. He strode across the floor, his long brown robe flowing around him. Fear dripped down Belle's spine as he approached Dax looking him up and down.

"I heard the news. They said you had returned but I didn't believe it," said the man.

"I told you he was still alive," said Aurora. "You gave up hope."

"No." The man shook his head. "Not hope. I never gave up hope." He stepped closer to Dax and the two men stared at each other. His long robe belied the fact that he'd been in bed when he'd received the news.

Dax walked forward, closing the distance between them. He placed his heavy hands on the man's shoulders. "Stil."

The two men embraced.

Dax pushed Stil to arms' length. "Look at you. A full-fledged Mage now."

"He's in charge at the mage towers," said Aurora.

"Second in charge," Stil corrected.

"With how the Head Mage has been going absent so frequently, you might as well be," she retorted.

Dax laughed. "You two are ever the same."

"Where have you been?" Stil asked. "What happened to you?"

Dax's muscles tensed. It was too soon for him to recount all he'd recently remembered.

Belle stepped forward. "Dax, I would like to get Chloe settled."

He turned to her and squeezed her hand, a look of gratitude playing across his features.

"Of course," said the king. "We have all the time in

Fairelle now to find out where Thaddeus has been these last years. It is late and we should all get some rest."

"I'll not get any rest," said Aurora. "I've waited five years, six months and two days for this moment. You think I'm going to sleep after all this?"

"Agreed," said the queen.

Dax threw his arm around Aurora's shoulder. "Your image kept me going all these years, little sister. I couldn't remember who you were, but I knew I had to find you."

She hugged him tight, her blonde hair cascading over his arms.

Chloe tugged on Belle's arm. She picked up her little girl and Chloe's head dropped onto her shoulder.

"You probably knew what kind of trouble she kept getting herself into and felt the need to come back and protect her like always," said Stil.

Brother and sister broke apart, chuckling.

"Dax, can I go to bed now?" Chloe yawned. "I'm tired. So is Alabrax."

"Wait," said Stil. "Did she call you Dax? As in, the Dax that helped Cinder?" He whirled on Alabrax. "Is that the dragon Cinder made?"

Dax nodded. "Dax is... a nickname. I lost my memory and so everyone took to calling me Kondak."

"Like the bear?" asked Aurora.

Dax nodded again and Stil clapped him on the shoulder. "We have much to catch up on."

Belle's stomach tied in knots. She wished that she had family who wondered where she and Chloe had been the past year, let alone years. People who cared about her and her well-being. People who sounded bells and trumpets when she returned. The Gwyns were always more than welcoming when she went to them but they had their own problems of late.

The thoughts made her cheeks heat with shame. She should be happy for Dax. Happy that he'd reunited with his family and his home, but somehow the idea struck her with sadness. Before she'd felt connected to him because of what they'd both been through, but now... now she wasn't sure.

"Come," said the queen. "Aurora, you and I can go down and get some tea to help calm our nerves while Thaddeus helps Belle and Chloe to their room."

"What about Alabrax?" Chloe asked.

The group looked at the dragon who had curled into a ball to sleep.

"He'll be all right for the night," Dax smiled. "We can find him a better place in the morning."

Belle gaped at all of the glittery surfaces in the castle. Never in her life had she seen so much finery. Even the queen's sleeping gown was more beautiful and expensive than everything Belle owned put together. Not that she owned anything anymore. What little belongings she had left were in the small satchel at her side.

The news of Dax's return had most definitely spread because it seemed every person in the castle had lined the hallways to bow or curtsey as he passed. Belle felt awkward as ever walking at his side, but as all eyes were on him and not her, she did her best to ignore the circumstances.

Finally, they reached the upper most level of the castle where half a dozen servants waited.

Belle stepped to the side as the king and queen said good night to Dax, hugging and kissing him repeatedly before heading off with Aurora.

"I am assuming you know where your room is," said Stil.

"I have a general idea."

"Then I will let you get some sleep." Stil turned to leave.

"Actually," said Dax. "I'm not all that tired. I wonder if maybe you might stay for a bit."

Stil smiled. "Of course."

"Let me just get Belle and Chloe settled and I'll meet you in my room."

Stil bowed to Belle and then excused himself, heading to the last door at the end of the hallway. Dax stopped at the room next to it and opened the large white double doors into a beautiful yellow and pink space. Belle gulped at the sight. She walked inside and set Chloe down. Chloe ran to a large golden clock on a table.

"Mama, look!" She reached out to touch it.

"Chloe, don't touch. You don't want to break it."

Chloe pulled her hand away and looked around. She ran to a large candelabra that sat on another table and reached for it.

"Chloe, please don't touch that either."

Dax squeezed her shoulder. "Belle, it's all right, she can touch things."

"This room is highly inappropriate for a child," she huffed.

Dax's eyebrows knit together. "Why?"

"Because... because everything in here begs to be touched and yet it cannot be."

He crossed his arms over his chest and a smile played at the corners of his mouth. "I grew up in a room just like this one and I promise there isn't anything in here that if broken cannot be replaced."

"Exactly," Belle blurted.

They stared at each other for a moment. He didn't understand. They hadn't been raised with such finery. It was like living in a hall of antiquities. Pretty things to look at, none of which could be touched. And just the idea that if Chloe did and it broke, that the value placed upon it was so little that they could just replace it with a wave of their hands was too foreign to her.

"We don't belong here," Belle whispered.

"Why would you say that?"

"I'm a common girl from a small village."

"So?"

"And you're a prince!"

Dax stared at her for a moment. "Isn't that what you said you always wanted? A prince to sweep you off your feet?"

Her cheeks heated. Since when did he want to sweep her off her feet? "Aren't you the one who said it wasn't all glittery dresses and fancy parties?"

"A title doesn't change who I am."

She crossed her arms over her breasts. "A werebear?"

He held up his hands and nodded. "I admit I should have told you that sooner. But I didn't expect us to—"

"To what?"

Dax glanced in Chloe's direction. "To become friends."

"I knew," said Chloe.

They both looked at her as she crawled up on the large bed and climbed under the covers.

"I knew all along." She closed her eyes and yawned.

Silence stretched between them as they watched Chloe drift off to sleep. For the first time in a long time, Belle entertained the idea of asking Chloe what their future held. If they would be safe with Dax or if they should run. Would Klaus come for them?

She pushed the what ifs away. She had never once used Chloe's gift. She'd promised herself, and Chloe, that she never would. She refused to break that promise.

"I'm sorry I didn't tell you," said Dax. "But honestly, can you think of a good way to tell someone something like that?"

Belle opened her mouth and then closed it again. Her shoulders sagged. She supposed not.

Dax stepped closer to her and pushed a strand of hair from her cheek.

"You and Chloe will be safe here. Just give it a little time for you to adjust. Here, you and Chloe could have a life. A real life with people who care about you. A place where you never have to be afraid. Don't dismiss that so easily."

"Are you asking me to marry you?"

"No. I'm asking you to realize you are worth loving and you are deserving of happiness. Same with Chloe."

Was he saying he loved her? She wasn't sure whether she wanted him to be saying that or not. And she wasn't going to ask.

Belle looked to her sleeping little girl. How many years had she dreamed of being a princess? Living in a castle. No cares, no worries. Safe and protected. For the first time in her life, looking at Chloe sleep in a warm, soft bed, she felt a small sense of peace.

"We will stay, for now."

"Thank you."

"But. You must promise me that you will not tell your friend Stil about Chloe's abilities."

"But Stil—"

"It's my only stipulation. He cannot know about her. If he finds out, he'll take her for sure."

"He would never do that."

Agitation rattled around in Belle's brain making her want to run right then. "That's right I don't know him. I know you and I am trusting *you* with her secret. If you don't promise, we will leave right now."

"All right." He pulled her into a hug. "All right. I won't tell him."

Despite everything, Belle clung to Dax. A bear shifter. A bear shifter prince, but in that moment, as she closed her eyes they were back in the ruined castle, just the three of them and he was holding her. The feeling of belonging swept over her; Chloe and Dax were all she had. She had to trust him. Dax was all that stood between her and Klaus with his sorceress and army of dragons.

Dax calmed Belle and said goodnight, showing her where he would be if she needed anything at all. Then he walked to his own room. For as difficult as it was to wrap his head around what he'd lost, and who he was, he could see in her eyes it was equally as hard for her. They may not be married or romantically involved even, but over the past week they'd become fast friends and confidants. Learning that the person you've opened up to isn't who you thought was more than a shock, he knew. He'd seen it with Zelle and Flint.

Dax stood outside the door to his old bedroom and stared at it. It'd been over five years since he'd stepped foot in there. Part of him hoped nothing had changed, the other part of him hoped it had.

Hand shaking, he turned the knob. Inside he found the room exactly how he remembered. Deep blues colored every surface. A stag's head hung on the wall above his bed. Several more, smaller animals stood stuffed around the room. It seemed cruel to him now that with the exception of the stag, he'd not killed even one of the other animals for food, simply for the pleasure of it. First thing in the morning he would have the maids take it all away. The sight, disturbing to him, would be even more disturbing to Belle and Chloe.

"Strange to see it all still here, isn't it," asked Stil.

Dax spotted Stil on the small couch near the fire. He closed the door and crossed to join him.

The old friends stared at each other for a long minute. His face still held the same brown mischievous eyes and boyish grin that Dax had grown up with. He'd sprouted facial hair since Dax had seen him last but then, so had Dax.

"It was Morgana wasn't it?" asked Stil.

Dax nodded.

"I knew when she took control of the dragon guard that she'd grabbed you too, but I couldn't prove it; and finding her has been impossible."

Dax nodded, having seen Morgana's power too many times over.

"But you escaped," said Stil.

"A couple of the dragon guard set me free. She wiped my memory as a parting gift though so that I couldn't find my way back here."

"But you did."

"Only because of—" he stopped. He'd promised Belle he wouldn't mention Chloe. "Because of a mere coincidence. Finding Cinder in the castle allowed me to find my way here."

"So where have you been all this time?"

"With the wolves up north. Then the vampires. I traveled around Fairelle a bit with my friend Flint Gwyn and then went to Ville De Fee."

Stil sat forward, a wry smile on his face. "Is that how you met Cinder? Through Flint Gwyn?"

Dax nodded. "She helped free his wife from a tower and told Flint that she could help me with my memory loss. I was there when she faced the trials."

"Wait!" Stil held up his hands. "The girl in the tower?"

"Zelle, yes."

"I made the powder used to get her out." Stil's mouth hung open.

"Isn't that interesting," Dax mused.

"And you were with Cinder when she performed the trials?"

"In disguise. The Gwyns helped Rome and I rescue her after she'd been kidnapped."

Stil leaned forward and hung his head in his hands. "How's it possible that our paths crossed but never met so many times over?"

It was strange, for sure.

"I was here when Cinder was kidnapped. I counseled Aurora extensively while you were gone. Tried to keep her from running off to find you. It would have killed your mother to lose you both."

"I thank you for that. I would never want anything to happen to my sister. Tell me," said Dax. "What has happened here since my disappearance?"

Stil blew out a long breath and sat back on the couch. "Too much to recount in one night. Morgana took the dragon guard and you as their captain. She turned them on us, forcing them to ravage the crops and eat the livestock. The entire kingdom had almost starved to death when about a year ago, everything stopped. The attacks. The killings. The plundering. All of it."

"She stopped because of Zelle and myself, I would assume."

"I don't understand," Stil shook his head.

"Zelle is Morgana's daughter. She'd been draining Zelle's power and using it to power the stones she uses to control the dragon guard. But that has stopped since you helped us free Zelle. I can only assume that Morgana's power is now weakening. In truth, I'd not seen her do anything in the last year. Cinder's stepmother and her uncle were two more of Morgana's children, but they're gone now as well. She can't have many children left out there."

"We had no idea that her influence had spread so far."

"Morgana is a cancer on this land. She needs to be destroyed," Dax leaned forward, his words falling like a lightning strike.

"I agree with you," said Stil. "But we must be smart, otherwise we could end up with another Fairelle war that blows an entire city into a wasteland."

CHAPTER TEN

Dax stood outside Belle's door the next morning more fatigued than he'd been since being with Flint. He and Stil had spent most of the night talking. He'd only gotten a few hours' sleep before rising with the sun. He stared at the door, trying to figure out how to help Belle see that the Draaklands were the best and safest place for both her and Chloe. He raised his hand and tapped on the door.

"It's Dax," Chloe called. Her tiny feet slapped on the floor as she ran to the door.

"Chloe, wait!"

The door flew open and Chloe stood in front of him in a beautiful tiny gown made of white satin and lace with a beautiful pink bow.

"Come help me." Chloe pulled him into the room.

Dax chuckled as the tiny girl dragged him in and slammed the door behind him.

"What do you need help with?"

Chloe pointed across the room. Dax looked over to find Belle standing by the bed, half dressed.

He turned away. "I'm so sorry."

"It's fine," said Belle. "It's just..."

He glanced over his shoulder. She half wore a beautiful champagne colored gown.

"I can't lace this up," she finally said.

"See," said Chloe. "She needs help."

Dax looked between them. "Oh. Of course." He crossed to Belle and she turned around for him to lace her up. Underneath the dress she wore nothing but pantaloons. Her soft peachy back made his fingers itch to touch her skin. To kiss her slender neck and—

"If you can't do it, it's all right. I'll just wear my regular clothes."

Dax cleared his throat. "No. I have it."

Trembling, he looped the laces through the holes and pulled them snug.

"Uh... how tight do you want it?"

"Not too tight. It's not like I'm trying to show off for anyone. Everyone already knows by now that I'm an unwed mother."

Dax stopped. "Don't say that. No one is talking about you."

She glanced over her shoulder at him. "You should have seen the maids practically giggling at me this morning. Eyeing Chloe. Wondering if she is yours, or if I'm—"

"Stop." He laid his hand on her shoulder. "You know you aren't whatever it is you were going to say. And I know you aren't that either. Maids, butlers, lords, ladies, stable masters, bar wenches, clothing merchants, all of them are going to gossip. About you, and about me. Where have I been? What have I been doing? Why did I leave? Why did I come back? If it makes it easier, I'll tell them you are my wife and Chloe is our child. No more questions."

She stared at him over her shoulder and for a split second, he thought she might say yes. Instead she shook her head and faced forward again. "I won't have my indiscretions messing up your life any more than it already has."

Dax snorted. "You think you have messed up my life? If anything, you've fixed it. If it hadn't been for Chloe I never would have gotten here." He continued to lace the dress to the top, trying to keep his mind off how he'd rather be dropping the gown to the floor and covering Belle with his body.

"If anyone here makes you feel like anything less than the highborn woman you are, you just tell me and I'll deal with it."

Belle nodded but Dax knew she wouldn't tell him. It had been the fit of frustration that had caused her to say anything in the first place. Either way, Dax would not have her or Chloe feel one ounce of embarrassment for who they were or what they'd been through. Belle had endured more in the past months than most noble women could stomach in their lifetimes.

He finished lacing her up and then stepped away. Belle turned and looked at him, making his breeches grow too tight. Her modest dress cut just low enough that he could glimpse the tops of her breasts. It hugged her curvy figure, accentuating every line to his great pleasure.

"Is something wrong?" she asked. "Something is wrong, isn't it? I look ridiculous. I knew I would. As soon as the servants walked in with all those dresses I just knew."

"Belle." He grabbed her hands. "You look beautiful."

"See Mama, I told ya." Chloe smiled and twirled in her dress.

"Let's go get something to eat and I can show you around," Dax said.

Belle licked her lips and ran her fingers through her wavy mane. "I suppose we should eat."

"I'm starving," said Chloe. "Do you have any tarts? Or oatcakes? Or eggs with squishy centers?"

"I'm sure we have all of those. Why don't we go see?" Dax picked Chloe up and she rubbed her face into his and kissed his cheek.

"Wait a moment." Belle looked him up and down. "Why is it that we have to wear these fancy gowns and you get to wear a plain blue tunic and breeches?"

"I, well... I mean..." Dax took a deep breath. "I have no idea. If you'd like I can unlace you and you may wear the clothes you came with, if you are more comfortable."

Belle patted down her dress and ran her fingers over the embroidery for a moment. "Seems a pity to just take it off after all the work we had to do to get me in it. I suppose I can wear it for a little while."

Dax fought the urge to smile and instead inclined his head. "Of course."

He turned and walked with Chloe to the door, no longer able to hold back his smile. Chloe giggled.

"Are you laughing at me?" Belle demanded.

"Who me? No," said Dax. "I make it a point to never giggle like a little girl when I can help it."

Belle frowned, and Chloe giggled again.

Dax opened the door and stepped into the hallway before breaking into a fit of laugher right along side Chloe.

"I can hear you," Belle called.

Dax and Chloe laughed harder.

BELLE FOUGHT TO NOT PULL AND PUSH ON THE DRESS, BUT she wasn't used to that kind of constraining material; no matter how soft and expensive.

They walked down the long hallway to the stairs with Dax pointing out every picture that hung on the walls and telling Chloe what they were about. Walking behind them and watching how Dax acted with Chloe made Belle's heart melt. She remembered a time when Klaus had been loving and patient with Chloe. Teaching her how to ride a pony and how to swim in the lake. The thought made her gut clench.

Memories from the night before flooded back. Seeing Klaus' face in the mirror. Knowing that he was coming for Chloe, not because he cared for her, but because he considered her his property. Belle wondered if he remained trapped between this mirror and the other? Destined to never surface again? For as much as she hated Klaus, the thought of him floating in nothingness for the rest of his life seemed harsh, even for him.

The group stopped on the floor below and Dax pointed

to a large portrait of an imposing man. The portrait stood close to eight feet tall and spanned four full-grown men.

"That's my grandfather Theodor," said Dax.

"He's really big."

Dax chuckled. "He was big, but not that big."

"That's your father's father, isn't it?" Belle asked.

"How did you know?" Dax looked at her.

"Because you favor him greatly."

Dax looked up at the portrait. "Do I?"

"Thaddeus, there you are." The queen strode down the hall toward them. "We wanted to let you sleep but our guests have become quite anxious to see you."

"Guests?"

The queen nodded and took his arm. "Many nobles have come to welcome you home. As a matter of fact, they've talked your father into hosting a dinner and a ball in your honor at week's end."

Dax looked down at Belle and then back to the queen. "MaMaw, I don't think I'm ready for something like that. And I need to check on Alabrax—"

"Your dragon is just fine. Aurora fed him and he went right back to sleep. As to the guests, I told your father you weren't ready, but you know how he gets when he is excited about something. He has to let everyone know."

They descended a staircase and stepped into a large dining hall. A dozen or so people sat at a large head table at the front of the room. A hushed silence fell over the group as they rose from their chairs and stared. Belle took a slow step behind Dax to avoid them looking at her. Then, in a sudden burst of noise, clapping and whooping filled the air.

Cheers and welcomes and warm wishes. She peeked around Dax's shoulder to see men and women rushing down from the table, toward them.

A man in a long blue robe approached them and shook Dax's hand vigorously, smiling from ear to ear.

"Your highness, it is so good to see you back."

"Thank you," Dax mumbled.

Another man rushed forward and shook Dax's hand. "Your highness I am so glad that you've returned to us. Draakland has not been the same since you left. A hole was left in the hearts of many of us due to your absence."

"Yes," came a feminine voice from the back. "A very large hole."

The gathering onlookers parted and a beautiful young woman with hair like walnuts and skin like fresh cream walked toward them. She stopped in front of Dax and curtsied.

"Violet." Dax's voice came out barely above a whisper, sending a chill sweeping over Belle.

The girl rose and stepped forward, offering Dax her hand. He raised it to his lips and kissed it. Belle's fists clenched tight. Another thing Dax had hidden from her? He had a girl all this time?

Belle stepped up beside Dax and reached for Chloe, breaking the connection between Violet and Dax.

"I'm so sorry," said Dax. "Everyone, I would like you to meet Belle and Chloe."

The group bowed and curtsied to her in turn, making her cheeks heat.

"Thaddeus saved them from some ruffians," said the

queen. "And now Lady Belle and Miss Chloe are staying with us."

The group nodded and smiled at Belle, but all of their graciousness only served to make her even more uncomfortable.

"Mama, I'm hungry," said Chloe.

Violet walked to Dax's side and took his arm. "Come. Let us all sit and eat together."

She pulled him forward before he could protest. He looked back at Belle with an apologetic smile.

"They make a good couple, don't they?"

Belle spun around to see Aurora standing over her shoulder eating an apple. Wearing a plain cotton frock with her hair tied up in a strap, Aurora had dressed just as Belle wished she was.

"Uh, yes, they do," Belle replied.

Aurora's eyes narrowed, and she cocked her head to the side and bit into the apple again.

"Liar. They would never make a good couple. I see it. Mother sees it. Dax knows it as well. But it's father who wanted the match. Maybe now that you're here though... maybe he'll see what we've all known for a years."

Belle rubbed her tongue over the roof of her mouth, unsure of what Aurora wanted her to say.

"Come on," said Aurora. "I'll take you two somewhere more comfortable to eat."

She hopped from the table she sat on and grabbed Belle by the hand. Belle followed Aurora to the door and looked over her shoulder to where Dax sat with Violet. He caught sight of her just as she disappeared out the door.

"Belle!" he called.

Aurora dragged her down the hallway toward a small staircase.

"Belle! Wait!" Dax raced down the hall after them.

Aurora stopped and turned. "Go back to your meal, Thad. All the pomp and circumstance is for you, not us."

"Aurora, let her go." He broke his sister's hold on Belle. "Belle, come, eat with me."

"You mean us, don't you?"

His eyebrows knit together. "Well, yes there are a lot of people in there—"

"I wouldn't want to break up your little reunion with Violet." The words came out cattier than she'd anticipated.

His brows furrowed. "It's not like that."

"Not like what? I saw how she looked at you."

His face mixed between amusement and anger. "I didn't remember her, or I would have told you."

"Like you would have told me about being a werebear?"

Aurora stepped forward. "What? You're a werebear?" She shook her head and smiled. "I suppose your nickname was very astute of me wasn't it? How amazing is that?"

Dax threw Aurora a tense look. "Not as amazing as you would imagine."

"Look," said Belle. "Chloe and I would be more comfortable eating somewhere... private."

He inclined his head. "If that is what you wish."

"It is." It was a half-truth. She really just wanted a private breakfast with the three of them, like they had in the castle. Reading and eating and playing games, but now that he was a prince, she supposed those days were over.

Belle realizing how attached she'd become to him in such a short time. Something she'd vowed she wouldn't do.

"All right. But I'm going to come find you afterward. I want to show you and Chloe something."

"We'll be in our room." Belle turned to go.

"Belle." He grabbed her hand.

She stopped and looked back.

He stepped closer, his gaze conflicted but set. "You may have seen how she looked at me, but if you'd seen how I looked at her you'd know there is nothing in my heart for her more than friendship. I didn't lie to you."

Belle wanted to believe him. Wanted to believe that he told her that because he cared for her instead. But she'd been cheated on before.

Slipping her hand away, she followed Aurora down the small stone stairs. It didn't matter what Dax felt for Violet, the fact that his father wanted it was all she needed to know.

"So tell me," said Aurora. "What is he like?" She dug into her sausage and eggs.

Belle looked at Chloe, who put an egg on some toast and bit into it with a smile.

"He's kind."

"He's always been kind. What's he like?"

Belle wasn't sure what Aurora wanted from her. "Why don't you tell me what he was like before he... left."

Aurora scooped more eggs and sausage into her mouth and shrugged. "Kind, like you said. He had the respect of his men because of his kindness, and also his generosity. He didn't yell at his men or beat them into submission. He encouraged them. Worked with them. It instilled a high amount of loyalty from them. But he wasn't all business. He also knew how to have a good time. A really good time. Women, drinking..." Aurora stopped talking and took a long swig of mead.

Belle pushed her eggs around her plate. "So, Dax has been with many women?"

Aurora shoveled more food into her mouth and shrugged. "I suppose. Does that bother you?"

It shouldn't. Belle knew it shouldn't, but she couldn't help that it did. She'd not seen Dax as a womanizer. Some men you could tell just by the look in their eyes. The way they watched women or the tilt of their smile, that they would bed anything with a cute face and a round behind. But Dax... he'd never once looked at her that way. He'd even said he wouldn't kiss her again unless she wanted him to. She had a hard time seeing a man like that as someone who went from woman to woman.

"It does bother you," Aurora finally said. "You care about him. He cares about you too, if it makes a difference."

"How would you know that? We've not even been here twelve hours."

"Because I saw him be more attentive to you and Chloe and what you needed in a couple hours together than he's been of his own needs, or any of us for that matter."

It was true. Dax had been concerned about little else than her and Chloe since their arrival.

"So, Dax was what? Captain of the Guard before he disappeared?"

"Before they all disappeared. He was Captain of the Dragon Guard."

"Dragon shifters?"

Aurora shook her head. "No. The Dragon Guard were dragon riders not shifters. Each rider bonded with a single dragon and rode them into battle."

"But... they're shifters now. When did that happen?"

Aurora shook her head. "No idea. Though I am assuming Morgana did it to them."

"And the castle guard. Do they ride the dragons now?"

"The dragons are gone. Except for the one you brought. We still call them the Dragon Guard though in hopes that dragons will return to us one day."

"Does Morgana have them?"

Aurora sighed. "Until you arrived we thought she did. But everything is so confused now. The riders are now dragon shifters, so where did the dragons go? Or worse, what did she do with them?"

It broke her heart to think what Morgana may have done to the dragons and to the riders; especially considering the lengths she'd gone to to try and get Dax to submit to her. "You knew her?"

"Everyone knew her, she made sure of it."

Belle swallowed. "What was *she* like?"

"Creepy. I never liked her. She used her body and sexuality on everyone she met, men and women. She appeared one day as the young new wife of one of my father's advisors. The man died soon after and she took his place over the guard and Thad. But soon, she'd wormed herself deeper and deeper into their ranks. By the time my parents decided she couldn't be trusted it was too late. Thad and the guard disappeared, and so did she."

Aurora stared at Belle for a moment. "She hurt him, didn't she?"

Belle didn't know what to say. The story wasn't hers to tell, and she didn't know how much Dax wanted his family to know.

"It's all right," said Aurora. "You don't have to tell me. It's written all over him that he's been through more than we will ever know."

"He's strong. Most men wouldn't have gone searching for their past after having amnesia. But all he's wanted for the last five years is to find out where he belonged."

"That's all I've wanted for the last five years too. I knew he wasn't dead. People told me to give up, but I never did."

Belle's gut clenched. "He's lucky to have a sister like you."

Aurora shook her head and bit into her toast. "It's us who are lucky to have him."

Of that, Belle had no doubt.

CHAPTER ELEVEN

It wasn't until close to noon that Dax could pry himself away from Violet, her father and his father. Every moment in Violet's presence reaffirmed to him that she was not the one.

She was sweet, completely ignorant of the evils flourishing in Fairelle, and so unlike he himself. The darkness he'd seen, the things he'd endured; all of them shaped the man he'd become in the last five years. He was no longer the carefree youth that spent his time playing cards with his friends and hunting in the mountains. He'd been through too much. Knew too much. Most of all, he didn't want someone who fancied him because of his title, but someone who wanted him despite his title.

He jogged up to Belle and Chloe's door and knocked. A moment later, Belle opened the door a crack, a stricken expression on her face.

"What's the matter? What happened?" he asked.

Belle looked over her shoulder and then shimmed out the door before closing it again. She looked around the hallway and then rubbed her brow.

"It's Chloe. She's had a... spell."

"Spell?"

"An episode. She gets them now and again and she... sees things."

"What did she see?"

Belle shook her head. "All she said is that something bad is coming and then... Then she blacked out." Belle shook like a frightened rabbit. "She's never done that before."

Dax pulled Belle into his arms and hugged her tight. He kissed the top of her head.

"I promised I wouldn't let anything happen to you and I meant it. You're safe here."

"I don't know," said Belle. "Maybe it's better if we leave. Right now, we are sitting geese. But if we go and don't tell anyone where, there's a chance that Klaus won't find us."

"And there's a chance he will, and I would never know. Just give it a few weeks. I know this is an adjustment. It's an adjustment for all of us, but I promise things will get better."

"How?" She pushed away from him and looked up into his face. "How do things work out for me here? What am I supposed to do?"

"Anything you want. You can rest. You can read. You can walk the grounds. You can learn to needlepoint."

Belle cocked an eyebrow at him.

"Maybe not needlepoint. But the thing is, you can do anything you want."

"Except leave," she said. "I'm a prisoner."

The words struck Dax in the gut. "I hope you don't truly feel that way."

Her shoulders slumped and she leaned back against her door. "I don't know how I feel. Everything is so mixed up. A week ago, I could scarcely scrape together enough money to feed my child. Now I'm wearing fancy dresses and eating as much as I want."

"Is that so bad?"

She wrapped her arms around herself. "I don't want to be stuck here. I want to do for myself. Provide for myself."

"I know that. But, why can't you do that here in Draakland? I could get you a house. You could set up a shop. Build clocks and gizmos and gadgets of every kind."

"But I haven't earned that. It would be just you giving it to me."

"Says who? Who says you haven't earned it?"

"Me." She looked at him hard. "I don't want to be indebted to you."

"Then let me loan you the funds. You can pay me back when you have it."

Chloe screamed from the bedroom and Belle and Dax threw the door open and rushed in. She sat bolt upright in bed screaming, her eyes wide and focused on the ceiling.

"Chloe. Chloe!" Belle shook her daughter, but Chloe continued to scream.

Finally, Chloe's scream died out and she fell back on the bed. "She's here."

"Who?" The quaver in Belle's voice was unmistakable. "Who's here?"

Chloe's eyes stayed fixed on the ceiling. "The woman in the red dress."

"Morgana?" Dax's throat dried.

Chloe nodded, but didn't look at him.

Dax sprinted from the room and ran down the hall. He jumped the stairs to the lower level and spotted a guard.

"Everyone on alert. We have an intruder in the castle."

The guard ran down the stairs barking orders as Dax back-tracked down the hallway and headed to the lower floor.

His father stood in the hallway. "What's going on?"

Dax ran from room to room, sniffing the air and looking inside, but nothing was amiss. He'd never, as long as he lived, forget her scent. He raced to the ballroom and threw open the door. Dax whistled and Alabrax warbled and got to his feet.

"What's happened," his mother asked.

"It's Morgana. She's in the castle."

"Where?"

"I don't know."

Alabrax lumbered toward him and snorted. Dax's mother yipped and jumped out of the way as Alabrax entered the hall.

"Alabrax, find her!"

The dragon hissed and stormed down the hall. Dax ran past him to the large double doors at the end.

His mother rushed to keep up. "I don't understand. Did you see her?"

"I don't need to. She's here."

Dax threw the doors open wide and his mother jumped

out of the way just as Alabrax reached them, jumped up on the balcony and took to the sky. He spread his wings wide and roared.

Dax ran to the railing and looked out over his kingdom. People ran and ducked for cover below at the sight of Alabrax. The dragon dipped low and searched the ground, snorting and roaring.

"Thaddeus, please," said his mother. "I don't understand. If you didn't see her, did someone else see her?"

Dax refused to turn, instead tracking Alabrax as he swooped from house to house and feeling the dragon's frustration as he searched. Dax's bear lumbered inside, wanting to be let out to find Morgana and rip her limb from limb.

"Sir." A guard strode to Dax's side. "Sir, we've searched the castle and there is no one here."

"Search again," Dax demanded.

The guard looked to the queen.

"Thaddeus—"

Dax whirled around. "Search again!" he roared.

The queen winced and backed up. The guard nodded and headed back into the castle.

A shift ripple coursed through him as his bear fought to be let loose. Dax breathed in deep and closed his eyes. He had to keep it together. Turning into a bear at that moment would create a panic that he wasn't ready to handle.

He opened his eyes to see his mother hadn't moved.

"I'm sorry," he said.

She nodded but said nothing. Dax wanted to comfort her and tell her everything nothing was amiss, but it wasn't. If Chloe had seen Morgana, then Morgana had been there.

Minutes passed, and Dax watched Alabrax search the entire village three times. Finally, a stately stride that could only be his father's walked up beside him.

"Son we've searched the castle three times. She isn't here."

"She was here."

"It is possible that she was. But she isn't now."

"No." Stil walked onto the balcony. "It's not possible."

They turned to look at him.

"I put a spell of protection over the castle after you arrived. If she'd been here, it would have alerted me." Stil gave them all a grim smile. "You can call off the search. You are all perfectly safe."

Dax looked over Stil's shoulder to see a maid with eyes like coals, standing expressionless, holding a knife to her own throat in the doorway.

"What the hell?"

"You will give Dax to me." Her voice came out monotone and flat as her vacant black eyes.

"Martha, what are you doing?" Dax's mother stepped forward, but his father grabbed her arm, stopping her.

"You have seven days to deliver Dax back to me. If you do not comply, I will rain down fire upon this city until every inch is nothing more than ash."

"Martha!"

"Seven days," the girl said in a voice not her own. Her eyes remained blank as she drew the blade across her throat.

Dax's mother screamed and Stil rushed to the girl, catching her before she hit the floor. Blood pooled on the stone tile and spread out staining the floor. Stil whispered as he poured a small vial of dust over the wound, but it was too late. The girl sputtered, coughing blood on Stil's robes and then her eyes turned from black to their original blue, and then faded. Silence fell over the group as they stared at the dead maid in Stil's arms.

"Why... why did she do that?" asked the queen.

"She didn't," Dax replied. "Morgana did. She has a way of getting into people's heads."

The queen shuddered. "So Morgana was here then?"

"No." Stil sprinkled dust over the blood on the floor and waved his hands over it. "She must have gotten to Martha some other way." The blood seeped into the dust and blew away.

"There could be more like Martha?" asked Dax's father.

"It's possible. Morgana has spies in every kingdom. We have to believe that Martha isn't the only one under her control, whether they know it or not."

Dax pounded on the railing as Stil called for two guards to carry Martha's body away. Damn Morgana. Why did she want him so much? What made him so special? It couldn't just be that he'd rejected her. He knew for a fact that Hunter and the dragon guard had rejected her as well, with the exception of one. There had to be more to it than just that... but what?

Dax whistled and Alabrax soared back toward the castle. His mind reeled with the idea that she'd been in the castle. Near his family. Near Belle and Chloe. He had to stop her.

"Dax." Belle walked out on the balcony, her eyes fearful. "What happened? Did you find her?"

Tension released from Dax's body just seeing her beautiful face. Alabrax landed on the railing and nuzzled Dax's cheek.

"No. It wasn't her," said Dax. He had no desire to upset Belle further for the day. He'd tell her about Martha after things had settled down.

"How is Chloe?" he asked.

"She's sleeping. One of the maids is with her and there are two guards outside the door."

"No!" Dax blurted. "Chloe shouldn't be trusted with anyone but our family."

Belle looked like she might panic.

"I'm sorry," he said. "I just mean—"

"I'll go sit with her," said the queen. "I used to love watching my children sleep."

"You don't have to do that, your majesty," said Belle. "I can go back."

Dax walked over and took Belle's hand. "Let her sit with Chloe. She's asleep and won't even know we aren't there. I need a few minutes alone with you. Please." His words came out needy and weak, but he didn't care. Everything was piling up inside him and tying him so tight that he wasn't sure how much more he could take before his control snapped.

Alabrax snorted and Dax pet his head.

Aurora appeared out of the shadows. "I'll see to Alabrax. Then I'll sit with Mother and Chloe. You two go."

Belle and Aurora shared a look. Dax led Belle back inside. He looked over his shoulder to see Aurora stroking Alabrax's neck.

"Are you sure Morgana isn't here? Chloe's never been wrong before," Belle said.

"It wasn't her. I promise. Stil put a spell on the castle. If she enters, he will be notified." He squeezed her hand. "I told you, I won't let anything happen to you here."

Belle looked at him pleadingly, like she wanted to believe him. Finally, she blew out a breath and nodded.

"What is it you wanted to show me?"

Dax squeezed her hand tight and walked back inside. "I think we both could use a little reprieve. I want to show you my favorite room in the castle."

BELLE WANTED NOTHING MORE THAN TO RUSH BACK AND SIT with Chloe, but the blinding headache that had accompanied Chloe's vision had forced Belle to give her little girl the last of the opia. Chloe would be asleep for several hours at least. And as there was nothing more she could do for her daughter, with the queen inside the room and guards watching inside and out, every precaution had been taken. Hell, a mage's spell protected the place.

Even so, Belle's gut churned at the thought that Dax's mother might find out about Chloe, but she had no good reason to refuse the woman's help. And doing so might have made her suspicious. For the first time in a long time, Belle decided that she needed to give up that moment of control and allow herself to trust in others.

At breakfast she'd gotten to know Aurora, as well as more about Dax's history. And though she wasn't happy about his past, she couldn't blame him for it. She needed to accept his past the way he had accepted hers. Interestingly, in her hour with Aurora, Belle had come to find that though she looked like a princess, Aurora possessed extensive knowledge of weaponry and fighting. His little sister had even taken it upon herself to train to protect her family in Dax's absence. Having assembled a new guard for Draakland, Aurora had become every inch the fighter that any man would be and then some, because she had to prove herself being a woman.

Belle took a deep breath as she ascended the staircase with Dax to the second floor. It wasn't possible to help Chloe at the moment, but she could help Dax. Relief had flooded his face when she'd walked out on the balcony. The wildness to his stare told her that he was fighting to hold it together. For as uncomfortable as this new environment was on her, it had to be overwhelming him. Gaining all those memories, a family, and an old life as well as a new one, combined with an evil bitch who wanted him for herself had to be a lot, even for him.

They walked hand in hand to a large door. Dax pushed it open and the scent of old parchment met Belle's nose. They stepped into the room and Belle gasped. The library in the crumbling castle had been large, but this... This went beyond anything she could have imagined. More books than a person could read in a lifetime stood before her, waiting to be taken off the shelf and rifled through.

"I spent more hours in this room than any other. But my favorite section is over here."

He pulled her between several rows of books until they

emerged in a small alcove dressed with soft floor pillows and a small fireplace.

"This was my section." He sat on the floor and stretched out on the pillows. He patted the pillow beside him and Belle sat.

"Lay back," he said.

Belle eyed him for a moment. What was he up to?

"I just want to show you something." He folded his arms over his chest.

Belle continued to eye him as she lay down next to him and looked up at the ceiling. "Oh my toth!"

An entire night sky painting covered the ceiling. Millions of individual stars mapped out the heavens above Fairelle. Belle stared at it, wondering how many hours it had taken to create. She recognized several of the star clusters from the night sky over Westfall.

Dax pointed to the right. "That constellation over there is Kondak Majorus. It's who I chose my name from, after..."

She looked over at him and his expression sagged. "What's it like?" she asked. "Being a bear shifter?"

"It's like... it's like having your deepest most basic instincts heightened and given a mind of their own; always wanting to get out and do what they want."

"But it's still you."

"It's me and it's not me. It's a part of me that I never knew existed before. My bear thinks in simple terms. Food. Shelter. Mating. Whereas I think of those things too, but I also think about—"

"Everything else humans think about."

He glanced over at her. "Right."

They lay together looking up at the night sky for several minutes.

"Can I ask you something?" Dax said.

"Sure."

"If I gave you gold and told you that you could leave today, right now, would you?"

Belle's chest squeezed tight. She opened her mouth to say yes, but the truth was, "I don't know."

Dax rolled onto his side and looked at her. "I would understand."

Belle licked her lips. "You told me that you wouldn't wish being a princess on anyone. What about being a prince? If you had the chance and could take a chest full of gold and run from here, now remembering who and what you are, would you?"

"If it meant I could be with you and Chloe, I'd go in a heartbeat."

She turned her head to look at him. Sadness mixed with desire in his eyes.

Without thinking she reached up and ran her fingers through his shaggy hair. She didn't know what they were doing. What their futures held, or even what tomorrow would bring. But what she did know was that despite her fears and her desire to run, she believed Dax when he said he would keep her and Chloe safe. The look in his eyes told her that he felt for her the way she'd begun to feel for him.

Her body warmed as he closed his eyes and pressed his cheek into her palm. It didn't matter that he was Prince Thaddeus of Draakland. To her, he was still Dax the were-bear. The man who had saved her, more than once. The man who read to Chloe at night. The man who had held her tight time and time again, and promised to keep her safe.

She pulled his mouth to hers in a soft kiss. He didn't move for a moment, and then rolled atop her and cradled her face. The feel of his large body had her tingling with need.

She licked across his bottom lip and desire bloomed inside her. His scent filled her nostrils. The scent of soap and leather. He kissed her soft and long, as if savoring her. She'd never been kissed like that before. Never been kissed as if he wanted nothing more than to please her.

He ran his hand down over her breast to her waist and squeezed her hip. The sensation sent shockwaves through her body. She moaned into his mouth, wanting more of him. To feel him inside her, making love to her. Suddenly she needed to feel him, to have him, to taste his skin.

He kissed down her neck. "Belle, we don't have to do this."

"Do what?" she kissed him again, reaching for his breeches tie.

"This," he said kissing down to the tops of her breasts.

"I want to," she panted. "I want you, Dax."

He kissed her again and then rested his forehead on hers, and blew out a breath.

"What's wrong?"

"I want you, I do. But this isn't the place."

"It's nice enough to me." She kissed him again and he responded, claiming her mouth.

A growl escaped him, and he broke the kiss and shook his head. "Anyone could come in at any moment."

Maybe Violet would walk in and see them and run out crying. "I don't mind."

He kissed her again and then nipped her chin. "But I do. I don't want anyone else to see you but me."

Belle sighed. A gentleman through and through. She'd denied herself release for more than a year and she'd not been with Klaus for almost as long. The desire to be held and loved ran deep down to her bones. In Dax's arms, she knew she'd find what she needed. Tenderness, passion, satisfaction.

He pushed the hair from her eyes and kissed across her eyelids. "You look tired."

She chuckled at the feel of the soft kisses he whispered across her skin. "I haven't been sleeping well."

Dax rolled on his side and pulled her into his chest. "Then why don't we take a few minutes here and just rest?"

"How can I rest when we know that Klaus and Morgana are out there spending every moment trying to get to us? I'm too pent up to sleep."

"Because for now, they aren't here. It's just you and me." He kissed her hair and pulled her closer. "Forget everything else and just relish in the peace and quiet of now."

She didn't want to rest, but in the warmth of his embrace Belle closed her eyes and breathed in his smell. A mixture of manliness and leather that relaxed her further. She imagined what it would be to feel like this forever. Cared for. Content. Safe. With Dax.

DAX STARED UP AT THE STARS WITH BELLE SNUGGLED against his chest. Never before had a woman intrigued him as much as she did. Tough but tender, he couldn't help but be drawn to her. He sucked in air, trying to push away the fear and painful memories. He wanted nothing more than to move on with his life, but that wouldn't be his fate. Not anytime soon, anyway. In the not so far off future they were going to have to deal with Morgana, Rasmuss and Klaus. He just had to figure out the best way to do it. But for the moment, he allowed himself the moment of bliss.

He'd known her less than two weeks and even so, he'd become more attached to her and Chloe than he had any of his other friends in Fairelle. Even with Flint, with whom he'd spent over six months as a constant companion.

Dax kissed Belle's head and pulled her closer to him. She wrapped her arm around his abdomen and he closed his eyes. He didn't know how long they had, but he refused to waste a moment of it worrying about things he couldn't do anything about.

DAX LAY WITH BELLE IN HIS ARMS FOR MORE THAN AN HOUR mulling over the problems at hand. The door to the library creaked open and Dax turned to listen. Soft footsteps shuffled through the rows of books and stopped just inside his alcove.

Stil took upon the scene and nodded to Dax. Dax returned the nod and looked down to Belle. Her light snore made him smile. He kissed her forehead and slid out from under her.

Stil walked out of the alcove and Dax met him a few stacks of books down.

"I've doubled the spell on the castle. There is no way Morgana can get in."

Dax nodded.

Stil stared at Dax for a minute. "Do you want to tell me how you knew she'd been here?"

Dax shook his head.

"Every exit is being covered. Every inch of the castle is spelled. You are safe."

"We came in through a mirror in the ballroom, I disabled it, but there could be another one in the castle somewhere."

"A mirror? I had no idea anyone else used them anymore besides us."

"You know about them?"

"We have them in the mage towers. They go all over. We use them for travel."

"You use the bloodstones?"

"What? No. A simple spell and some dust from where we wish to go are sufficient."

Interesting. "So technically if she knew the spell and had some dust, she could use any mirror to get here."

Stil's eyebrows drew together. "Well... yes. But she isn't a mage so how would she know that?"

A memory surfaced. "Rasmuss."

"Who?"

"Rasmuss. He's the mage that locked Zelle in the tower. He used a powder and a spell to blind Flint."

"I don't know a mage named Rasmuss and I know all the mages in the towers."

"He's a master of disguise. In Zelle's tower his appearance changed from young to old."

"That's troubling," said Stil.

Belle cried out in the alcove and then quieted. Dax walked back and looked at her, but she still slept.

"You care for her."

Dax looked at his friend. "I care for both her and Chloe."

"More than as a friend."

Yes, though he wasn't ready to admit that to anyone.

"Your mother and father are worried about you."

"Is that why you're here? They asked you to talk to me?"

"Something like that."

Dax stared at Belle's sleeping form. "For five years I had no identity or past. I traveled from place to place with no real sense of home. But for some reason when I look at Chloe or hold Belle in my arms, I feel more at home than I ever did living in this castle."

"Are you regretting coming back?"

Dax turned and looked at his friend. "It's good to know who I am."

A smile spread across Stil's face. "You didn't answer the question."

Dax turned back to Belle. "Who I used to be and who I am are two different people now. I'm not sure the new me belongs here."

Stil placed his hands on Dax's shoulders and turned him around.

"You are the prince and you belong here. Who you were then or who you are now, it makes no difference. This is your home and your family. They will just have to learn to get used to the new you."

Dax gave Stil a tight smile. At least those words were true. Because if they didn't accept the new him, they weren't going to accept Belle, and if they didn't accept Belle and Chloe... Their stay in Draakland would be short indeed.

CHAPTER TWELVE

Dax watched over Belle until she awoke with a start an hour later.

"My toth, how long was I asleep?"

"A couple of hours."

Belle jumped to her feet and pushed at her hair. "Chloe."

"It's all right," he said. "I had Stil check on her and Aurora."

Belle strode across the alcove and passed him. "You promised you wouldn't tell him about her."

"I didn't." He followed her through the stacks. "I told him she was napping."

She didn't stop as she hit the door and bolted into the hall.

"Belle, she's fine." He took the steps two at a time to try and catch up.

She practically ran down the hallway to her room.

Giggling floated out to them and Belle threw open the door.

"Mama!" Chloe ran to Belle's arms and Belle hugged her tight.

Dax looked to Stil, who stood in the middle of the room with the dragon book from the other castle laying open on the floor.

"Stil pretended to be a dragon," said Chloe.

"Did he?" Belle's voice shook.

"She said she had a headache and you'd given her some opia," said Stil. "I used to get those a lot when I was a child as well. Mine were followed by nose bleeds though."

"Mine don't do that yet," Chloe replied.

"Yes, well, the headaches are a recent development," Belle interjected. "I'm sure it's just all of the excitement from everything that's happened."

"It could also be from the altitude," said Stil. "We are quite high up here. If you'd like, I have a friend who's a healer. I can ask her for some herbs that might help."

Belle smiled at Stil but her body remained tense. "Thank you, but I'm sure she will be fine."

"Thad?" Aurora stood in the doorway. She looked to Belle with a tight smile and then to Dax. "Lady Violet is in the garden. Father is meeting with her father."

"I can entertain her," Stil offered. "I have a couple more hours to spare before I have to head back to the towers."

"I'm afraid my father would like Thad to do it."

Dax's gut clenched. He needed to speak with his father. He had no intention of leading either Violet or her father on with the hopes that there would be a union between their families.

"Aurora," said Belle. "Would you mind taking us down to the kitchen to get something to eat?"

Dax looked to Belle but she adverted her eyes.

"Of course," said Aurora.

Belle took Chloe's hand and the three walked out. Dax touched Belle's arm as she passed and she stopped, but didn't look at him.

"You have duties. We'll see you later."

"Belle—"

"It's impolite to keep a lady waiting." She continued out the door and out of sight.

"Go after her," said Stil.

Dax shook his head. "It wouldn't do any good."

"You don't know that."

"Unfortunately, I do. All of this is a lot for Belle and there are things... things she is afraid of that won't be made better by me going after her. She needs to work this through herself."

Stil shook his head. "I have no idea what you just said."

"Of course you don't. You aren't even allowed to court or marry."

"True, we mages are supposed to keep to our studies and not be concerned with lesser matters of love. But I've watched both Cinder and now you fall in love, and I think I know a bit more than you realize."

"Come on," said Dax. "Father will expect me to put on something appropriate to entertain Violet."

He walked out of Belle's room and strode the few feet to his own. Two rooms separated by walls. They reminded him of how his and Belle's relationship felt. Every time they came to a point where they might move forward, something happened to throw a wall between them.

Dax pushed open his door and stripped off his tunic, flinging it to the floor. He strode to his wardrobe and pulled it open. He thumbed through his tunics and settled on the least luxurious. He'd become so accustomed to the feel of normal linen in the last five years that wearing the bright silk felt wrong. That, and the fact that he'd put on enough muscle in his absence that he now found everything a size too small.

"What's that?"

Dax looked to where Stil pointed. A large white box sat on his bed.

"Looks to be a present," said Dax.

"I wonder who sent you a present?"

Dax pulled the tunic over his head. "Probably my mother. Or it could be a joke from Aurora."

Stil chuckled. "I still remember her presents to you. A bed full of frogs once."

"And a bowl full of snails."

"How about the Festivus tree full of lady beetles?"

Dax snickered. "I spent a year picking them out of my wardrobe."

"Yes, but she was so proud of herself for cutting down the tree herself."

"That she was."

Dax crossed to the bed and looked down at the box.

"Do you dare open it?" asked Stil.

"I'm not sure," replied Dax. "It could be anything."

Stil stepped forward and reached for the box. "I should

check it for spells."

"Don't bother. It's probably just another present from one of the dignitaries that were here this morning. I got a dozen more over there in the corner."

"Maybe we should stand back just in case," said Stil.

Dax looked at Stil. "Fine."

Stil rolled up his sleeves and cast a spell removing the satin bow and flipping the lid off the box. They both jumped back waiting for something to happen, but nothing did.

Finally, they walked to the bed and looked in the box.

"A rose?" said Stil.

A single white rose lay on a bed of greenery. Dax took the rose from the box and looked at it.

Stil pulled a small card from the box and handed it to Dax.

Dax looked at the blank card. He flipped it over and then handed it to Stil, who looked at it quizzically.

"Seems you have an admirer," said Stil.

A chill ran up Dax's spine. "Seems I do."

Dax turned the rose in his fingers and a thorn pricked him. A bead of blood welled on his finger and smeared onto the stem.

"See, that's why I've never liked roses," said Stil.

"Me too." Dax's eyes widened as his blood soaked into the flower and traveled up the stem to the petals. The white rose suddenly turned deep red.

Stil grabbed the rose from Dax's grasp and tossed it back in the box. They took a step back as the box turned from white to crimson, as did the bow.

"Shite!" Stil stared at the card on the bed. Red writing appeared on the card.

A pit grew in Dax's stomach as he lifted the card and read it.

A week in time is all I give
Come to me and as a man you'll live
Stay in your castle warm and snug
And in one week's time you'll be no more than my rug.

"What the hell does that mean?" asked Stil.

"I have no—" Dax's bear roared to life. Without his consent a shift ripple coursed through him. Dax fell to the ground as his limbs snapped and broke. His bear, untethered, forced his way through Dax's skin. The pain broke every bone, snapped every muscle, pulled every tendon in an unnatural direction. Not all at once, but one by one, prolonging the pain. Dax's vision blurred and then he unleashed a glass shattering roar.

He fell in a heap, sweaty and raw. His body shook with strain as his arm bones broke and then his leg bones. Dax cried out as his body contorted and he flipped on his stomach. His shoulder broke and then the other. Bone by agonizing bone, his body shifted and changed from man to beast. His bear roared and paced and clawed his way to the surface with each excruciating change to their form.

"Dax!" Stil rushed to his side. "Dax! Are you all right?"

Another onslaught of pain ripped through him. Everything went fuzzy, and as his back broke and his spine shifted, everything went black.

"But he's a bear," said the queen.

"Yes," said Stil patiently. "He was cursed by Morgana."

The king swore. "That stupid witch. I should never have let her stay here. I knew I should have thrown her out as soon as she turned up on the castle steps, begging for help after her husband's death."

The queen squeezed his arm. "You were just being a good man."

"And look what it's cost us. Our son is a beast and all because he refused her."

Belle looked at Dax's large white face. Chloe snuggled into his side and hugged Dax close.

She looked up at Belle. "He's not dreaming, mama. His mind is blank."

Belle nodded and motioned for Chloe to be quiet.

Aurora pet Dax's head. "I should have killed that bitch myself," she mumbled. "Look at what she's done to our kingdom. Taking our dragon guard. Crippling our food supply, and now this."

Belle knelt beside Aurora. "He'll change back. He did last time."

Aurora smiled at her. "You're good for him. You keep him grounded."

"That's not what I'd call it."

"He cares for you. It's obvious to everyone. He's changed, not for the worse I might add. He's less selfish. More... grown up."

"That's all him and has nothing to do with me," Belle swallowed. "He's a good man. Better than most."

She reached out and touched his soft face. At her touch, he roused and yawned.

"He's waking," Aurora called.

Dax's eyes opened and he looked around at the scene. He rolled over and tried to stand, but fell back down. He tried again and again he fell.

"Easy," said Belle. "Stil said you fell hard when you collapsed."

He huffed and tried a third time. He got to his feet for a moment before falling again. Belle snatched Chloe away just as Dax's heavy body plopped back on the floor.

Belle's heart galloped. This wasn't good.

He growled and she touched his face. "It's all right. We're gonna figure this out."

Dax nodded his shaggy head.

"Can you change back?"

He shook his head.

"What do we do?" the queen exclaimed. "He can't stay like this."

"The note said if he went to Morgana that she'd change him back," said Stil.

Dax growled.

"Not an option," said the king. "Can't you do anything?"

Stil shook his head. "This isn't my magick wheelhouse. This is daemon magick. Only a daemon could help with this."

"Where the hell would we find one of those willing to help us?" asked the king.

Dax chuffed.

"What is it?" asked Belle.

He tried to speak but it came out a mix of warbles and snarls.

"I... I don't understand."

Dax growled and tried again, but again nothing.

"Do you know someone who can help?" Belle asked.

Dax nodded.

"Cinder isn't daemon," said Stil. "It can't be her. Her half-sister is part daemon, but we have no idea where she is and she has no magick or knowledge of the arts at all."

Dax shook his head.

Belle wracked her brain. "The Gwyns."

Dax looked at her and nodded.

"Snow?"

He shook his head.

"Erik?"

Again, no.

"Flint?"

Dax nodded and pawed at the floor.

"The girl in the tower," said Stil. "The one Flint saved. His wife... what's her name?"

"Zelle," said Belle.

Dax nodded and tried to get up.

"You know these Gwyns?" asked the queen. "Would they come here?"

"The Lords Gwyn are the only family I have. And Dax is their family as well. If we can get them a letter, they will come." Belle pet Dax's head.

"I can do one better," said Stil. "I can go get them myself."

CHAPTER THIRTEEN

Dax lay on the floor trapped inside his mind. Belle, Chloe and Aurora had kept constant watch over him since he'd awoken, but he could see the fear written over both Belle and Aurora's face. Only Chloe's gentle smile kept him from losing his mind.

His anger against Morgana had increased in the past hours. But if she thought that meant he would give in to her, she had another thing coming.

Chloe lay against Dax's side, twirling her little fingers in his fur. He appreciated the simple comfort that the child brought him.

A group of footsteps rushed down the hallway and he lifted his head. Aurora opened the door and Dax's heartbeat quickened. Stil walked in with the king and queen, followed by Cinder, Flint, Zelle, Erik, Snow, Sage and Adrian. He stared at them all and shook his head.

"Don't act like that," said Erik. "You had to know that we'd all come when we heard the news."

"You couldn't keep us away." Cinder walked toward him, and Dax rose to his feet. She hugged him tight and then the rest of the group gathered round; all touching him and murmuring their thoughts.

Through the gap in the crowd, he watched as his parents clustered in the corner with Aurora. Their faces full of fear and exhaustion.

A moment passed, and then Snow and the Gwyns went to Belle and Chloe, hugging her tight and asking what she was doing there.

"We're going to sort this out," said Adrian. "And then we'll make sure that Morgana pays for what she's done."

Dax nodded.

Zelle stepped forward, her white hair flowing down her arms. She knelt and set her hands on his shoulders.

"I can feel her magick flowing over you," she said. "It's like the armband I used to wear. It's locking you inside your bear body."

Flint set his hand on Zelle's shoulder. "Can you break it?"

Zelle concentrated, her face scrunching up and her hands running over his muzzle.

"Break it, no. But change it, maybe. My magick was used to make this spell, so I may be able to alter it."

"How so?" asked Aurora.

Zelle turned to face her. "Morgana is my mother."

The queen gasped.

"Don't worry," said Stil. "Zelle isn't like her mother."

"Far from it," Zelle replied. "I was her prisoner once, too. She used my magick to forge bloodstones of great power. The stones are what she uses to create spells by combining my magick with her own. I have powers that she does not, however. I am a soulbinder. It is possible that I can bind Dax's human soul to another human soul here in Fairelle, forcing him to stay in human form as long as the two are together."

"Is it dangerous?" asked the king.

"Not particularly," said Zelle. "It just..."

"Just what?" asked Aurora.

"It will link the two people so that the person receiving might feel what the giver is feeling. That can be uncomfortable in some relationships therefore it is usually something one would only do with their spouse. But as Dax isn't married—"

"I'll do it," offered Aurora.

Dax shook his head. *No way.* And as much as he loved his little sister, he did not want her knowing what he felt.

"I could do it," said Adrian. "Dax and I have been linked before when he stayed with me in Wolvenglen."

"But we don't know how long it could take to break the curse," said Sage. "Are you prepared to stay here for an extended period of time?"

"I'd offer," said Stil, "but I have still have my responsibilities at the mage towers. I couldn't be here all the time."

"And I'd be no use during the daytime," said Sage.

"Let me be the one," offered his mother.

The group looked between each other. Dax appreciated all of their offers, but it was more than he could ask anyone.

"I'll do it."

The entire room looked to the corner where Belle stood holding Chloe. Her cheeks flushed and she set Chloe on the ground.

"Dax has helped both Chloe and I enough. I owe him," Belle said.

Dax shook his head. He didn't want her to do this out of obligation. He'd put her through too much already.

Belle stared at Dax. "Could everyone give us a minute, please?"

Aurora began to clear the room as Chloe took Zelle's hand and headed out the door. Belle waited until it closed before turning a chair toward him and sitting. They stared at each other for a long moment.

He had so many things he wanted to say to her, starting with: No. This was too much to ask. What happened if she wanted to leave? He didn't want her to feel obligated to stay. And he didn't want her knowing his thoughts.

"I know what you're thinking," she said. "We don't know each other that well and this is a big commitment."

Dax opened his mouth to speak but only gibberish came out.

"You don't want me to do it out of obligation. I get that. And the truth is, I am doing it out of obligation, partly. But I'm also doing it because it's the right thing to do. Everyone here cares about you. We don't want to see you stuck in this form for the rest of your life, and the only way to get you out of this is to have you help us and for you to help us, you have to be human. You don't want to be tied to your sister or your parents. Stil can't and neither can any of your other

160

friends, so that leaves me. Does the idea scare me? Yes, it does. But I'm willing to do it and you need to let me. Because you can't tell me that if it needed to be done for me or Chloe, or any of the other people that stood in this room, that you wouldn't do it in a heartbeat. No questions asked."

She was right. He'd have done it for the Gwyns, or Cinder, or Sage, Adrian, his sister, Stil… any of them. And if they were going to stop Morgana, he needed to be human.

Belle waited until he nodded.

"Good." She stood and strode to the door. "So," she said to Zelle. "How do we do this?"

BELLE HID HER HANDS TO KEEP EVERYONE FROM SEEING HOW much she shook. She did not want to be doing this.

Chloe took her hand. "It's going to be all good, Mama."

Belle threw her a smile. Being around so much magick and so many magick users set Belle's nerves even further on edge. For a split second, she wished she'd never left her cottage. Not that she wanted Klaus back in her life, but she had enjoyed the peace and quiet, away from prying eyes.

Zelle knelt on the floor in front of Dax. "The first thing I'm going to need to do is force you back into your human form." She looked at the king and queen. "You might not want to be in here for this."

"We're not leaving," said the queen.

Zelle looked at Flint and he shrugged.

Zelle held her hand out to Belle. "Sit by me. I want to

try and do this as fast as I'm able. I don't know how long I'll be able to hold him in human form before binding him."

Belle let go of Chloe's hand. "Chloe, sweetie, why don't you go stand with Auntie Snow."

Snow held out her arms to Chloe and the little girl ran to her.

"You're cold," Chloe said, laying her hand on Snow's cheek.

Snow smiled. "I am."

Sage touched Chloe's face. "You are very beautiful."

Chloe giggled. "Your daughters will be, too."

Sage and Snow exchanged a strange expression and Belle bit back the excuse she wanted to make for Chloe's words.

Belle knelt in front of Dax and Zelle squeezed her hand. "This won't hurt you. I promise."

Belle managed a small nod.

Dax looked at her and she could swear she could hear him telling her that she could back out if she wanted. She breathed in several times and tried to relax.

"I'm not going anywhere," she said.

Zelle placed her palms on the sides of Dax's large head and stared deep into his eyes.

She began chanting in a language Belle didn't recognize. A purple light glowed from her hands as she continued speaking, almost to herself.

A minute passed with nothing happening and then suddenly, Dax shook his head and growled. Zelle's chanting grew louder and she pushed her hands deeper into his fur.

Dax jerked his head and tried to stand, but couldn't. He fell to the floor and tried to get up again.

"Dax, stop." Belle laid her hand on his shoulder.

He chuffed and then growled as Zelle's chanting grew louder still. A crack split through the room and Dax roared. His legs broke and he fell in a heap, making the floor shake.

"Stop," said the queen. "You're hurting him."

Zelle continued.

Dax's breathing came in and out in large bursts. He whimpered as excruciatingly, one by one his bones split and broke apart. His roars rang out, quaking every surface of the room. A vase fell to the floor with a crash and Dax tried to get up once again. Belle watched on in horror, unable to move as his muzzle flattened and then grew out again.

A harrowing cry escaped Dax and the queen screamed.

Belle looked over to see a giant wolf standing where Adrian had been a moment before. The wolf's clothing dropped to the floor in tatters as he padded over to Dax and lay next to him, placing his head on Dax's.

"What's he doing?" the queen demanded.

"Adrian can communicate with Dax while in wolf form," Flint replied. "He's trying to help."

Adrian's presence seemed to ease Dax.

Dax's limbs shook and shortened. The hair retracted, and his human limbs appeared. Again, his muzzle flattened and his hazel eyes lit on Belle. Tears dripped from the corners and she moved forward to touch his face.

"I'm here. I'm right here. You can do this." He grabbed her around the waist and she scooted closer to him trying to hold her own tears at bay. She lifted her head to the ceiling and begged the gods to help him.

Zelle's body shook with strain and she broke from chanting and sucked in a deep breath. White fur again began to grow on Dax's arms.

"Don't stop," said Aurora. "He's changing back."

"I... I don't have... enough strength," Zelle breathed. Flint dropped to the floor and hugged her tight.

"You can do this. You can. I've seen you do more."

"I'm too weak," she said.

"Use me," he said.

She looked up at him. "I don't want to hurt you."

"No, use me." Cinder strode forward. "Use my magick. I can handle it."

Cinder crouched on the floor and grabbed Zelle's arms with her hands.

Dax cried out as his arm broke again.

"Hurry," said Erik.

Zelle leaned in close and breathed in from Cinder. Cinder gasped like a woman drowning and Zelle breathed in again. A haze swirled around her, tinged with red in places. Cinder's face paled and her lips took on a bluish tinge. The sight made all the blood drain from Belle's body. It looked as if Zelle sucked the life right out of Cinder. Dax's spine snapped and he cried out.

Belle held him tighter. "Hang on, Dax. We're going to fix this." She kissed his blond head, forcing herself to be strong for him.

Zelle breathed in once more and Cinder's face went ashen.

"I think that's enough," Belle managed. "We have to hurry."

"Zelle, darling, you need to stop." Flint pried Cinder's hands from Zelle's arms and eased Cinder onto her back.

Dax roared again as his legs snapped and fur sprouted across his limbs.

"We're losing him," said Erik.

Stil rushed forward and carried Cinder to the couch. "She needs mead. Now."

The queen nodded and hurried from the room.

Zelle laid her hands on Dax once more. Her eyes glowed with an eerie red light and she chanted stronger than ever. Dax's arms and legs snapped back to human. His facial bones shifted, and his lips drew back into a human's mouth. He cried out and then breathed in again through his now human nose.

His body shrunk and the fur disappeared as his ribs cracked and shifted, and then his shoulders, and finally his spine. The sight made Belle's stomach roil. How anyone could endure such pain was beyond her.

Dax lay in a sweaty lump on the floor. Adrian backed away as Erik grabbed a blanket off the bed and covered Dax from the waist down. Dax let go of Belle and rolled onto his back. Belle wrapped her shaky arms around herself, trying to keep from crying out, or screaming or worse; running from the room.

Zelle's eyes drained back to her natural purple color and she relaxed. "We have but a minute." Zelle looked at Dax. "This... is going to hurt."

"I think you're a bit late for that," Dax replied, his voice like gravel.

Zelle crawled over to Dax and laid her hands on his chest. "I'm afraid this is the difficult part." She reached out and wiped the sweat from his forehead. "No matter what happens, you cannot move."

Dax nodded.

Zelle looked at Flint and then to Erik. "Hold him."

"I can do this," he said.

She nodded to Flint. He grabbed Dax by the arms. Erik grabbed Dax's massive thighs.

Zelle looked to Belle. "It might help if you spoke to him during this."

"Me?"

"He needs you," said Zelle.

Dax strained against Erik and Flint's grips. He cried out and his cry became a roar.

"Hurry," said Zelle. "We're losing him and I don't know that I have the strength to try again."

Belle scooted to Dax's head and bent over his face. His warm breath hit her cheek and beads of sweat dripped down his hairline.

Again, Zelle began chanting, but this time the words weren't strong or forceful; they were sweet, tender, even.

Belle stroked Dax's head and looked on as Zelle pointed her fingers at Dax's chest and then began pressing them into his skin.

His body trembled and Belle looked at his face. Tears streamed from his eyes.

"I'm here," she said. "I'm right here."

Dax whimpered, watching as Zelle's fingertips pierced his skin. He threw his head back and pulled against Flint's grip.

"Don't let him move," Zelle ground out.

"Hey. Look at me. Look at me." Belle turned Dax's head so that he faced her. His entire body shook. His eyes reddened and went glassy with strain. His waxy, pale skin was almost as white as his fur had been minutes before.

"So, I was uh... thinking that maybe we could take Chloe and go for a stroll through the kingdom. I've never been in one this big before, so I wondered if maybe you would take us down there. I hoped that maybe there would be a toyshop that we could see if there's a doll or maybe a stuffed bear for Chloe. I think she'd enjoy that." Belle spoke so fast that she could barely keep the words from tumbling out of her mouth. Anything she could do to keep his focus away from Zelle digging her hand into his chest. He sucked in a deep breath and held it. Belle glanced over at Zelle and caught a glimpse of her entire hand inside Dax's chest. Belle bit back the scream that clawed its way up her throat and looked at Dax again.

"And... and... and maybe— maybe I could see if there is a place I can get some parts to fix my blunderbuss. I can make the bullets —"

Dax roared and heaved, and his whole body contracted in a spasm of agony. Belle bit the inside of her cheek. She wanted to scream at Zelle to stop. To push Flint and Erik off Dax and hold him tight.

Dax's gaze connected with hers again and she heaved a sob, unable to hold it back.

"I'm sorry," she whispered. "I'm so sorry." More than anything she wished she could take away his pain. She ran her fingers through his soft hair and kissed his forehead. "I'm sorry. I'm sorry. I'm here, Dax. I'm here."

A light glow emanated from his chest and then Zelle held a small, golden ball in her hands.

"You have to take it," said Zelle. "Usually I would do it, binding the two of you together, but you are just an anchor. You must take this piece of him willingly and accept it fully."

Dax's eyes opened and closed, clinging to consciousness.

"We don't have much time and if you think that you won't be able to fully accept it, tell me now because there is no doing this a second time." Belle met her stare full on. "If you don't take it, this part of his soul will be lost forever." Zelle held the golden ball out to Belle.

A part of his soul would be lost? What would that mean for him? A chill raced over her skin. She didn't want to hurt him. She didn't want him to suffer. Something inside of her clicked and she held her hands out for the ball. Zelle tipped it into Belle's hands and warmth spread from her palms all the way up her arms. In an instant the most beautiful peace overcame her. A peace she'd never felt in her life. Safety. Security. Love. It invaded her senses and encompassed her entire body. She needed this. She wanted it more than she'd ever wanted anything. To feel that safety and love. To know such peace. To be part of someone else and their life. To fully and totally surrender to letting someone in.

Without knowing why, Belle lifted the golden ball to her chest and pressed it into her breast. All of the air whooshed out of her as the ball burst inside her, burning its way through her skin. Her entire body filled with golden light and she lifted off the floor. Every nerve ending lit with warmth and a smile spread across her face as she looked down at Dax.

Then, in an instant the light disappeared and she dropped to the ground, cracking her head on the wood.

"Belle!" Dax reached for her and her vision grew fuzzy, and then dimmed.

She was complete.

CHAPTER FOURTEEN

"Thaddeus you should rest," said the queen.

Dax stared at the sleeping Belle. She looked so small in his large bed. He rubbed the back of her hand with his fingertips willing her to wake up. His bear paced inside him so close to the surface that Dax wasn't sure Zelle's spell would be able to hold him at bay.

"She's going to be just fine," said Aurora. "You should sleep. The pain is written all over you."

Pain? They knew nothing of pain. The word pain did not even begin to describe what he'd been through and yet, even as his head hurt so horribly he was sure it would split open, it paled in comparison to what he'd experienced just an hour before. He continued to stare at Belle. She had to be all right. She just had to. He'd never forgive himself if anything happened to her.

"Thaddeus—"

"Leave me," he bellowed.

The queen blanched, and the king's expression hardened.

"Dax," Erik's voice came out a low warning.

"He didn't mean it," said the queen.

He should apologize. He knew he should apologize, but he didn't have the energy.

"Mother, why don't you and Father go have something to eat?" said Aurora. "Maybe have something prepared for Thad's friends? I'll make sure he sleeps."

Dax continued to watch Belle and a minute later, his door closed. A weight lifted off his shoulders at having them no longer stare at his back. Though he'd put on a tunic, there was no doubt that everyone had seen his scars.

Aurora stepped up and squeezed Dax's shoulders. "She's strong and has much to live for. You for one. And Chloe. She'd never leave Chloe."

Silence stretched out unbearably. Dax bounced his leg up and down on the floor, willing Belle to open her eyes.

"Go," said Erik. "I'll stay with him and make sure he rests."

Dax glanced at Aurora and caught her sad expression. "I'll sleep. I promise. Go. Check on Mother. Give her my apologies."

Aurora nodded. "You should apologize yourself. It wasn't I who was rude."

"Dax knows that. But I think we should all try to be a little bit more tolerant of each other considering the situation," offered Erik.

"And who are you again?"

Dax looked at Erik and saw him do something he'd

never seen before. Standing up straight, Erik assumed a height beyond his own, swathing himself in an air of royalty.

"I am Lord Erik Gwyn of Westfall. Myself and my brothers have been friends of your brother's for several years now, and have been extended family to Belle since we were children."

Aurora's eyes narrowed as she took him in.

"Stop sizing Erik up," said Dax. "He's as much a king of his lands as father is of ours."

Aurora continued to eye Erik, but more with an air of respect than anything.

"Aurora, please. I don't have the patience to deal with this today." He was pretty sure he wouldn't have the patience to deal with it tomorrow, either. Or the next day or the next. Or any day until the curse had been broken. "Please check on Chloe. I'm sure she is with Snow and Sage, but can you make sure she's eaten?"

Aurora looked at Dax and he saw for the first time the woman she'd become in his absence. The leader he had been. The protector of her family and a force to be reckoned with.

Aurora strode from the room and as the door closed, Dax dropped his head to the bed. He didn't know which was worse, how he'd been an hour earlier or how he was at that moment.

Though he may be locked in his human body and anchored by Belle, he could feel his bear nearer to the surface than he ever had before. For the first time, he felt like an intruder in his own body. Every instinct he felt was not his own, but his bear's. All he wanted was to hunt and to eat and to —

"Do you need anything?" asked Erik.

"I need her to wake up."

Erik walked over and patted Dax's shoulder. "She will. Belle's been through a lot. More than most women could handle. But she lives for Chloe. That won't change. She'll wake up for Chloe and now for you, as well."

Dax snorted. "I wouldn't be too sure of that."

"Dax, she voluntarily took a piece of your soul and put it inside her. I don't think she would have done that unless she cared for you."

Erik's words sounded rational, but Dax's bear did not care about rationalities. Erik couldn't understand what was going on with him. But there was one person.

"I need Adrian," said Dax.

Erik nodded. "I'll get him. Stil took him to find some clothes."

"Please also see that Cinder and Zelle are all right," said Dax. "I don't think I could bear it if they were hurt because of me."

Erik chuckled. "I think you need to stop underestimating the females in our lives. They are far from damsels in distress."

He strode from the room, leaving Dax alone with Belle. Dax got up from his chair and sat on the bed next to her. Her hair fanned out around her peachy face. He brushed it from her eyes and ran his palm down her cheek. He could feel her in there. Sleeping. Dreaming. Peaceful. Happy. It eased his worry knowing she merely slept, but he wanted her to wake. He needed her to wake. To see him. To tell him she was all right. To tell him *he* was all right. That they would get through it, together.

He leaned in and smelled her hair before pressing his lips to her forehead. Dax growled. Gods above if anything happened to her because of Morgana, he would rip the stupid daemon limb from limb with his own teeth and eat her heart.

Dax backed away from Belle. The ferocity of his rage startled him. He had to keep control of his bear. He couldn't let his baser instincts take over.

Dax caught Adrian's scent before he even knocked and opened the door. Dax turned to his friend and his bear roared to life. He didn't want Adrian anywhere near Belle.

Without thinking Dax sprang at Adrian and bellowed. Adrian caught him mid leap and slammed Dax to the floor. His eyes flashed golden and he held Dax down by the throat.

"Easy," said Adrian. "Easy, brother."

Dax struggled against him. "Get off me. Get off."

"Dax. Dax!"

Dax looked up at Adrian, his heart racing. What had he done? Why had he attacked Adrian? Adrian wasn't a threat, he was a brother in arms. A friend.

Dax grabbed Adrian's arms. "Adrian... What's happening to me? My bear. I... I can't keep him caged. It's like I'm in here but I'm not in control. I don't even know why I attacked you."

Adrian's grip eased on Dax. "It's the curse. We may have made your form human, but that doesn't mean that your bear isn't still awake in there controlling your every move."

Dax laid back and gripped his hair tight, pulling on it. "I feel like I'm going insane. I'm starving, and I want to hunt and I want to mate. It's never been like this before. Not ever. I feel like I'm turning into..."

"A beast?" Adrian rolled off Dax and placed his hand on Dax's chest. "Magick is a tricky thing, I've learned. Trying to change it can lead to... complications. You needed to be human and you are. But that's just appearance. I was in there with you earlier. I felt you slipping in and out of control. It's never been like that in your head before. When we were in Wolvenglen, you were always in control. Bear was your form not your spirit. But now..."

Dax grabbed Adrian's hand and squeezed. "I'm afraid. Afraid that if I don't break this curse, there will be nothing left of Dax the human. I'll be a beast forever."

Adrian nodded. "A valid fear. But we're all here for you. We're here to make sure that does not happen. Every wolf in Wolvenglen is ready to fight at my command. Every vampire will come to your aid with Sage and Snow. The Gwyns, the humans of Westfall, the fae. If it comes to that, they will fight. They will fight for you and they will fight to eradicate this evil from Fairelle once and for all."

"Dax?"

Dax jumped to his feet, making his head spin. Belle sat up and looked around. He rushed to her side and kissed the back of her hand as elation flooded him.

"You're awake."

"I think I passed out," she chuckled.

He brushed his knuckles across her cheek. She was awake. She was all right. She stared at him and cupped his cheek, making his bear purr.

"I can feel your concern," she said. "It's strange. Almost like I feel it for myself."

"I'd die if something happened to you because of me."

She smiled. "I'm fine. I actually feel better than fine. I feel better than I have in a long time." She studied his face. "You, however, look terrible. Let me get out of your bed and you can get some sleep."

"No."

"No arguing. Get up here." Belle patted the bed and scooted over. Dax looked back at Adrian and then laid down next to her. His pillow smelled of her scent, only a thousand times stronger. Her warmth still clung to his duvet and pillows. He wanted to pull her close like he had in the library. To hold her and rub his scent all over her. To make love to her and —

Whoa! Stop right there, he told his bear. *We are not going there. She does not need that.*

Belle pulled a blanket over him and tucked it around him. He sunk into his bed and every bone in his body sagged with exhaustion. She patted his cheek and stared at him for a moment. Then she rolled over and got up.

"Where are you going?"

"To check on Chloe."

He hated to seem needy after all she'd done for him, but having her close eased his bear somewhat.

No. She needed to see her daughter. And he needed to

let her do it. Whatever he went through with his bear, he'd just have to deal with it on his own.

"You rest and I'll be back soon with some food, all right?"

"Are you sure you should be up? You smacked your head pretty solidly."

She rounded the bed and stopped. "I feel fine. If something changes, you'll be the first to know."

Dax nodded, afraid that if he did anything more than that, he'd beg her to stay and she'd see him for the weak beast that he was turning in to.

"I'll stay with him until you return," said Adrian.

Belle thanked him and headed to the door. Dax tracked her as she went. She stopped and looked back at him, smiled again and then continued out.

He threw his head into his pillows and growled in frustration. Closing his eyes eased the pain in his head. He had to get control of this. He had to- otherwise he feared what he would become.

"How is he?" asked Snow.

"Is he all right?" asked Flint.

"Has he said anything?" questioned Erik.

"All right, let's just give the woman some air." Aurora stepped between them like a personal bodyguard, shielding Belle from everyone.

"It's fine," said Belle. "Believe me, when it comes to being questioned by the Gwyns it could be much worse."

Belle joined the group at the kitchen table where they ate. Chloe hopped into her lap and Aurora sat at her side. Belle hugged Chloe close and kissed her hair. A servant set a plate of food in front of Belle, and she picked up a biscuit, smothering it with butter and jam as the Gwyns and Sage looked at her.

"What happened for you to be here?" Snow asked.

Belle recounted for them what had happened with Klaus, and how Dax saved them in the woods. She told them about Morgana and finding the mirror. Finally, how they'd ended up in the castle.

"We knew it had to do with the dragons," said Erik. "We'd been saying it for months. But Dax didn't want to just walk back into the dragon lands without a reason."

"Very wise of him," said Aurora.

"What are the dragon guard?" asked Flint.

Aurora lifted the sleeve of her dress revealing a brand upon her forearm.

"I've seen that before," said Belle. "Dax has one on his shoulder."

Aurora nodded. "Every dragon rider has one. Or they did, until they were captured."

"How did that happen?" asked Erik.

She shrugged. "We are hoping Thad can tell us. He and his riders went out to hunt Morgana after she fled from Draakland. No one returned. Not the riders. Not the dragons. Not Thad."

"So, the dragons... they belong to you?"

Aurora nodded. "The word 'belong' denotes ownership. We never owned the dragons. We had a mutual agreement with them. They protected Draak, and we provided for them. It had been that way for hundreds of years. But then something happened and Morgana stole the dragons and turned them against us."

"The collars," said Flint. "It's how she controls them. Magickly binding them to do her will."

"But they defied her when we fought. They refused to attack Dax," replied Erik.

"Because he was their captain," said Aurora. "He'd bonded to their leader."

"But what did Morgana want here?" asked Sage. "Why did she come to Draakland of all places?"

"Because of the prophecy," said Aurora. "What number are we on now? Five?"

When the prince without a name, a memory or a past,
Returns to claim the throne on which a spell was cast,
The bonds he will but heal with friendship strong and true.
The north and south shall once again reforge the old alliances
    like new.

"Makes sense," said Sage. "Dax is the one from the prophecy. The prince without name or memory. Morgana knew her children might fail. By coming and taking Dax and the dragon guard, she insured that the prophecies could never be fulfilled."

"But why not just kill him?" asked Erik. "Why take him and chance him escaping?"

"Because Morgana still wants to win. She wanted to take over the dragons and the riders and win them to her side."

"But the riders are gone, and she still has control of the dragons. What did she need the riders for?" asked Snow.

"For the bond," said Aurora. "Riders and their dragons share a special bond. With the bond a rider can move faster, be stronger. They move with a speed no one can match and are practically impervious to being hurt."

"But what does she need people like that for if she had dragons? The dragons alone can decimate all of Fairelle."

"Because she doesn't just want to decimate all of Fairelle." Zelle joined the group and Flint went to her and embraced her tight.

"You should be resting," he said.

Zelle set her head on Flint's chest. "I saw what Morgana wanted when I was in Dax's mind. She wants to rule Fairelle, yes, but she wants more than that. She wants to go to Shaidan and kill my father. She wants to reopen the rift. Reclaim the Daemon realm, and flood Fairelle with daemons."

The group looked at each other and Belle grabbed onto Chloe. It was crazy. The whole thing was crazy. Vampires, werewolves, fae, dragons, princes, princess warriors, mages, magick. It was too much to believe, and yet she couldn't deny the reality slapping her in the face.

"What do we do?" she asked.

"We do what Dax has done for each and every one of us. We keep him safe. Make sure Morgana doesn't get her clutches on him," said Flint.

"And what about the curse?"

The group looked around the table, none of them knowing how to answer.

"He can't stay like that," said Belle. "We can't stay like this. You know what the card said, he's going to get worse."

"We'll figure out a way," said Zelle. "I bought us some time. Not a lot—"

"But enough." Snow reached across the table and squeezed Belle's hand. "He's strong. He'll make it through this."

Belle nodded, but she wasn't as sure. It was true, he might very well make it through without the curse being broken. Question was, who would he be in the end?

CHAPTER FIFTEEN

D ax awoke the next morning with a hunger
gnawing in his gut larger than any he'd experienced before. His head pounded, and his bear
roared to be fed.

Barely getting on his clothes, he made his way down the
back staircase to the floors below. Once down on the lower
level, he headed straight for the kitchen. Maids curtsied and
moved out of his way as he lumbered past. Butlers bowed
and asked how they could help him; but all Dax could focus
on was the food.

Smells of bread, rolls, meat, fruit, roasting vegetables
and more floated out to him, calling his name and beck-
oning him forward. By the time he hit the kitchen door he
could scarcely contain the overwhelming need. He scanned
the bustling arena of people. Everyone hurried about
mixing and chopping and plating food.

Dax strode into the kitchen and grabbed the nearest

plate, gobbling down the eggs and toast. The kitchen help stared at him but said nothing. As he finished the food, his body cried out for more. He grabbed the next plate and devoured that as well. Then he grabbed the next, and the next and the next.

"Your highness, is... is there something we can get you?" asked the cook.

Dax's head whipped up at the pig rolling on the spit. "More."

"More?" asked the cook. "What more can I get you, your highness?"

"Food!" Dax slammed his fist on the counter. "Get me more food!"

The servants shared a look and then backed away. Dax scanned the terrified faces, his bear roaring for more. The hairs on his neck prickled and his bear fought for control, wanting to shift, but the spell held him at bay.

Enraged, Dax roared at the ceiling and then swiped at the barren plates, sending them crashing to the floor.

"What the hell is wrong with you?" he demanded. "I want more food!"

BELLE AWOKE TO A POUNDING ON HER DOOR AND JUMPED from the bed. Her heart raced as she looked at the clock, which told her it was too early for someone to be pounding. She glanced over at Chloe, who sat up and rubbed her eyes.

"Go back to sleep, Sweetums," Belle said.

Chloe yawned as there another pound hit the door and then someone tried the handle.

"Belle!" yelled Aurora. "Belle, open up!"

Belle rushed to the door, her heart racing, and pulled it open.

"You need to come with me," said Aurora, still in her nightdress.

"What's wrong?"

"It's Dax," said Chloe, walking to her side. "He needs you, Mama."

Aurora stared at Chloe and Belle. Belle swung Chloe into her arms and together the three rushed to the back stairs. She'd just left Dax a few hours previous. After eating, she'd put Chloe to bed and had gone in to sit and read to him for a while as he rested. Then after he'd fallen into a deep sleep, she'd returned to her own room. With everything he'd been through, he couldn't have been awake for more than a few minutes, how much trouble could he get in?

They reached the bottom floor and servants stood gawking in the hallway, whispering and pointing at the kitchen. The king and queen crowded the doorway as did Erik, Flint and Adrian. A roar sounded from inside the kitchen and everyone backed up a step.

"I tried to talk to him," said Adrian. "It didn't work."

"Dax is hungry," said Chloe.

Belle looked at her daughter and then at Aurora.

"We can't stop him. He won't listen to reason," said Aurora. "He's destroyed just about everything in there."

Belle looked at Flint and Erik. "He won't let us near

him," said Flint. "I've never seen him like this before."

Belle nodded. She could feel him in there. The rage, the hunger, the fear. All of it mixed inside Dax, one emotion battling against the next.

All eyes went to her. She was his tether, they were counting on her to keep him sane. Problem was... she had no idea how to do that.

Belle set Chloe on the floor and the little girl took Erik's hand. A crash sounded from inside the kitchen and Belle blew out a breath. She steadied herself and stared straight ahead as she walked past the entourage.

She stepped to the kitchen door and stopped. Broken glass and debris scattered the floor. Food spread over every surface. Half eaten fruit, bitten vegetables, a leg of meat strewn wastefully on the ground. Back in the cabin, it would have been over a month's worth of food and then some. Her gaze traversed every surface and landed on Dax's bulky form bent over half a pig that had been ripped from the spit. He tore into the animal's flesh, making her stomach roil. She crept across the floor, careful to not step on the glass. She halted several feet from him when she kicked a bottle and it rolled to Dax and hit his foot.

He whipped around and stared at her, his eyes wild, food smeared across his face. He looked at her like he didn't even know her, and Belle forced a smile upon her lips.

"Hungry?" she asked.

He blinked and wiped his mouth with the back of his sleeve.

"You know, pig is much better when it's cooked. I could cut a few pieces and fry them for you."

He didn't speak, simply stared at her, blinking.

She took a step forward and he growled. She threw up her hands. "Easy, Dax. Easy."

She could feel him in there. His conflict, his hunger. The battle inside him with his bear coursed even worse than she had imagined.

His eyebrows furrowed and he shook his head. When he looked at her again his eyes had softened. Belle took another tentative step toward him and he sucked in a breath. She stepped closer and his body began to relax. She reached for him, her hand hovering in the air inches from his face. Then Belle knelt beside him and their eyes connected. She felt the moment his bear backed away and Dax took control again.

Shame rounded his features. "Belle." He pushed his cheek into her palm and then grabbed it and kissed it. She cradled his face. Sadness coursed through her as the realization of what he'd done crashed down around his features.

"Belle." He looked at her. "What's happening to me?"

She pulled him into her arms. He hugged her tighter than she thought possible.

"It isn't you, Dax."

"You can't know that."

"I do know that, because I know you. You are kind and gentle and well-mannered. You would never eat meat without utensils."

He chuckled and looked up at her, and then over her shoulder. "They're scared of me. My own family."

She cupped his face again and forced him to look at her. "No. They aren't scared of you. They are scared for you. Like I am."

"You're afraid I'll be like this forever."

She could lie to him, but what was the point? "Yes," she said. "Afraid not for me, but for you. I feel what is happening inside you. How it is tearing at your soul. I fear that at some point you won't be able to deal with the guilt and you'll..."

"What?"

"Leave."

His eyes told her that he'd thought about it already. Thought about leaving. Thought about giving in. Thought about ending it.

"Promise me," she said. "Promise me that you will not do any of the things that you are thinking of doing to get you out of this situation. We are here. Flint is here. And Erik and Snow and Zelle and Cinder and Stil and Adrian. We are all here, and we won't stop working until we've broken this curse and set you free. Do you hear me?"

He nodded.

"Say it. Say that you hear me, and you won't do anything. Promise me Dax."

"I promise."

She couldn't tell him that she needed him. She couldn't tell him that she wanted him. She couldn't tell him that to lose him now might break her in a way that she could never fix. To tell him those things would be to admit that she had fallen for him. That she cared for him. That... she loved him.

Dax stared at Belle. Shame and anger at what he'd done and what was happening to him ripped through his body. For the moment he'd gotten his bear to back away, but he could still feel the beast, close to the surface, wanting to be let out. Waiting for the moment Dax's resolve slipped so he could take over, even if he couldn't shift.

Dax sat by the pig, his stomach feeling like it might explode. He didn't want to get up from the spot though the fire burned too warm and the stone floor ached his knees. He didn't want to see the fear and sadness on his parents' faces for coming home and not being what they expected. Who they expected. He didn't want to think of the servants cowering before him as they had minutes before when he'd torn through the kitchen out of control.

"I think you should clean up," said Belle. "Then if you are still hungry, we can grab a bite at the table."

He loved how well she took to her new job of looking after him, but he hated that she had to do it. Belle had her own worries, she didn't deserve to have his heaped upon her as well.

"Cleaning up would be a good thing, but you don't need to take care of me. I know it's early. You and Chloe should go back to bed."

Belle chuckled. "I think that is quite impossible at this point. Why don't you wash and then we'll see how you're feeling. Perhaps if you are feeling up to it, we could go down into the city and you could show me around."

"You wanted to find a toy shop, did you not?"

She smiled. "I didn't know if you could hear me when I said that."

"I think getting out for a bit is exactly what I need today."

"Then let's do it. You clean up and Chloe and I will get ready as well, and then you can show us around Draakland."

He pulled her to her feet, wanting to hug her again. To feel the comfort of having her body pressed against his, but he dared not, for fear of what he might do.

Belle brushed the glass from her nightdress and he helped her over the shards to the doorway.

Dax hung his head unable to meet anyone's eye. "I apologize for my outburst," he said. "It was uncalled for."

His mother walked to him and wrapped her arms around him. His father joined and then Aurora. Dax fought to keep his emotions at bay as they stood in a group hug. They'd been close before he'd disappeared. The four of them. They'd done things together every single day. Eaten together. Walked together. Talked together. It had been his own parents who had tutored him and his sister growing up. His parents who had raised them. Where other nobles had employed servants to raise their children, his parents had insisted on doing it themselves.

His mother stepped back and looked him dead in the eyes. "This isn't you, Thaddeus. We know that."

"We will do anything to help you break this curse," said his father.

"And kill Morgana," finished Aurora.

"Aurora!" Their mother gasped.

"Don't you think it's time we took the fight to her? I'm tired of sitting around, waiting to see what she does next."

"She's right," said Flint. "Sitting here will do us no good."

"But rushing in is unwise," offered Erik.

"Then we make a plan," said Sage. "We sit down and formulate the best plan of attack."

"Agreed," said the king. "I'm tired of hiding. It's time we do something about this and before we lose our son again."

It warmed Dax to see so many coming to his rescue, but he wouldn't let anyone get hurt because of him. Not the Gwyns, not Sage, and definitely not his father or sister.

"Then let's all take the morning to think of anything we can. We will meet in the great hall at noon and all present ideas," said Erik.

The group nodded.

"Can I present an idea, too?" asked Chloe.

Everyone looked down at her and chuckled.

Dax picked her up and she rubbed her cheek on his. "How about if you and I and your mommy get cleaned up and then we go down into the city for a bit?"

Chloe nodded. "You need to wipe your face. You're a messy eater."

Again, everyone laughed and Chloe threw her arms around Dax and squeezed his neck tight.

"You're going to be fixed," she whispered. "Mama will make sure of it."

Dax's gaze traveled to Belle. He squeezed Chloe tight and watched as a myriad of emotions crossed Belle's face. He wanted to believe Chloe's words that Belle would make sure he got fixed. But he wasn't sure if the child's words were those of prophecy, or those of comfort.

CHAPTER SIXTEEN

Belle strolled next to Dax holding Chloe's hand as she ate a sweet bun from the bakery they'd visited. She tried to ignore the stares and whispers and curtsies and bows as she and Dax passed, but it wasn't easy. She wanted nothing more than to run back to the castle and hear everyone's ideas, but she knew that Dax needed a break, as did Chloe.

Dax stepped next to her and squeezed her hand. "Is it really that bad?"

She looked up at him and wanted to lie, but she wasn't able to. "I don't like being looked at."

Dax chuckled. "I would have thought you'd be used to it by now."

She cocked an eyebrow at him.

"What I mean is, you're so beautiful. I can't imagine you go much of anywhere without attracting attention of every man within seeing distance."

Her cheeks heated. "I try not to notice whether or not men stare at me. I want to be admired for my mind, not my face."

"Would it bother you if I admired you for both?"

She peeked up at him quizzically. His words surprised her. He'd never been so forward with her before.

"Only if you don't mind that I admire you for both," she finally replied.

He smiled and took her hand. His large, warmer than usual fingers, wrapped around hers and the sensation made her grin. Klaus had only ever held her hand when he wanted to drag her somewhere or show people she belonged to him. Not the way Dax held her hand; comforting, protective yet not possessive.

They walked several more minutes with Dax pointing out different shops. Everywhere they went shopkeepers cheered and bowed and offered him goods for free. Mostly he said no, but at a flower shop he stopped and plucked a single sungold for Belle. Snapping off the stem he placed it in her hair behind her ear. His fingers lingered on her cheek and she couldn't help but see the desire that burned in his eyes.

"You look beautiful, Mama," said Chloe.

"She always looks like that," replied Dax.

Belle looked at Chloe and then to the flowers in the vases. She walked to a beautiful peony the color of the sky. "May I?" she asked.

"Of course," the shopkeeper replied.

Belle picked up the flower and handed it to Chloe. Chloe's eyes lit up like little jewels and she thrust it to Dax.

"Put it in my hair."

Dax knelt down in front of Chloe and broke the stem. He pushed the large flower behind her ear. "Just as beautiful as your mother."

Chloe threw her arms around Dax's neck and kissed his cheek. "I love you, Dax."

He looked up at Belle and her heart squeezed. She couldn't remember how long it had been since Chloe had done that with Klaus. A year? More?

Dax hugged Chloe back. "I love you too, sweetie."

Belle's chest constricted and she had to turn away. Why couldn't Klaus be like that? Why did he have to be so selfish? So angry? So mean? Why couldn't he just be decent and good? The answer slapped Belle in the face. Because that wasn't who Klaus chose to be. In that moment the truth she'd denied for years finally struck her. He wasn't ever going to change because he didn't want to, and because she allowed him to be that way.

It wasn't her fault he was a selfish, abusive, bastard. But it was her fault for letting him treat her badly for so long. For not leaving sooner. But no more. She refused to be a victim any longer. She refused to let her daughter be a victim. Chloe deserved a father who treated her as a precious jewel. A father who provided for her and protected her, even from himself if need be. Not a man who treated her like property.

"Mama, why are you crying?"

Belle looked down to find Chloe staring at her.

"Belle, are you all right?" Dax's hand landed on her shoulder.

Belle nodded and smiled, swiping the tears from her eyes. "I'm fine. I just got a bit of dust in my eyes. It's nothing." She took Chloe's hand. "I think we promised to find you a toy shop, didn't we?"

Chloe nodded vigorously.

"Come, it's right around the corner," said Dax.

CHLOE RAN AROUND THE SHOP POINTING AT EVERYTHING AND taking things off the shelf one by one to see what they were. The toy maker happily obliged Chloe in helping her pick something out.

"Do you want to tell me what happened back there?" Dax asked.

Belle swallowed and smiled as Chloe showed them another doll.

"I finally came to the realization that Klaus is never going to change."

"No, he isn't."

"I mean, I knew that deep down, but still, in my heart I'd hoped... Even if it was just for Chloe. But he won't. Ever since I've known him he's been selfish, overbearing, possessive. In the beginning I didn't mind because he and Jamen were the ones to get me away from my drunken father who used to beat me and abuse me... in more ways than one."

"Belle—"

"I thought, well, with Klaus at least I knew no one would mess with me again. No one would hurt me again. I thought with him I could be me. I could be strong. But within a year of moving in with him, I realized that I'd just gone from one form of abuse to another. It's not all his fault though, I mean, he hurt me but time and time again I went back. After the lying, cheating, stealing, I still went back. I could have stayed with the Gwyns but I didn't. I kept thinking I could change him."

"Belle, what he did to you was not your fault. Your misplaced optimism about him did not make it all right for him to do the things he did to you or Chloe. To say that you were at fault for letting him treat you that way is like a dog saying it deserved to be kicked because it loved its owner so much."

Dax turned her so that she faced him.

"Belle. You are beautiful and strong and an amazing woman. You are what Fairelle needs if we are to keep going." He paused and licked his lips. "You are what I need."

He scooped his fingers into her hair and cradled the base of her skull. Her stomach flopped as he pulled her body in contact with his.

"I will never let him hurt you again. I will never let him hurt Chloe again. I will do everything in my power to keep you both safe and happy for as long as you want."

Belle ran her hand up his muscular arm. She wanted to believe Dax. She wanted to beg him to keep them safe. To open her heart to him and see what it felt like to let in someone who wouldn't hurt her.

Dax moved closer and his lips lingered above hers. "Stay," he said. "Stay with me Belle and let me take care of you. You and Chloe."

Belle closed her eyes. She wanted to say yes. She wanted to wrap him in her arms and feel him making love to her.

His lips brushed hers.

"Mama, I found it!"

Belle pulled away and looked to where Chloe stood. In her arms she held a large stuffed dragon.

"It's just like Alabrax," Chloe announced.

Belle nodded and headed for her little girl. "Yes, it is."

"It's one of a kind," said the toymaker. "It has articulating legs joints and if you pour hot water in its mouth, it smokes."

"Amazing," replied Dax. "What do I owe you for it?"

The toymaker held up his hands. "For the beautiful little princess, I couldn't possibly charge for the toy. It is my gift to welcome her to the kingdom."

Belle stepped forward. "Oh, Chloe's not—"

"Not going to be able to put such a wonderful gift down. Thank you," said Dax.

Belle bit her tongue. She didn't want the people in town to think Chloe was a princess and she didn't want Chloe thinking it either.

Belle tugged on Dax's sleeve. "May I talk to you for a moment?"

Dax looked down at her and she pulled him several feet away from the scene, but he put up a hand before she could speak.

"I know what you are going to say and what does it matter? You came with me through the mirror. I want you to stay. She looks like she could be mine. Is it such a bad thing if people think I'm her father?"

"What happens when they find out you aren't?"

He squeezed her arm. "Who is going to tell them? You?"

Belle looked to Chloe. Pretending Dax was her father would bring Chloe a life Belle could never have dreamed of. And protection of her gifts that Belle wouldn't be able to get anywhere else.

"You think your parents are going to just let you say you are her father?"

"They don't know she's not. I haven't said a word."

"Aurora knows she isn't yours."

"Aurora won't say anything if I tell her not to."

"And what happens when she gets older? What happens if we stay with you in the castle and one day, she decides she wants to leave? Or marry? Do you think your parents will allow such a thing if they think she is your child?"

"They won't have a say in it. You are her mother. It's your decision."

"Just like they don't have a say about who you marry? About Violet?"

Dax's mouth clamped shut and his gaze turned sad. "You know I don't have feelings for her."

"But does that matter to your parents?"

"It matters to me. And that is all that matters. Six years ago, I would have done it. I would have married the girl and kept her happy and had her keep my bed warm in return. In time I would have even come to love her, but I would never have been in love with her. Not the way I am—" He stopped and looked over to Chloe. "I'm not marrying Violet. I don't love Violet. I made that clear to my father and

Violet. After so many years she wants different things for her life as well. But that's beside the point. The point is, in this small instance, with a toymaker, does it really matter who he thinks Chloe is? For dragon's sake, if people think she is my daughter isn't she more protected than ever?"

He was right. Dax had a hundred armed guards at his beck and call. He had a dragon. And he was a bear. Was there anywhere safer for Chloe?

"Did you just say, for dragon's sake?"

Dax snorted. "I guess I did."

"All right."

Dax kissed her, sending shivers through her body. Then he walked over to Chloe and lifted her up. "What a great choice."

"Look its legs move!" Chloe moved the toy's legs. "When we get home can we put hot water in him and see him smoke?"

Dax nodded. They walked to Belle and Dax took her hand in his, carrying Chloe in the other. She'd wanted this for so long she had no idea how to feel. Her entire life she'd wanted one thing; a family of her own. With Dax, she might actually get it. Belle's chest constricted at the thought and she smiled.

CHAPTER SEVENTEEN

Klaus slammed a cup against the wall. "Dammit!"

Morgana growled behind him. "Please. You think your daughter and girlfriend are so special? What about me? Do you know what I've been through?"

Klaus turned in time to see her drape a scarf over the blood-drenched bowl they'd been staring into moments before. Belle and Dax. Dax and Chloe. Chloe and Belle. Together like one happy family.

"The time it took me to perform that spell on him drained more than a little of the magick I still possess. You think things are bad for you losing a pretty piece of curvy tail? You have no idea what will happen if I run out of what I need to power the stones."

"I don't care one whit about Belle. If Dax wants her, he can have her. But Chloe is mine. My blood. She's more important to me than—"

"Than what?" Morgana's eyes flashed.

"Nothing," he muttered. Klaus wasn't stupid. Morgana wasn't a woman you upset without expecting some painful repercussions. "So what do we do now?"

Morgana gave a mirthless laugh. "We? We. Since when did you and I become a 'we'?"

A chill raced through Klaus. He'd known for months that he'd gotten in too deep with Morgana. Even he couldn't sate her sexual appetites, and her temper was even more uncontrollable. The mood swings between wanting sex and wanting to exact revenge were enough to have him running back to Westfall if he hadn't been so afraid of her finding him and dragging him back.

She tapped her fingers on the small table. "I need to show him I meant what I said. I don't know how he's back in human form, but he needs to know that I will not let him go without a fight."

"Why do you want him so much?" In all the time he'd spent with her, Klaus had found her obsession with Dax to border on the edge of madness, but he'd never understood why.

Morgana turned her red gaze upon him. "Why I want him is none of your concern. The thing you need concern yourself with is proving to me how I am going to get him back because if you don't, you are of no use to me. If you are of no use to me then you are nothing more than baggage. And I don't like baggage."

The strange red mist swirled around her hands as she stared at the mirror that stood in the corner of the room. He'd seen it every time they had sex, every time she administered punishment, and every time she became angry, like the mist he'd seen swirl around Zelle when she killed his friends. Klaus was no fool. He knew that when the mist arrived, it was time for him to make an exit.

"I should leave you to your planning," he said. "I know that the recent developments must be quite vexing."

She didn't look at him but continued staring at the mirror. "Vexing... vexing... vexing." A smile crept across her face and she turned to him again. "For someone so stupid, every once in a while, you remind me why I continue to let you breathe."

Klaus wasn't sure if she meant it as an insult or a compliment.

She sauntered over to him and kissed his cheek. "Thank you for reminding me what I had been trying to accomplish before I became so distracted by Dax's re-emergence. You say he is vexing me? Well, I shall show him how vexing I can be in return."

She planted her hand on Klaus' chest and pushed him back until he fell on the bed. Morgana crawled up his body and licked the side of his neck. "What if I gave you another child?" she asked. "A son."

Klaus froze. A child with Morgana would be... what? Not all human. And not his for damn sure. And he'd be tied to her forever.

She continued to kiss across his chest and ripped his shirt open.

"I... appreciate the offer. I know that is a huge gift, but I couldn't even think of having another until I am able to get Chloe back."

She licked her way down to his waistband and undid the tie. "Why? Why is she so important to you? She's only human. What I offer would be so much more."

Klaus grabbed her hair as she ran her tongue below his waistband and shimmied his breeches off him. His head swam with the need to flip her on her stomach and drive into her.

"I— I love her. She's... special. She sees."

"Sees what?" Morgana licked his length and his fingers gripped her white hair tight.

"She... she... sees the future."

Morgana stopped moving and her gaze whipped up. "What did you say?"

Klaus's mind and body clashed as he tried to remember what he'd said. Morgana sat up and he groaned.

"What do you mean she sees the future?"

"I... she..." Had he said that? Dread washed through him. In all of the months at her side, in her bed, at her beck and call, he'd sworn he would never tell her.

"She what?" Morgana demanded.

"She nothing. I meant she makes me see the future. Look to the future. Be a better man." He fought to keep his face passive.

Quicker than light she had her hand around his throat. She squeezed harder than he thought her petite form capable of.

"You're lying." Her eyes glowed red and she squeezed tighter. "Tell me the truth and I may not kill you."

The air sucked out of Klaus' lungs and his head began to feel too much pressure. Even so, he would not give Chloe to Morgana. He grabbed at her wrist trying to push it from his throat, but it didn't budge. He bucked his hips but she stayed planted atop him.

"I'm... not lying..." He barely squeezed the words out as dark spots formed behind his eyes.

He tried in vain to force her off, but she held him fast. He fought against her, trying to flip over but she pinned him down, her body impossibly strong and heavy.

"Tell me!" Her face shrank and changed taking on a skeletal appearance. Her eyes glowed brighter and her teeth lengthened into several long sharp rows.

Klaus clawed against her hold as his head felt like it had filled with bricks and would explode at any moment.

She leaned in close and smiled with a mouth unnaturally too wide for her face. "You will tell me. One way or the other."

His hand dropped to the bed as the pressure in his head became too much to bear and everything went black.

KLAUS GASPED AND SHOT UP ON THE BED. HE SUCKED IN several deep breaths and grabbed at his throat. He glanced around the room and found Morgana sitting at her vanity brushing her hair. She glanced at him through the mirror and smiled.

"You're finally awake."

She set the brush down as Klaus continued to suck in breath. He needed to get out of there. Klaus had known she was a little off, but the most recent development had him realizing that she had completely lost it.

"Everything is in place and ready to go, we were just waiting on you, my darling." She sashayed toward him.

"Me?" he croaked. "What do you need from me?"

"You are going to go get your precious Chloe, of course."

A chill raced through him. "No, I think... maybe she is better off with Belle for now."

Morgana smiled at him and ran her finger down his cheek. "Oh darling, that wasn't a request."

She pushed a stone on her red ring and Klaus's body exploded in pain. Every nerve lit up as if set on fire. His chest constricted so he couldn't breathe. His mouth opened in a silent scream and every thought vanished as pain and lack of oxygen took him to the edge of consciousness.

Just as the blackness seeped into view, the pain stopped and he sucked in gulps of air. He rolled sideways and pitched onto the floor, dry heaving. A cry escaped him as his muscles twitched and spasmed. A tear escaped his eye as snot and spit dripped onto the floor.

Morgana knelt beside him, her hand on his back. "There is no use fighting it Klaus." She produced a vial from her sleeve. "One way or another you will help me." She ran her fingers through his hair and kissed his temple. "I wish it didn't have to be this way... Actually, never mind. If I am being honest, I'm glad we've arrived at this point. Your betrayal in not telling me about Chloe had me angry enough that I almost let you die; but then I figured, what good does that do me? I'd be satisfied for a moment that I'd ended you, but you are so much more valuable to me compliant and alive than you are dead and worthless."

Klaus reached up and ran his fingers over the collar at his throat. His stomach pitched and he gulped down the bile that rose deep within. Weakness shook his limbs.

She ruffled his hair. "So, let's try again. Tell me the truth about Chloe."

Klaus shut his eyes and sucked in a breath. Willing himself to tell her the truth and end his anguish. "I misspoke. Chloe is just a normal little girl."

"Hmm..." Morgana tapped something on the floor and he opened his eyes. "You see this potion? It's going to make you do whatever I want you to. I don't even have to use the collar to control you once I make you drink this. The thing is, I'm not ready to give it to you. First, I want you to know, really know what it feels like to betray me."

Pain shot through Klaus and he dropped to the floor. His face smashing into the stone and his nose exploded in pain. His body convulsed as blood poured from his nose, dripping into his mouth.

Chloe's smile floated into his mind. His body constricted like he'd been piled under a dozen horses. Spots appeared in his vision obscuring Chloe's angelic face. His body jerked and twitched as the excruciating pain overtook him. He wouldn't give her up. He wouldn't. No matter what Morgana did to him. He would never give up Chloe.

CHAPTER EIGHTEEN

Dax pulled at his collar fighting the urge to rip it off. He did not want to be there, and he did not want to be having a party for all the nobles in the land. A hand skimmed up his leg and his bear growled.

He chewed his lip fighting to keep his composure.

"What do you think of that?" asked the royal tailor.

"I think it fits him beautifully." Dax's mom walked to him like a living doll and pulled on the fabric here and there.

After returning from the city, Dax and Belle had met with everyone else to try and figure out the best way to attack Morgana. In the end, since they had no idea where she was, they decided that they would send a troop of the guard into the hills to search areas they hadn't covered yet. Granted, there were many terrains out there that were still undiscovered, but it was the best they could do under the circumstances. Even so, it still left Dax feeling useless.

He wondered for the millionth time if the reason his mother had always been so particular about his clothing was because Aurora never allowed their mother to dress her. From the time she had been three years old, Aurora had made it quite plain that she would wear what she wanted or nothing at all.

He remembered all too well Aurora arriving to a royal feast in nothing but her pantaloons when she'd been younger than even Chloe.

Where their mother insisted Aurora wear pink, Aurora always chose blue. The fight between them had continued even that morning. The tailor had brought many different shades of pink fabric. But Aurora had insisted that if she was going to be forced to wear a dress, that it be in the fabric of her choosing. Dax had chuckled when Aurora had chosen a fabric brought for him. A deep, bluish purple that matched Aurora's eyes.

A pin pricked him in the leg and Dax roared at the tailor. The man scrambled away in fright.

"Why don't we take a break," offered the queen. She snapped her fingers and a maid approached. "Will you get Lady Belle and Miss Chloe, please?"

The maid curtsied and left.

Dax grumbled. "I don't need Belle. I need to not be dressed up like a dancing bear and paraded in front of people I don't care about."

His mother smiled. "Is that what we're doing?"

Dax pulled the fabric from his body and moved away from her to sit in an overstuffed chair. "I can't do this. I need to get out of here."

"Do you think that's wise?" asked his mother. "Just leaving again? What good would that do?"

"I don't know. But I can't do this. Being cooped up. Confined."

"No one is confining you. If you want to go out, go out. There's no reason for you to sit around here brooding and sulking."

Dax bounded to his feet in an instant. "Is that what you think I'm doing? Brooding? I was cursed by a witch. Tortured. I forgot who I was and spent almost six years trying to figure it out where I belonged. Then, I finally got back here only to be cursed again to be a bear until I return to the witch who cursed me. And the only way I can stay human is to have part of my soul put inside a woman who — who…"

"Who what?"

Dax turned to find Belle standing in the doorway, arms crossed and an eyebrow cocked.

What had he been about to say? Even he wasn't sure.

"You know what I think?" She stepped forward. "I think you need the frustration run straight out of you."

"Yes?" he asked. "And just how do you think we should do that?"

A smile pulled up the corners of Belle's mouth.

"Are you serious about this?" asked Dax.

"Absolutely," Belle replied.

Dax stared at the forest. She could feel him fighting to

keep control of his bear. And she had the idea that the best way to do that, was to tire his bear out.

"Are we doing this or not?" asked Adrian.

"Oh, we're doing this," said Belle.

"I'm not sure this is a good idea," said Dax.

"Why?" asked Aurora. "Are you afraid you might hurt someone?"

"I think he's afraid he'll hurt himself," replied Flint.

Everyone chuckled.

"All right," said Belle. "On the count of three, everyone is going to run into the forest. Flint, you are going to make Dax wait sixty seconds before he is allowed in and then blow the whistle letting us know he's on his way. As he finds us, he will tag us and we will come back to Flint."

"And me!" Chloe beamed, waving a small golden flag, holding Erik's hand.

"This is childish," said Dax.

"You mean like how you've been acting?" Stil replied.

Dax grumbled but didn't respond.

Adrian clapped Dax on the shoulder. "You love running in the woods. It's in your blood. Trust Belle."

Adrian winked at Belle and stripped off his shirt, forcing her to look away.

"What if he doesn't catch us?" asked Aurora.

Dax snorted. "Trust me, I'll find you."

"Yes, but will you catch us?" asked Sage.

"All right," Belle said. "Ready? One, two, three!"

Belle shot into the trees with Zelle, Flint and Cinder cheering behind them. Sage took off fast as light and hit the trees first. Adrian dropped onto all fours and ran into the forest next. She caught a slight glimpse of his wolf form disappearing behind a rock. Aurora continued straight ahead with Alabrax flying up above the treetops.

Belle took off to the left. She raced into the trees and ducked under a low hanging branch and then jumped over a rock. Her heart pounded as the blood pumped through her body. She breathed hard and slowed. She looked up at the enormous trees. They were twice as wide and three times as tall as the trees in Westfall. The thick branches looked almost as big as the bed she used to sleep in. She wondered for a split second if she could hollow one out and make a house inside. If she did, she was sure no one would ever even notice.

The whistle blew and she took off again. She wondered who Dax would go for first.

Belle made her way deeper into the woods and the sounds of water rushed up to meet her. She followed them until she came to a large pool with a beautiful waterfall. A bed of rainbow flowers the size of dinner plates covered the entire grove. She'd never seen anything like it. Belle walked into the spacious clearing and tiptoed through the waist-high flowers to the edge of the pool. The water twinkled in the afternoon sun, giving off an iridescent glow. She dipped her hand in the cool water and drank from it. A roar sounded not too far off and she stood and turned. Alabrax bellowed and then everything went silent again.

The only thing she'd been able to think to do to help Dax run off some of his excess energy was playing the childish game. It'd been two days since their venture into town, and almost five total since they'd been in Draakland.

Every day since the curse she witnessed him trying to hold it together for everyone else, while feeling his rising distress and anxiety. There was very little time left until the bear took over permanently and none of them had any idea what to do. Getting rid of some of his mounting frustration seemed as good an idea as any.

CLOSE TO THIRTY MINUTES LATER BELLE HEARD A RUSTLE IN the trees. She stood at the water's edge waiting. Something moved closer and closer. For the first time, Belle feared what could happen to any and all of them having run into the woods for a mere game, when Morgana and Klaus could be just waiting for them to let down their guard.

She looked around for somewhere to hide and backed up toward the water. The closer the noises got, the more anxious she became. It had been a stupid idea. What had she been thinking leaving the safety of the castle? Closer the thing stalked. Then, she felt it. The anxiety, the thrill, the desire.

Dax stalked into the clearing. His shirt slashed in several areas and slight cuts marred his skin.

"Are you hurt?" she called.

He didn't answer. Eyes fixed he headed straight for her. His body rolled like that of a giant predator. She moved back a little and her shoe sunk into the wet dirt. He tracked her movements and she fought to pull her foot from the mud, but it stuck tight. She swayed on the spot as she tried to keep her balance. Stepping out of her shoes, she pitched backward toward the water.

She yelped as a strong hand clamped around her arm and pulled her upright. Dax stared at her, his body hot where it touched hers. His eyes scoured her face and she could feel him once again fighting to keep control.

"You found me." Her heart thudded so rapidly she feared it might hop out of her chest.

Dax leaned in and sniffed her neck, making her body shiver.

"I've been searching for you," he said.

Belle closed her eyes as his arm slid around her waist and he pulled her in closer to him. He brushed her long hair from her neck and sniffed her again.

"I... I've never been anywhere like this before," she managed. "It's so..."

"It's the dragon breeding ground. The dragons used to come here to breed and nest. Their lair is just behind the waterfall. The flowers are called Poisoned Passions. They are believed to be the main ingredient in love potions. It's said that if someone drinks it, they will fall in love with the first person they see."

Belle gave a nervous laugh. "Then I better stay away from them." Her body flooded with desire, but her head told her to be wary. His powerful body wrapped around hers in a cocoon of heat. He sniffed and rubbed her body making her skin sensitive.

The smell of his skin made her head swim.

Dax laced his fingers in the hair at the base of her neck and massaged it in his large palm.

"I caught you," he whispered before clamping his mouth down on hers.

Fear and desire mixed inside her as his tongue swept into her mouth. She moaned and ran her hands up his strong arms. Dax's kiss deepened and he growled, grabbing her rear. She jolted at his rough touch. But he didn't stop. Instead, he kissed down the side of her neck to the top of her breasts. Belle's mind and body collided as his hand pulled at her dress, lifting it up.

"Dax, slow down," she managed as he guided her to the ground.

He kissed her rougher, his whiskers scratching her face. She tried to slow his kisses but it only seemed to spur him on. He nipped down her neck as his hand ran under her skirt and skimmed the edge of her pantaloons.

"Dax... Dax, slow. Go slow."

He kissed over the top of her dress again and bit her nipple through the silky fabric sending a jolt of pain across her chest. Fear trickled down her spine like ice water. She pushed at his chest, but he didn't budge.

"Dax, that's enough." He continued down her body, kissing across her stomach and then lower. Belle scooted out from under him as his weight lifted. His gaze went straight to her, wild and non-human.

She'd seen that look before. In Klaus' eyes before he lost it.

"Dax, stop." She scurried away from him.

He growled and lumbered back and forth on all fours. She dashed away again but he continued to track her through the tall flowers.

"Dax—" She didn't even get out his name before he roared and ran straight at her. Belle screamed and jumped to her feet. She raced through the flowers for the trees. "Dax, this isn't you!" she yelled. "Stop! This isn't you! I know it isn't."

She hit the forest edge and sprinted for a rock. Leaping off it she caught a large tree branch and swung upward. Her dress snagged on the branch, ripping the hem as she backed against the tree. Dax raced into the forest at full speed, sniffing the air and growling.

Belle caught sight of the piece of torn fabric clinging to the branch and went to reach for it, but stopped herself as he stalked toward the tree where she hid. She looked up to see if she could climb higher without him noticing. She reached up, but the next branch hung a foot out of reach. He stopped and sniffed the air again before his head swung toward her tree. His gaze locked on hers and Belle stifled a cry.

He took two giant strides and just as he leapt at the tree, a blur slammed into him, knocking him to the ground. Dax roared and then another black blur joined the fray. *Sage and Adrian.*

They pinned him to the ground and Adrian roared back at Dax. Dax shoved the two off of him and the three circled each other in a match of dominance.

Sage raised his hand. "Dax. You need to stop this. You can control it. Don't let the curse win."

The trio continued circling.

"Don't let her win," said Sage. "Morgana has taken enough from all of us. Don't let her take you too. Think of Belle. Of Chloe. They need you. We all need you."

At the words, Dax stopped moving and his body relaxed.

He blinked several times and then looked around wildly. He said something and Sage looked up at her. Dax followed Sage's gaze and his entire body sagged as tears formed in his eyes. Belle could feel the crushing weight of Dax's guilt and sorrow for what he'd done. True and honest remorse. She knew he would never hurt her if it wasn't for Morgana's curse. He wasn't like Klaus. All Dax had ever done was try to protect her and Chloe. Provide for them and care for them. None of which Klaus had ever done. Klaus had hurt them out of selfishness. Dax was completely the opposite.

"Belle."

She shook as voices rushed toward them. Erik appeared at the foot of the tree as did Cinder, Stil and Aurora.

Erik followed Dax's gaze. "Belle, are you all right?"

She nodded and her cheeks heated at all the eyes upon her. She lowered down from the tree with Erik's help. The group stared between her and Dax. A million questions hung in the air.

Shoulders slumped; the pain for what he'd done was written all over him. Belle moved toward Dax.

"I'm so sorry," he whispered.

She reached for him and he backed up a pace.

"Dax," she tried.

"I'm sorry. To all of you." Without a word he turned and fled.

"Dax!" Belle started after him but Sage caught her around the waist.

"Let him go."

"But he needs me."

Sage nodded. "That he does. But not right now. Right

now, he needs a moment to come to grips with what's happening to him and what it means if we can't find a cure."

"I keep telling you lot that we need to just go in there and kill her," said Aurora.

"And I keep telling you that that is a suicide mission," replied Stil.

"Well I'd rather die than see my brother in this much pain," she retorted.

Stil shook his head. "Even I don't believe that."

Aurora looked at Belle, but Belle didn't know what to say. She had no idea what to do. They weren't strong enough to face Morgana, it was true. But one thing was for sure, they had to get Dax back to being himself. If they didn't, she feared what he might do to save them all from what he would become.

CHAPTER NINETEEN

Belle lay in bed reading Chloe a book, with her mind on nothing but Dax. She hadn't seen nor heard from him since he'd run away in the woods earlier that day. Eating dinner with everyone had been agonizing, seeing his place vacant, and the talk had been of nothing more than everyone speculating on things they could do to break the curse, which made her ache worse to see him.

She'd just finished the book and tucked Chloe into bed when a soft knock landed on her door. Belle rushed to it and threw it wide to find Aurora standing outside.

"Sorry. I know you're putting Chloe to bed, but I thought you'd want to know that he's back."

Belle's grip tightened on the door as she looked down the hallway toward his room. "How did he look?"

Aurora paused. "Terrible."

Belle's gut clenched. "Will you stay with Chloe?"

Aurora nodded and Belle walked into the hallway. She

strode toward his room in her nightgown, not caring if anyone caught her. She reached his door and raised her hand to knock, but stopped. What if he didn't want to see her? It didn't matter, he needed to see her. Needed to know that she didn't blame him. That she understood it wasn't him. She needed to make sure he wasn't beating himself up.

Footsteps floated up a small staircase off to the side and she looked to see two maids bringing up buckets of hot water. They curtsied when they spotted her.

"For the prince?"

The maids nodded.

Belle knocked on the door.

"Come," Dax called.

Belle opened the door and looked around. He lay on his bed staring upward. Belle motioned the maids in and pointed to the bathing room. The maids carried the buckets in before curtsying and leaving. Belle closed the door after them and stared at it for a moment. She could do this.

She padded to the bed and stared down at his large, dirty form. Red blotches stained his cheeks and deep shadows bruised the puffs beneath his eyes. His clothes were torn in too many places to patch, but she supposed it didn't matter. He had enough money to buy whatever he wanted. But not what he needed.

"How are you feeling?"

Dax sat up like a shot from her blunderbuss. His eyes bloodshot. "Belle."

She could feel the conflict he wore like a shroud around his heart. She walked to his side and reached out to touch his face. He didn't move as she pressed her palm to his cheek and then cupped his face in her hands. He wrapped his arms around her and she stepped between his thighs as he buried his face in her stomach.

"Belle I'm so, so sorry. I would never hurt you. I need you to know that. I need you to believe me. Please. Please believe me."

She tipped his face so that he looked up at her. "I do." She ran her fingers through his hair and stared into his soft hazel eyes. She wanted nothing more than to kiss him and hold him, and tell him she believed him. That she trusted him. That she forgave him.

She took his hands and pulled him to his feet. Like an obedient cub, Dax followed her as she led him to the bathing room.

DAX HAD SPENT THE LAST SIX HOURS RUNNING, AND running, and running some more. He'd not even stopped to breathe, let alone anything else. By the time he'd exhausted his bear into submission he'd barely been able to drag his aching body back to the castle. But none of the physical pain compared to how his soul ached for what he'd done to Belle.

He'd been unable to control his bear. Her idea of letting him run off his bear's energy had been a great one. Having him chase people had not. He'd struggled to keep it together finding the others, but by the time he'd caught Belle's scent, his bear had taken over. Moving purely on mating instincts his bear had pulled him to the secret grove and right on top of Belle. Now, as she led him into his bathing room, he knew no words could ever be enough to explain to her the pain he harbored.

He stood by the tub, his entire body sagging to get in as she poured three of the buckets in and then turned to him. Her compassionate expression only made him feel that much worse. She'd been through hell with Klaus. To think that he'd done anything even remotely close to the same thing made him want to rip his own throat out.

She pulled her beautiful brown hair back from her face and tied it behind her head. Then she rolled up the sleeves of her nightdress and walked to him. He wanted to apologize again. To hold her and swear he'd never hurt her or Chloe. To promise that they were going to break the curse no matter what it took.

She stepped up to him until their bodies almost touched. She moved her hands to the hem of his shirt and slid her slender fingers underneath it. She ran her palms up over his chest and then pushed the shirt over his head.

Dax stood there afraid to touch her. Afraid to speak. Afraid to move. She tossed the shirt in the corner and then untied his breeches. She pushed them down over his hips and he grabbed her wrist. She stopped and looked up at him. She didn't speak, neither did she ask permission, she simply waited. Dax removed his hand from her wrist and she slid his breeches to his ankles. She knelt, and he lifted one foot and then the other. Pulling the breeches off him she tossed them with the shirt.

She stood once more and looked up into his face. He

fought the urge to cover his nakedness, but with Belle, it seemed natural to be bare in front of her.

She walked to the small stand in the corner and grabbed the bar of soap as well as a towel. Dax stepped into the hot water and sat before she came back. Belle knelt on the floor and dipped the soap into the water. Dax tried to relax as she took his right arm in her grasp and ran the soap over it. She cleaned the dirt and blood from his knuckles where he'd pummeled a tree for several minutes. Though the wounds had almost healed already, the blood still remained. She dipped a small towel into the water and wiped at his knuckles with a mother's tenderness. Then she rubbed the soap on the towel and scrubbed up his arm and down into his armpit.

Dax lay in the tub, allowing Belle to clean him, their eyes always on each other, neither speaking. He reveled in the feel of her nimble hands on his skin. Relishing in the softness of her touch. When she finished with his arms, she soaped across his chest and then down to his stomach. Her eyes met his again as she worked down his left thigh. Dax gripped the edges of the copper tub as her hand slid up his thigh, inching closer and closer to the erection he could not hide.

She leaned across him and her breasts brushed his chest as she ran the towel down his other leg. Dax ground his teeth together. The scent of her need washed over him and he couldn't help but wonder why she would even want him after what he'd done.

Belle's hand slid up his calf and behind his knee. Dax's fingers dug into the metal as she inched her way back up his thigh to his hip. Her breast brushed his chest again and the thin cream nightdress dampened from the bath water darkening it, and allowing him a glimpse of her deep colored nipples.

Dax closed his eyes. He'd never wanted someone so much in his life, but there was no way in hell he'd do anything without her asking.

He sucked in a breath and her lips brushed his. He didn't move. She brushed his lips with hers again, light as a whisper, and then she was gone. Dax held back a groan as his erection throbbed.

She rounded the back of the tub and pushed him up so he sat forward. Belle ran the towel over his still sensitive scars. She traced them with her fingertips. Memories bombarded him.

Stretched tight on Morgana's bed. The slice of her talons as she stripped his flesh over and over and over.

Belle's lips fell on his shoulder and she kissed her way across his shoulder blade. Following the route of one of his deepest scars, she kissed over his back, ending at the other shoulder. Then she kissed up the side of his neck to his jaw. He held his breath as she kissed across his jaw and up his chin to his lips. She kissed him soft and playful. Her tongue darting into his mouth for a moment before withdrawing again so she could kiss up the other side of his face and across his temple to his forehead.

She pushed him back again and picked up the last bucket of water. Pouring a small amount on his hair she then ran the soap over it. Leaning against the side of the tub, Dax closed his eyes as she worked her fingers through his hair, making his scalp tingle.

She pressed her fingertips into his scalp and worked the soap through it. Then, as sleep threatened to overtake him, she stopped and poured the rest of the water over his head. She stood and took a step toward the towel, but Dax caught her fingers in his. He couldn't articulate the way he felt for her at that moment. The service and forgiveness she offered by what she'd done. No one had ever done more for him.

Belle entwined her fingers with his, and then without warning stepped into the tub. She straddled his broad chest and sat down. He ran his hands up her thighs over the wet nightdress.

She hooked her arms behind his head and her body crushed against his as she kissed him again. Dax's hands slid up to her waist and rested there as every instinct inside said to take her and make her his. But he fought the urges running through him as she kissed him. She controlled all of him. His body and his undeserving soul.

BELLE WANTED TO RIP EVERY STITCH OFF HER BODY AND make love to Dax right there in the tub. He wanted her too, but she also felt his trepidation. She appreciated his concern for her, but she was no withering flower. She knew he meant her no harm. Now, she just had to get him to know it too.

She ran her hand down between their bodies and gripped his length. He was bigger than she thought possible.

At the feel of her hand on him, his fingers dug into her waist.

"Dax, take off my gown," she whispered.

He ran his hands under the fabric and up her back. She slid her arms from the fabric as he pulled it over her head and dropped it to the floor. For a long minute he stared at her bare body but didn't move. Finally, she pulled his hand from her waist and placed it over her breast. His large hands made her feel delicate and small.

She leaned in and kissed him again, and this time he responded more forcefully than before, but still tentative.

He squeezed her breast and kissed down the side of her throat. She closed her eyes as he kissed down to her breasts and pulled one into his mouth. His tongue flicked her nipple and she raked her fingers through his hair.

"Dax," she moaned. "Make love to me."

He continued to suck at her flesh, making her run her hands down his arms. She tangled her fingers with his and kissed the top of his head. He smelled of soap and the forest.

Gradually, she rubbed her most sensitive area down over his erection. She moaned again, wanting him so much her body throbbed.

"Dax."

He sat back and squeezed her hands in his. "Are... Are you sure?"

She kissed him hard. "Make love to me."

Dax grabbed the edge of the tub and stood with her wrapped around his waist. He steadied himself, and then kissed her and swooped her into his arms.

He carried her from the bathing room out to his room, trailing water behind them. When they reached the edge of the bed, he set her on her feet and pulled down the covers. He slid in between the sheets, his large, muscular body waiting to see if she would join him.

Belle slipped off her dripping pantaloons and stood at the edge of the bed. He took in her entire form, and then took her in again. Not even a twinkle of apprehension sparked within her. She slid into the bed next to him and he covered her with the sheets and blankets.

He brushed a hair from her face and then leaned in and kissed her. Belle scooted closer to him, allowing the heat of his body to seep into hers. Grabbing his arm she pulled him on top of her. He kissed down her neck to her shoulder as she guided him to her core.

"Wait."

She stopped. "Do you not want to?"

He chuckled for the first time in days. "I want to more than you could know, but..."

"But?"

"I just need to make sure you know that it's all me here with you. I'm in control."

She smiled and touched his cheek. "I know that."

"I just..."

She pulled his mouth to hers. "Dax. If I have to ask you to make love to me a third time, I might just get up and walk out."

He smiled and kissed her again. Thrusting his way inside her was easy as she was more than ready. She gripped his shoulders as he filled her and made her body shudder.

"Belle," he panted. "I don't... know how long I can hold out."

She bit his powerful shoulder as the first wave of desire shot through her core.

"Me neither."

She raised her hands over her head and he locked his fingers with hers. Their gazes connected and he rocked his hips into hers. Belle's body shook as he rocked against her again, sending a wave of pleasure through her.

"Dax," she panted his name as he rocked into her again sending another wave of pleasure through her.

Soon his rhythm picked up speed and she hooked her legs with his. Her entire body shot with jolts of electricity as his gaze stayed on hers. Pleasure built in his eyes as her own body responded and her breathing quickened.

He closed his eyes and panted her name.

She spiraled closer to the edge as his body pulled taut and he growled.

"Look at me," she said.

Dax's eyes opened and he kissed her forcefully, rocking into her. She moaned and then climaxed. His forehead rested on hers as he growled low in his chest and she fought for breath. In that moment everything in the world floated away and she saw nothing but him. Felt his heart beat in time with hers, her body tensing around his, pulling him deeper inside her and locking them together.

When the climaxes tapered off, Dax fell on top of her, kissing her soft and slow. He pulled her into his arms and kissed her face all over. A tear leaked from her eye at his tenderness and he kissed it away.

"Was it that bad or do you just regret it?" he asked.

Belle bit his chest and smiled up at him. "Neither."

He kissed her hair. "Then what?"

She didn't want to say it. She didn't want to feel foolish in front of him. Not now. Not after everything they'd been through. She didn't want to ruin it.

"Tell me," he begged.

"It's just for the first time in my life, I feel like I'm—"

"Right where you belong," he finished.

She nodded and bit her lip waiting for him to laugh.

Instead, he pulled her tight against him and hugged her. "I know what you mean."

CHAPTER TWENTY

Dax awoke the next morning to the feel of Belle's body molded into his back and her arm draped around his waist. He reached down and set his hand atop hers where it laid on his hip. His bear roared to be fed, but somehow, he didn't fight to take over. He too was satisfied with the most recent development in Dax's relationship with Belle. Dax closed his eyes and reveled in the feel of her body against his.

He'd been with women before; many women. Before he'd been taken, he'd had his pick of any woman he wanted and so he'd rarely found his bed empty on the weekends. Never before, in any of his many escapades, had he ever wanted any of them to stay or be there when he awoke. But with Belle, he didn't want her to leave.

It was strange how he'd known her a few short weeks and yet all he wanted was to be with her. He loved the way she stood up to him. The way she took care of him. The way she... completed him. He paused at the thought that he might be in love with her.

Belle had made it quite clear that she didn't want any part of royal life, and yet she'd taken to it as if born there. She kept their private life private. She didn't fuss or make a scene when things weren't going the way she wanted. She was quiet, respectful and even gracious. She possessed more poise and grace than he'd seen in the majority of the fae candidates Cinder had fought against the year before in the competition for Prince Rome's hand.

Belle stirred and kissed his shoulder. He loved the feel of her lips on his body. Even when she traced the scars on his back he felt not an ounce of insecurity about it. She had a way of making him feel good about himself, despite what he was becoming.

Her hand slid down between his legs and he reached back and grabbed her rear. So many times in the dark hours of the night they'd made love. And if not making love, they'd caressed and traced, kneaded and teased each other as if nothing else in the world mattered but the two of them in that moment.

Belle stroked him and his body responded. He rolled over and kissed her.

"Good morning."

She smiled and pushed her tousled hair from her face. "I believe it is."

He kissed her again, once more trying to understand how she had forgiven him. The way she'd bathed and taken care of him the night before had been the most tender and erotic thing he'd ever experienced.

She rolled on top of him and he got a full view of her beautiful body in the morning light. Long thick hair cascaded around her shoulders and down her back. Her breasts heavy and ripe. A slender waist that bowed out into glorious creamy hips, perfect for hanging on to. He loved every curvy inch of her strong body. Every second he saw her was a second he drew closer to never wanting to let her go.

She slid down on him and he sucked in a breath. She grabbed onto the headboard and slid down on him again. Dax trembled with need and his bear sat up and took notice. Suddenly his instincts began to take over. He wanted her. His bear wanted her. Not slow and gentle like they had been all night, but fast and hard.

She slid down on him again and he grabbed her hips.

"Wait. We have to stop," he said fighting against his rapidly emerging adversary.

She looked deep into his eyes. "What do you need?"

"I need to stop. My bear—"

"No," she said. "What do you need?"

He didn't want to tell her what his bear wanted. Didn't want to risk hurting her or upsetting her.

"I can't... I don't want to hurt you. I couldn't bear it if—"

She kissed him forcefully making his bear growl with delight. "You won't. I won't let you."

As if knowing exactly what he craved she kissed him again, and then kissed down his throat and bit his neck. His bear lurched with need and Dax gripped her rear. Belle dug her nails into his skin as she slid down on him. Dax pulled her mouth to his and he plunged his tongue into it as he rocked her hips against his firmly. He tangled his fist in her hair and pulled her head back, making her breasts press against his face.

He pulled one of her creamy mounds into his mouth and sat up. Pulling her hair with one hand he yanked her body into his with the other. She cradled him against her breast as he drew their hips together again. Harder and deeper he plunged into her, needing to feel every inch, needing to fill her.

Belle moaned and then called his name, making him wind closer to the edge of climax. He thrust into her until the bed shook. She let out a breathy moan and her body tightened around his. Her nipple ripened in his mouth as he nipped at it. She wrapped her arms around his head and clung to him as she cried his name. The sound of it on her lips ripped his last shred of restraint. He climaxed; his entire body tensing. His bear roared as the euphoric rush of release crashed over him again and again.

He dropped Belle's breast and clamped his mouth on hers. She responded in kind and he ran his hands over her body until his fingers tangled in her hair. He pulled her head back and kissed down the side of her throat, licking every velvety inch. The salt of her skin made him want her that much more. The scent of her skin made him want to take her again. He rolled her over and rubbed himself along every inch of her body. He wanted her. Not just there and then, but forever and for always. He wanted her to be his and no other. He needed her to be his. Because one thing was already absolutely clear.

He was hers.

BELLE'S ENTIRE BODY TINGLED. HE'D BEEN FORCEFUL, BUT HE hadn't hurt her. He'd been able to control it, just as she knew he would.

"Belle." He kissed her again. "I need to tell you something."

She could already feel the words he wanted to say and butterflies shook her stomach.

He looked into her eyes and kissed her soft. "I love you, Belle. I love you and I need you. I need you and Chloe. Stay here. Stay with me, forever."

Belle's mouth opened and then closed again. She knew what her heart wanted her to say. Knew what her body wanted her to say. But she also knew what her head told her to say.

"I know you want to say yes. I can feel it. I also know you're scared. I'm more scared than you can understand. But I also know how I feel about you and it's like nothing I've felt for anyone else. If you don't want to say yes now, then just promise me. Promise me that you will think about it."

Her chest squeezed. "What about Chloe?"

"What about Chloe?"

"I... I don't want her to be treated as less because she isn't yours."

"I haven't told anyone that. Have you? We haven't said anything. And I love Chloe as if she was my own. Nothing could ever change how I feel about you or her. Not even if we had our own children. She would still be mine. My first-born. Always. And you know I will protect her at the cost of my own life. I will never let anyone take her because of her gifts or because they think she belongs to them."

She did want to say yes. Become a princess. Never have to worry about money or feeding Chloe again. But more than that, she wanted Dax. Only Dax. But with Dax came an obligation that she could never walk away from. If she did this with him, there was no turning back. No running. It was her, and a prince, and a kingdom forever.

He kissed her forehead. "I know you want me, too."

"Dax I do, but—"

A roar sounded outside the castle. Dax's head whipped to the window.

"Alabrax?"

Dax listened intently and then shook his head. A bell sounded outside, then another, and another.

Dax jumped from the bed.

"What is it?"

He threw open his wardrobe and grabbed a tunic and breeches. He ran into the bathing room and retrieved her nightdress and tossed it to her.

"Hurry."

"What's going on?" She yanked the still damp and chilly fabric over her head.

He grabbed her hand and pulled her to the door. "Dragon attack."

Dax ran with Belle at his side as his mother and father descended the staircase.

His father looked Dax and Belle up and down as Belle tried to braid her hair out of the way. Aurora stepped out of Belle's room holding Chloe's hand. His father's calculating gaze didn't miss a beat. Dax pulled Belle into his side and kissed her head. A flash of light appeared and Stil walked out of the middle of the hallway.

"The alarm sounded," he said.

Erik, Flint, Zelle, Cinder, Sage and Adrian ran up the stairs to meet the group.

"They're headed this way," said Sage. "Dozens, just like in the Wastelands."

"Where's Alabrax?" asked Cinder.

A roar sounded outside the window at the end of the hallway. Dax raced for it as Belle went to Chloe.

He threw the window wide. In the distance a horde of dragons flew toward the town. Down below in the city, people screamed and ran for shelter.

Dax scanned the area for Alabrax. He caught the dragon's small form racing out to meet the oncoming group.

"Alabrax!" Dax yelled, but it was no use, he'd flown too far away already.

Cinder joined him at the window. "Alabrax!" she screamed. "Dax get him back, he'll be ripped to shreds."

Dax tried to catch Alabrax's thoughts, but they were jumbled and confused. They looked on in horror as he soared out to meet the dragons.

From the left a loud crash sounded down below. Dax

looked to see a second set of dragons approaching from the west.

"Get the guard!" he shouted. "They're headed for the town!"

A dragon swooped down and bellowed fire at the nearest building before lifting back into the air.

Aurora joined him at the window and hurried away. "Fire rake, nine o'clock," she yelled down the hallway. "Get my water cannon loaded."

Aurora jumped over the railing to the floor below as Dax's mother screamed. "Stop her!"

Dax ran to the stairs and looked over the railing, but Aurora had already disappeared.

"I'll go." Stil blew powder in the air and did a quick spell before stepping through a hole and disappearing.

Screaming and chaos ensued all around. Belle stood by her bedroom door holding Chloe.

"Belle, you and Chloe stay in your room. Erik, Flint, you're with Belle and Chloe. Sage, Adrian with me," Dax ordered.

"Cinder, Zelle see if you can coax Alabrax back to safety."

"What do you expect us to do?" Zelle asked.

Dax shook his head. "Charm him." He raced down the stairs to the floor below and then down the next set of stairs to the main floor. He sprinted out the front doors onto the large terrace. Servants and guards raced to and fro. A huge stream of water shot from a turret above him and he looked up to see Aurora straddling a huge metal tube spraying water at the dragon, drenching it and the building below that had caught fire.

Dax darted to the railing and looked out at the city below. Another dragon had landed on the baker's shop and shot ice at the people below.

Dax grabbed a guard as he passed and pointed. "Take that thing down."

The guard nodded and rushed off barking orders. Dax felt helpless watching the dragons. Once upon a time he would have been riding one of those dragons, fighting against invaders, and now he stood unable to do anything but watch.

Alabrax's thoughts caught his attention and he looked northeast. The smaller dragon flew ahead of the rest of the pack straight toward him. Dax backed up from the railing with Adrian and Sage as Alabrax dove from the sky and landed in front of him. Alabrax walked to Dax and turned as a large bright green dragon headed for the railing. Sage and Adrian backed up again, but Dax stood his ground. The animal gripped the railing in his strong talons on landing and roared.

"Dax, move away," Adrian yelled, but Dax couldn't move. He knew the dragon.

"Constrixtus," Dax called. The animal hissed and roared again as he folded his wings in.

Alabrax roared back at the dragon, shielding Dax.

Dax set his hand on Alabrax's shoulder to calm him, but it was Dax's bear that needed the calming. Dax moved forward as Constrixtus watched him, hissing and lumbering from foot to foot.

Dax held out his hand. "Constrixtus. You know me. We've ridden together. You and Malius, and me and Flix."

Dax continued forward with Alabrax at his back. He fought to keep the fear that threatened to make him run away, at bay. His bear fought to claw its way out and defend itself, but Dax pushed the bear down.

Dax got within a foot of the dragon, knowing very well that if the beast opened his mouth he was dead. The acid spray from Constrixtus was even more deadly than that of the dragon that had sprayed Flint at Zelle's tower.

"Constrixtus." Dax's hand hovered in the air as he waited for the animal to make a move. "Where is Malius?"

Finally, the animal bowed his head and nudged Dax's palm with his nose. Relief flooded through him and the air around the dragon shimmered. Dax stepped away as the animal shrank and morphed. Dax couldn't believe his eyes as the dragon's wings turn into arms and his clawed feet shift into legs. Dax stepped forward as the man that emerged tumbled forward into Dax's arms.

The man flipped over and looked up at Dax. Dax could barely comprehend what had happened. "Malius."

"Prince Thad." Malius grabbed onto Dax's shirt. "I... don't have long," he panted. "She... already knows that I have shifted."

"But how is it possible? You and Constrixtus. You are one?"

Malius nodded. "She merged us... two beings, one body." He grabbed Dax's shirt. "She's coming... I have to warn you... She's coming."

"Who?" Dax asked. "Morgana?"

"She wants... You... must protect—"

Malius' collar lit up and his body lurched from Dax's arms. His muscles strained as his body pulled taut as if being yanked upon at every limb.

"Malius! Malius." Dax looked around for something to use as a weapon. He spotted Sage and ran at him. Reaching into Sage's boot he grabbed the knife Sage kept there and raced back to Malius.

"Hold him!" Dax yelled at Adrian.

Adrian and Sage joined him and grabbed Malius as Dax shoved the blade under the green stone in the collar and he tried to pry it free.

"Stay with me, Malius. Stay with me, dammit!"

Malius' face went from red to a deep purple. His eyes bulged from his head and his mouth stayed open in a silent scream.

Dax pressed on the stone trying to pry it free. Malius' body slumped to the ground and Dax continued to pry at the stone.

"Dax, he's gone," said Sage.

Dax shook Sage off and fought to get the stone out of the collar still. Aurora appeared at his side grabbing Malius' shoulders and shaking him.

"Malius. Malius." She shook him again, but Adrian's hand landed on her shoulder.

"He's gone princess."

"No. Malius. Is Fader alive? Is he all right? Malius!"

Dax's hand dropped from the collar. He stared at Malius' dead body for a moment and a deep sadness spread through him. He reached up and closed Malius' eyes before resting his hand on his friend's chest. He remembered the first day Malius had begun the trials to become a dragon rider. He'd been no more than a teen and Dax had been sure that if the boy made it through the trials, there wasn't a dragon among them who would accept him as a rider due to his age and inexperience. To everyone's surprise Constrixtus, one of the dragon elders, had chosen Malius to bond to.

A guard arrived with a blanket and Dax covered Malius. Alabrax nudged Malius' foot with his nose and warbled. Dax stood and pet Alabrax's head, knowing the animal didn't understand. Cinder arrived with Zelle and Dax's parents, as well as a large group of the guard. Dax looked out over the city to find two buildings with their roofs gone and bolts of ice stabbing the streets down one pathway. He heaved a sigh as the dragons retreated away.

"Why are they leaving?" asked Sage.

"They could have done significantly more damage," said Adrian. "We didn't even kill one of them."

"I think they left someone behind, Prince Thad," said a guard.

"What do you mean?" asked Dax.

The guard shook his head. "Someone said they saw one of the dragons drop someone off in the city. We have men scouring the kingdom but there is no way to know for sure."

"Morgana," said Aurora.

"I don't think so," replied Stil as he joined the group. "She wouldn't be so reckless to arrive in daylight and she wouldn't send the dragons away. She'd keep them here as cover for whatever she had planned."

"Malius said she was coming. That she wanted someone."

"Who?" asked the king.

Dax shook his head. "He didn't say."

Dax looked down at Malius again. He couldn't believe Morgana had done to the dragons and the riders what she had done to him. She'd made them into shifters.

"Come on," said Dax. "Let's get him off the ground where anyone can gawk at him. He deserves that much."

Two guards carried Malius into the castle.

"I need to examine his collar," said Stil. "If I can figure out how they work, I might be able to figure out a way to counteract it."

"I can help you," said Zelle. "I can tell you everything I know about the magick used to make it."

Stil nodded and the two walked inside.

Servants stood around looking at the scene. The queen clapped her hands and as if they wore collars of their own, they turned and headed back to their duties.

"We don't need everyone straggling about," said Dax's father. "We have much to do before people begin arriving for the party tonight."

"You can't still be going through with it," said Aurora. "Not after what has just happened."

"Of course I can. We have people coming from all over the kingdom to see Thaddeus and applaud his return home."

"But father, we were just attacked," Aurora protested.

"Even better reason to carry on. The Captain of the Dragon Riders has returned to us and we need him now more than ever. The people need to see him. Need to know that he is ready to take up his mantel again. With a dragon like Alabrax at his side, it will give people hope."

Aurora's jaw clenched at the same time her fists did and for a moment Dax thought she might throw a punch at their father.

"Alabrax isn't a show piece," said Dax. "I won't subject him to a being on display for people to see."

"But Thaddeus—"

Dax whistled and Alabrax backed up and hissed. Dax nodded and Alabrax took to the sky. Climbing the side of the castle he headed for the top tower.

"Alabrax can be spotted just fine from there. Anyone who wants a closer look at him is welcome to go up."

Dax's father's expression took on a hard-edged but Dax refused to budge.

Dax turned to Aurora. "I'll be in Belle's room. Let me know as soon the search of the city is complete."

Aurora nodded and Dax strode past his parents and back into the castle. His father could put him on display and parade him around for everyone to see, but he'd be damned if he'd let his father do it to Alabrax or anyone else he loved.

CHAPTER TWENTY ONE

"I t's Klaus. I know it is." Belle paced in her bedroom.

Dax walked to her and pulled her into his arms, surrounding her in warmth. "Belle, you need to—"

She pushed away from him. "Don't you dare tell me to calm down."

"I wasn't. I was going to tell you to trust me." His eyes held concern but also compassion.

She wanted to trust him. Wanted to believe him that he would protect them. But Morgana had snuck into the castle once already. How could she trust that Klaus wouldn't get in as well?

Dax stepped up to her and rubbed her arms with his strong hands. "The entire guard is here. I am here. Aurora is here, Adrian, Flint, Erik, Zelle, Cinder, Stil, Sage. All of us are here and we are going to make sure that both you and Chloe are safe."

She bit her lip and looked over at where Chloe played

with her stuffed dragon. "I should just go. Take Chloe and run. I could wait a few months and then contact you. Tell you where we are..."

Dax's gaze saddened, and he nodded. "If that's what you want, I won't stop you. I'll give you everything you need. Money to buy a house and keep you two for years. Whatever you need. You know how I feel and what I want. If going is what you need to feel safe, then I will support you."

She didn't want to go. As much as she hated to admit it, she didn't want to be even one foot away from Dax for the rest of her life. Her resolve set and she shook her head.

"No. I don't want to be afraid anymore. I don't want to run anymore. Klaus has already taken too much of my past, I won't let him keep controlling my future."

Dax smiled and tipped her chin, kissing her soft. "Good. Because with a piece of my soul inside you, I'm pretty sure you wouldn't have made it out of the kingdom before I came running after you."

Belle chuckled and wrapped her arms around him. Her fingers barely touched across his broad back. He kissed the top of her head and she allowed herself to melt into him and just be held.

Together they watched Chloe. She looked over at them and giggled.

"What's so funny?" Belle asked.

Chloe giggled again. "I told you Dax would be our friend."

Dax chuckled and it rumbled in his chest, making Belle laugh as well.

"That you did, Sweetums."

Chloe nodded. "You should listen to me more. I know things."

"Is that so?" Belle and Dax walked hand-in-hand to Chloe and sat next to her on the floor. "What kind of things do you know?"

Chloe looked up at them and gave a knowing smile of wisdom far beyond her years. Her eyes glassed over, and Belle set her hand on Chloe's hand squeezing it and bringing Chloe back to the present.

"No, sweetie. That isn't what I meant. I didn't mean for you to... look."

"Oh. All right." Chloe smiled again.

Dax picked up the dragon and flapped his wings. "Chloe, the other day, you knew that Morgana had been here."

Chloe nodded.

"How did you know that?"

Chloe's face scrunched up and she thought for a moment. "Because she isn't supposed to be here."

"Here in the castle?"

She shook her head. "She isn't supposed to be in Fairelle. She doesn't belong here. Like Auntie Zelle and the others."

Dax and Belle exchanged a look. "The others?"

"Rasmuss and Sabine and Ursul."

"Sabine is trapped," said Dax.

Chloe nodded. "But she's awake. Waiting."

"All right." Belle took the dragon from Dax and handed it back to Chloe. "That's enough of that. How about you get your shoes and I take you to the big library and we have some food and I can read to you."

Chloe nodded and ran to put her shoes on.

Dax grabbed Belle's hand and she looked at him. "I'm not going to push you or Chloe, but you know you can't hide her forever, right? Sooner or later people are going to find out."

"Why do they have to?"

Dax looked to Chloe and then back to Belle. "Because she is young and she holds power she doesn't understand. At some point, if she doesn't learn to control it, something bad could happen. You said she already had headaches and nose bleeds. The other day she blacked out."

Her mama bear roared to life. "I won't let anyone take her."

He squeezed her. "And neither will I. That's not what I'm saying. But..."

"But what?" She wasn't sure she wanted the answer.

"But what if she could help us get rid of Morgana and her kind for good?"

"I won't use her."

"You know that's not what I mean."

"I'm ready." Chloe's shoes pattered on the floor as she ran back and threw her arms around Dax and hugged him tight.

Belle's chest squeezed as Dax hugged and then tickled Chloe, making her shriek with laughter. Belle smiled at the sight of her daughter so happy.

She knew Dax would never use or hurt Chloe, but there were people out there that would. She would die before she let that happen. But... what if he was right? What if Chloe's gift could help them defeat Morgana? Bring peace to Fairelle once and for all? Belle sighed. That was a lot of pressure to put on such small shoulders.

CHLOE SPUN IN A CIRCLE, LAUGHING AT THE BEAUTIFUL silvery dress that had arrived for her an hour earlier. Maids came in and helped curl and pin both Belle and Chloe's hair before helping Belle into her own plum colored gown. She stared at herself in the mirror, unable to believe where she was. Her entire young life she'd dreamed of being carried off by a prince one day and yet she'd never believe it might happen for her. Being with the Gwyns had been the closest Belle had ever thought she would get to royalty.

She smoothed down the front of the dress and tried in vain to pull the bodice up higher to cover more of her breasts. She was neither used to low-cut style, nor the tightness in her waist.

A knock sounded on the door and her stomach clenched. She still wasn't sure how ready she was to go down amongst a ballroom full of nobility.

A maid opened the door and Dax stood in the doorway. Belle's breath caught at the sight of him. His hair had been slicked back and he'd shaven off his scruff into a tidy goatee. He wore a tunic of deep blue brocade and matching breeches. His lapel had been adorned with several medals and his boots shone like they were made of dark glass. For the first time, in that outfit, she could see him as Prince Thaddeus of the Draaklands.

The maids curtsied and excused themselves as Dax entered and closed the door. They stared at each other for a long moment before he walked toward her.

"You look amazing," he said.

"As do you."

He gave her a one-armed hug and kissed her. "I'm thinking we should skip the party and you should let me get you out of that dress."

She smiled. "And I am thinking that I could be persuaded to go along with that plan."

Dax smiled again, and she rubbed her palm over his cheek. His soft smooth skin felt strange.

"What do you think?"

She tugged on his goatee. "It suits you."

"As that dress suits you."

"Is that a present for me?" Chloe jumped up to join them.

Dax laughed and pulled two small boxes from behind his back. "Why yes, one of them is for you. The other is for mommy."

Dax handed Chloe a small silver box and held out a gold one to Belle. Chloe squealed with delight and clambered up on the bed to open it.

Belle looked at her own box and then at Dax. "You didn't have to get me something."

"I wanted to."

"Oh mama, look!" cried Chloe.

Belle walked over and peered into the box. Nestled inside, lay a beautiful golden necklace with a large blue teardrop gem in the center, the same color as Chloe's eyes.

"Can I put it on?" Chloe asked Dax.

Dax nodded. "It's why I brought it."

Chloe clapped and hopped off the bed. Dax knelt in front of her and took the necklace from the box. Chloe held up her hair with her chubby little hands as Dax fastened the necklace on. Then she ran to the mirror.

"It's so beautiful." Chloe twisted and turned in the mirror looking at herself. She looked down at the small gold bracelet on her hand and jingled it once. She walked back to Belle and held out her wrist. "Can I take this off now?"

Belle's chest squeezed. She remembered how happy Chloe had been when Klaus had given her the bracelet. How proud of it she'd been, showing it off to everyone she met. It pricked at Belle's heart to see Chloe no longer wanting it, but at the same time, it made her glad that someone so much better wanting to take Chloe as his own. Dax was like no other. Strong and brave, loyal and kind. Under his roof, Chloe would learn what a real man and father should be.

Belle nodded. "If that's what you'd like."

Chloe nodded and with shaking fingers Belle took off the bracelet, feeling a door shut on her old life. On who she used to be. And another opening on what she could be. Belle took the bracelet and placed it on her nightstand. She looked at it for a moment before returning to Dax.

"Open your box, Mama."

Belle opened the golden box and inside lay a matching set of diamond earrings and a necklace. Belle couldn't breathe at the sight of them. She opened her mouth and then closed it. Aside from the gift of Chloe, no one had ever given her more.

Finally, she looked at Dax. "I... I can't."

"Of course you can. They are jewels befitting the rarest of them all."

She looked at the jewelry again and her stomach lurched as the reality of who Dax was crashed around her. "Truly. I can't. They are too much. I... I think I might need to lay down."

"Breathe. I know this is a lot and this party is too soon. Trust me, I don't want to be down there any more than you do. It's not who I am. And it's not who we are together." Dax grabbed her hands in his. "I'll tell you what. You and Chloe come down for just an hour. If it's too much, then you two and the guard will come right back up here."

She stared at him wanting to beg him not to make her.

"Please Belle. I need you."

She could feel his trepidation adding to her own. But she'd taken on the role of his soul-binding partner so she could help him control his bear. And if she didn't go down and something happened, she would never forgive herself.

"Very well."

He smiled and kissed her. "Thank you."

"But I'm not accepting such a lavish gift." She pushed the box toward him.

"Fair enough. You wear them for me tonight, and then as soon as you are done, they will go back into the royal vault for safe keeping."

"So you can give them to another female friend?" She smirked, but his eyes grew serious.

"I will have no other, Belle. I told you as much. I'll never hurt you the way he did."

She touched his cheek, still not used to the feel. "I know."

He kissed her palm and she wanted more than anything to beg him to not go to the party. To stay like they were, just the three of them, up in their rooms. Playing with Chloe, making love, being... a family.

CHAPTER TWENTY TWO

D ax squeezed Belle's hand tight as he carried Chloe down the stairs toward the barrage of voices that floated closer to them. His bear sniffed the air wanting to trace and categorize every scent. Food, wine, flowers, burning candles and most of all— people. Lots of people. Hordes of people.

Nervousness skittered over him, but having Belle by his side eased him somewhat. They descended the last staircase and rounded the corner to the grand ballroom. Outside the door stood his gathered friends. They grinned when they caught sight of the trio. Snow walked up and hugged Belle tight, whispering something in her ear.

Belle smiled.

Flint approached and clapped Dax on the back. "Falling in love looks good on you, brother."

Dax hugged him back. "You too."

Erik hugged Dax as well. "I think this is where I'm

supposed to say that if you hurt her, I'll kill you, but I know you too well."

Dax chuckled, as did Belle.

Chloe showed off her new necklace as Stil and Aurora exited the party and joined them. Dax couldn't help but snigger at Aurora's half dress. It was quintessentially Aurora. From the back, one would think it a formal ball gown. It had the bodice of a dress, but in the front it split open at the waist like curtains pulled aside for her to show off her pants and boots underneath. Made in blood red brocade. He could just imagine the tantrum his mother was having over it.

Aurora kissed his cheek. "Father is having a fit because you aren't in there yet. You better hurry."

Dax nodded.

"The guards returned from the area of forest we sent them to."

"Anything?"

Aurora shook her head.

"What about the person dropped off by Morgana?" asked Erik.

"Nothing yet," said Aurora. "It's very well possible that in all the chaos someone made a mistake. Even so, we've tripled the guard for tonight. Everyone entering the castle has been checked against the list. No one is resting until we know you are safe."

Dax appreciated everyone's vigilance. But he knew that if Morgana wanted at him, she would find a way to get to him.

Aurora hugged Belle. "Great Grandmother's wedding set looks beautiful on you."

Belle shot him a look. "What?"

Dax took Chloe's hand and pulled Belle forward before she could protest. "We need to go in."

"Dax." Her voice was a warning that made him laugh.

"You look amazing." He nodded to Aurora, who took her other arm so she couldn't get away. The look Belle shot at him told him she knew what he was doing. He winked at her and together with their friends at their backs and the guards on either side, they walked to the wide open doors.

Dax took a deep breath and surveyed the scene. His bear paced and huffed and grumbled at the sight of so many people. Belle squeezed his arm and he looked down at her.

"I'm right here."

He nodded and wished her words comforted him more than they did. The musicians stopped playing and the entire crowd turned to stare. A trickle of sweat rolled down between his shoulder blades. He could do this. They were just people. All they wanted was to look at him and clap him on the back, nothing more.

The crowd parted as his mother and father stood from their thrones at the far end of the room. Aurora took a step down, pulling Belle and Dax with her. As the group passed everyone bowed and curtsied. Dax took a deep breath and kept his eyes trained on his parents. His mother smiled and by the time they reached her, everyone in the room had begun to cheer. Dax's mother kissed his cheek and then hugged Belle.

Dax shook his father's hand and then turned to the crowd. They stood for several minutes letting the cheering continue until Dax's bear could stand it no longer and a growl escaped his chest. Dax's father glanced at him and then stepped forward to address the crowd.

Belle scooted closer and rubbed the small of his back. "Take a breath."

"That's the problem. I can smell everything and it's making my bear beyond twitchy. I don't know if I can do this."

"You can, and you will. And as soon as you are done down here showing off your pretty princely costuming, we will go back upstairs and I'll let you unwrap me layer by layer."

Dax held back a groan and couldn't help but chuckle. She wiggled her eyebrows at him and just the thought of her naked made his bear want to leave all the more.

"Prince Thaddeus!"

Dax had missed his father's entire speech. Dax handed Chloe to Belle and stepped forward to wave at the crowd. Before he could say a word, they surrounded him. Hands clasped him. Palms touched his arms, his chest, his shoulders. Bodies pressed in on him from all sides, suffocating him. His bear fought and paced closer to the surface than ever. Suddenly the crowd parted as Erik, Adrian and Sage strode to his side.

Dax fought to keep his composure as Adrian's hand landed on his shoulder like a vise and squeezed. "Breathe, Dax."

"I can't," he said through gritted teeth.

"Breathe through your mouth. You can't smell that way."

Dax nodded and followed Adrian's advice.

It eased his tension a little.

Dax's father brought forward several of his royal advisors. They shook hands with Dax, but their gazes remained more on Sage than anyone.

"May I introduce my good friends, King Sageren of Tanah Darah, King Adrian of Wolvenglen and Lord Erik Gwyn of Westfall," Dax announced.

The men nodded in polite complacency.

"You should eat," whispered Sage. "It helps with the cravings amongst other things."

Dax nodded but couldn't think of eating anything.

"We heard you have a baby dragon," said one of the advisors.

"Uh, yes. Princess Cinder made him. She's over there with my sister."

"You sure have made a lot of friends in your time abroad," said another advisor.

Dax snorted. "Time abroad? Interesting way to put being kidnapped and tortured before losing your memory and wandering for five years to figure out who you are."

"All right." Erik stepped up and shook hands with all the advisors. "Gentlemen if you will excuse us, Prince Thad hasn't eaten today and I'm afraid that tends to make him a bit grumpy. If you'll excuse us?" Erik bowed to Dax's father. "Your majesty?"

Dax's father looked between them before his gaze

landed on Dax, and then he smiled and waved his hand. "Of course."

Guilt and shame struck Dax. He couldn't help but see the disappointment in his father's eyes. The eyes that wished he'd go back to who he'd been before Morgana. The obedient son. The carefree son. The unsullied son. Unfortunately, Dax would never be able to give that to his father and his father would have to accept that, or his father would have to learn to live with disappointment.

Adrian and Sage steered Dax to where Belle stood with Chloe. Dax picked Chloe up and she threw her arms around his neck.

"You're doing great," she whispered before kissing his cheek.

Dax took in the fresh scent of Chloe's hair and it soothed his bear. He opened his eyes to see a cluster of women watching him and whispering. Dax lifted his head from Chloe and nodded to the women before taking Belle's hand and walking toward the tables of food. He let everyone see him with Chloe and Belle, ignoring their whispers and wagging fingers. He knew the spectacle made Belle uncomfortable, but the more people saw them together, the better it was for both of them.

THE EVENING PROGRESSED SLUGGISHLY. BELLE, DAX, Chloe and their friends, including Aurora sat at a large table in the corner talking and keeping each other company. Every once and a while, someone would approach and wish Dax well. Twice his mother dragged him over to see distant relatives, whom he hugged and thanked for coming.

Finally, the music stopped and Dax's father called to him. Chloe stayed with Flint and Zelle as Dax and Belle walked front and center once more.

"I want to bring back a custom from when Thaddeus used to live with us. A dance, Prince's choice. All eligible young women will step forward."

"Father—"

"Husband," said the queen.

His father paid them no mind. "Women form a line on the right side of the room. All eligible young men, line up on the left. After the Prince has made his choice, all other young men may choose."

The guests arranged themselves about the room. Dax looked back at Belle whose eyes wore a pained expression.

"Get in the line," Dax urged.

Belle shook her head.

"Belle, please."

She shook her head again. "Go. Do this for your father."

"I won't."

His father stepped up to them. "Thaddeus, it is tradition. You must choose."

"I have chosen father. You just refuse to see it."

His father looked at Belle and then at Dax. "Thaddeus... she has a child."

Dax's jaw set and he nodded. "Yes, she does. Our child."

"I know that isn't true."

"You're wrong. Chloe is my daughter and Belle is whom I choose. If you don't like that, I'm sorry. I'll do whatever I need to, to protect them both. Even if it means I leave the Draaklands."

"Thaddeus." His mother gasped.

Dax glared at his father and then walked out into the center of the ballroom. Every eye in the room rested upon him, making his bear lumber from foot to foot. Neither of them fancied that kind of attention.

He turned in a circle and then assumed the customary stance. Holding his hand out wide he passed it down the line of young eager women, including Violet, until it pointed at Belle, who still stood next to the queen. Every person in the room turned to her, waiting to see what she would do. Belle's cheeks tinged a deep shade of rose and conflict set in her eyes. He didn't care. He chose her. He would always choose her. The question was, would she choose him?

He waited, hand out stretched until she set her shoulders and strode onto the floor. When her hand slipped into his, he all but kissed her right there.

He slid his hand around her slender waist and stared at her as all of the others paired up.

"I thought you might leave me to dance alone," he chided.

"I don't want to come between you and your father," she replied.

"It's his choice whether or not he will try to come between you and I. Not the other way around."

"But you've only just found him."

"And that will never change. But I am not the young man I once was, and he will either learn to accept that, or he won't. The choice is his."

The music began and Dax and Belle lead the way. Around and around they danced, filling the entire floor. His eyes fixed on hers, all he saw was Belle. Soon, other dancers swung in around them, dancing to the same music, but separate from them. Dax smiled at Belle imagining what it would be like to dance with her forever. To never hold another. Never kiss another. Never make love to another. And for the first time, he felt peace at the thought of being with one person for the rest of his life.

BELLE FOLLOWED DAX EASILY AS HE LED HER THROUGH THE steps. She'd learned to dance with the Gwyns and had been better than even Snow herself. As she swung around in Dax's arms, she felt a sense of pride she'd never felt before. Pride in herself. In who she was as a person and what she deserved.

When the song ended Dax bowed to her as she curtsied, and then he pulled her in tight and without a word, lifted her chin and kissed her.

The gasps, whispers, and giggles all but filled her ears as she allowed his lips to linger on hers and then she pulled away. Chloe raced up to them and hugged their legs.

"I get to dance next," she said.

Belle laughed and kissed Chloe's head. "Of course."

Belle backed away as the music picked up and Dax set Chloe's feet on his own and twirled her around. Belle felt a presence to her right and she looked over to see Dax's mother at her shoulder.

She wrapped her arms around herself as Dax danced with Chloe.

"My grandmother's jewels look beautiful on you."

Belle fiddled with the necklace and looked over at Dax's mother. "I... I didn't know."

"Of course you didn't. But Thaddeus did." The queen continued to smile at those who passed them.

Belle wasn't sure how to respond.

"Your little Chloe is beyond precious. And Thaddeus is wonderful with her. He will make a wonderful father. There was a time when I wasn't so sure."

Again, Belle had no words.

The queen nodded to a man and woman as they bowed to her in turn. "Thaddeus used to be his father's twin in every way. To be honest, it used to worry me. But I see him now as the man he's become, and he is no longer just like his father." She paused. "And that I think, is a good thing."

Belle looked at the queen, who continued to stare straight ahead for a moment before turning to Belle.

"Thaddeus has chosen you and I can see why. You are beautiful, smart, brave. All the things a princess needs to be. He loves you. And he loves Chloe. My husband doesn't like that right now, but one day he will come to understand that you are exactly what Thaddeus needs." The Queen squeezed Belle's hand. "Hang in there until he does. Please. For Thaddeus's sake."

Belle's chin quivered at the queen's kindness. She nodded her head and the queen squeezed her hand again before hugging her and kissing her on both cheeks.

Belle could swear that more people stared at her after the queen's kiss than had after Dax's.

The song ended and Dax walked back to Belle with Chloe.

"What was that about? Did she upset you?"

Belle shook her head and blotted her eyes. "Quite the contrary. Everything is perfect."

Chloe yawned. "Parties are hard work. I'm tired."

The group chuckled and Belle looked at the large brass clock. "I should get her to bed."

Dax nodded. "My father wants me to introduce Erik to one more advisor and then I'll be up." He leaned in close and his breath warmed her ear. "Don't fall asleep before I get there."

She smiled. "I promise."

Dax motioned to the guard. "Princess Chloe needs to go to bed. Please take at least six men and escort them to their room. Stay there until I arrive. No one else is to enter but myself, my sister or Stil."

The guard nodded and Belle headed to say goodnight to her friends.

"Do you want us to come with you?" asked Erik.

"No. You enjoy the party. We'll see you in the morning."

Erik and Flint hugged her and Chloe in turn. Snow did as well.

"Why don't I walk up with you?" asked Aurora.

Belle agreed and the group walked out of the ballroom and up toward the bedrooms.

"Did you have fun?" Aurora asked Chloe.

"I've never had so much food. And my feet hurt from walking and dancing."

Aurora laughed. "Wait until you have to do it in heeled shoes. That's even worse."

Chloe made a face.

They reached their bedroom and Belle opened the door. They walked inside and Aurora instructed the guard to wait by the door.

Belle undressed Chloe and got her into her sleeping gown.

Chloe climbed up into bed as Belle tried to reach the laces on her own dress and undo them.

"See," said Aurora. "That is why mine laces up in the front."

Belle chuckled. "There's nothing quite so humiliating as having to ask someone else to get you out of your own clothes."

Aurora walked over to her and undid the laces of Belle's dress. "True. Unless that person happens to be a man."

Belle looked over her shoulder and Aurora gave her a wicked grin that made her blush.

"And you would know this first hand?" Belle asked.

"No," said Aurora. "But I am hoping to remedy that soon."

Aurora gave the laces one last tug and the dress slid down Belle's shoulders. She caught it before it fell off.

"And do you have a specific man in mind?" asked Belle.

Aurora's expression saddened. "There was one. His name was Fader. He was a dragon rider. He disappeared when Dax did."

"Is he dead?"

She shook her head. "I do not know. But I intend on stopping Morgana and finding out for myself."

Belle's heart reached out to Aurora. But it explained her unnatural zeal to find Morgana and kill her. Belle headed for the bathing room where her dressing gown hung.

"Mama, I can't find my dragon," Chloe called.

Belle scanned the room but the stuffed animal was nowhere to be seen.

"Did you leave it in Dax's room?" Belle asked.

Chloe yawned. "Maybe."

"I'll go." Aurora headed for the door.

"Aurora?"

She stopped.

"Thank you," said Belle.

Aurora nodded. "It's what family is for."

"No. I mean it. Thank you... for everything. You've been very kind to us and to me especially."

Aurora's eyebrows knit together. "Is there any reason I shouldn't be?"

Belle smiled. "I suppose not."

Aurora gave another curt nod and walked out the door. Belle headed into the bathing room and felt around in the dark for her nightgown. She fumbled and then felt a piece of cloth and tugged on it. It didn't budge. She tugged on it again and suddenly Chloe cried out.

"Mama, run!"

Belle ran for the bedroom but then the grip of a cold, calloused hand grabbed her wrist. Belle jerked away as terror washed through her. She knew that hand.

Belle stumbled for the outer room, knocking into the tub and sending a shard of pain down her leg. She opened her mouth to scream when the same cold hand clamped around her mouth and dragged her back into the bathing room. Belle screamed and kicked but a second hand clamped over her nose, suffocating her.

"Chloe. I have to get Chloe. Chloe. I have to get Chloe. Chloe. I have to get Chloe." Klaus chanted, his voice flat and emotionless.

Belle gouged at his hands with her nails, but he squeezed her harder. She pulled at his arms and reached back for his face as her knees buckled and she fell to the floor.

"Chloe. I have to get Chloe."

She tried to plead with Klaus as tears dripped from her dimming eyes. She fought to keep at him, but her limbs grew too heavy and her head felt like it might explode from lack of air. Finally, her arms gave out and everything grew fuzzy.

She pulled on Klaus one last time, ripping a part of his sleeve away. The last thing she heard was, "Chloe. I have to get Chloe."

CHAPTER TWENTY THREE

Aurora searched her brother's room for the stuffed dragon. It had to be there somewhere. It wasn't like the thing was small. She looked under the bed and pulled back the covers and pillows. She huffed and glanced around the room. Her gaze lit on the bathing room and she walked to it, but couldn't see into the darkness. Going back to the front room she lit a candle in the roaring fire and then returned to the bathing room.

In the corner near the tub she spotted a dark fuzzy leg and headed for it. She reached down and pulled the stuffed dragon out. Aurora shook her head. Silly toy.

She brushed it off and walked out. Blowing out the candle, she set it on the mantle. She strode toward the door but paused, seeing the mess she'd left. The old Thad would have told her to leave it because the maids would clean it, but Dax... Dax was not Thad.

She set the dragon down and headed to the bed. The

least she could do was straighten the covers and pillows. Not that they would stay straightened for long. It was obvious to everyone now that Dax and Belle were not just spending *time* together. She'd spent the previous night in Belle's room with Chloe when Belle hadn't come back. Not that Aurora minded. Chloe was the sweetest child she'd ever met, even if she was a bit odd with some of the things she said.

Aurora finished straightening the bed, grabbed the dragon and strode out the door.

She closed Thad's bedroom door and walked toward Belle's room where the guards stood immovable. She stopped in front of them and they neither moved nor looked at her.

"What's wrong with you? Open the door."

They didn't move.

"Did you hear me? Open the door?"

Again no one moved.

A chill raced down Aurora's back. She poked one in the chest and he fell backward stiff as a board and knocked into the others. Like toy soldiers they fell to the ground in a heap.

Aurora dropped the dragon and jumped over the bodies, throwing the door open. She looked to the bed but Chloe wasn't there.

"Belle! Belle? Chloe!" She raced into the room. They were nowhere to be seen. She ran to the window and looked out but couldn't see anything. "Belle!"

Coughing sounded in the bathing room. Aurora ran to it and Belle stumbled out of the bathroom her dress hanging off her.

"Klaus! Klaus took Chloe!"

Aurora unhooked her skirt and flung it to the floor. She raced to the stairs and jumped to the lower landing. She pointed at a guard. "Secure the castle!"

She jumped the next railing and ran for the ballroom.

Dax shook hands with the advisor.

"I look forward to hearing more about what ideas you have for improving relations with the other kingdoms," the older man said.

"Seems he's done most of the heavy lifting already," said his father.

Dax gave a tight smile and nodded.

"My family looks forward to improved relations with the Draaklands as well," said Erik.

"Move. Move. Get out of the way!"

Dax turned to see Aurora pushing through the dancers on the floor. The half skirt gone, she was in just her bodice and pants. A wave of dread crashed over him as she advanced. The sounds of booted feet pulled his attention to the outer hall. Dax's bear whined.

He headed for Aurora, meeting her in the middle of the dance floor. He didn't stop as they headed toward the exit.

"Where's Belle?"

"She's upstairs in her room."

"What's going on?"

"Klaus. He attacked her and took Chloe."

Dax stopped and his bear roared to life. He looked at

Aurora and then bounded up the steps taking them four at a time. Belle rushed down in her regular clothes and boots. She bumped into him but didn't stop. She pushed past him and kept going.

"Belle, wait."

"He has my daughter."

Dax rushed to keep up with her as their friends joined them. "Belle!"

She stopped and looked at him.

"Is she wearing the necklace I gave her?"

"What?"

"Did she take it off before bed?"

Belle shook her head. "No."

Dax looked to Stil.

"I'm on it." Stil pulled a stone from his pocket the same color as the stone from Chloe's necklace. He said a few words over it and the stone glowed. He walked in a circle and then to the front stairs. "I got her."

"What is that?" asked Belle as they followed Stil down the stairs.

"I had Stil put a spell on Chloe's necklace and the one you wore. To track them in case something happened."

"I have the castle blocked off," said Aurora. "The guards are searching."

"He's gone already," said Stil. "The light is faint. They're most likely already out of the city."

"But we don't know which way he went," said Dax.

Belle burst from the front of the castle, pushing past guests and partygoers. She turned and looked up at the top of the castle. "Alabrax! Alabrax!"

Dax whistled and the dragon emerged from a tower and stretched. He looked at them and climbed down the castle, dropping to the ground.

Nobles screeched and ran, but Alabrax kept his gaze on Dax.

Belle stepped up to Alabrax and held out a piece of cloth. "He took Chloe. Find him."

Alabrax looked at the cloth and looked at Dax. Dax nodded and Alabrax sniffed it and hissed.

"Find him," said Dax.

"Tell him to carry me," said Belle.

"Belle, he's never had a rider before."

"Tell him!" she screamed.

Dax's bear paced. She wasn't a trained rider. And she and Alabrax hadn't had a lot of interaction. If Alabrax got upset, he could buck her off and kill her.

"I'll carry you," he said.

"Don't be silly."

Dax turned to Zelle. "Remove the binding."

Flint stepped forward. "We're at the end of the week. If you do that there's nothing to control your bear."

Dax continued to look at Zelle. "Do it."

"Dax, no," said Belle. "I won't let you sacrifice yourself for—"

"For our daughter? For the woman I love?"

Belle searched his face and then he turned to Zelle again. "Do it."

Zelle stepped forward. "If I do this, it's can't be redone."

"But what happens to his piece of soul?" asked Belle, putting her hand over her heart.

Zelle shook her head. "I don't know."

Everyone froze.

"The light is growing fainter. We have to move," said Stil.

Belle walked to him. "Dax."

He kissed her hard. "I love you Belle. No matter what happens, remember that. I love you and I love Chloe." Dax walked to Zelle, looked down at her and nodded.

"No. Wait—" Belle stepped to him but Zelle thrust her hand onto Dax's chest and the mist flowed around her.

"I release you," Zelle whispered.

Dax's bear roared and his bones began to break before he could even suck in a breath. Within an instant he was on all fours, his body growing and expanding. His clothes ripped and dropped to the ground in shreds.

He turned in a circle and his bear stood up on his back legs and bellowed for all to hear.

"Hurry," said Zelle. "I'll show you how."

Dax fought to explain to his bear. Belle pulled up on Dax's back and Zelle showed her were to hold on.

"Hold tight," said Zelle. "Move with his shoulders."

A wolf howled off to the left. "*I'm here for you*," said Adrian.

Dax nodded and Sage stepped up next to him. "Let's get moving."

Dax looked to Alabrax who took to the air and headed toward the castle gate.

"I'll get my horse," said Aurora.

"I'll need one too," said Stil.

"And us," said Erik and Flint. "As well as weapons."

"You don't think you're leaving us here, are you?" asked Snow, flanked by Cinder and Zelle.

Dax's bear stopped listening and bounded down the castle steps and out the gate. He looked to the sky and spotted Alabrax heading north. His bear wanted to go right and head for the woods. Dax wrestled for control of his body.

"*If we don't go with them, we die,*" said Dax to his bear. "*Chloe dies. Bell dies.*"

"*We need to move, Dax.*"

He looked at Adrian. "*I'm trying.*"

Adrian stood in front of Dax and leveled his gaze on him. "*Get control. Make him understand.*"

"*What do you think I'm trying to do?*"

"What are we waiting for?" screamed Belle.

Dax relaxed. "*All right,*" he said. "*You're in control. It's up to you. Just know what you are giving up if you don't listen to me. You are giving up the love of your life. Happiness. Peace. Family.*"

Dax stopped fighting and gave in to his bear. The animal shook his head and waited before bounding up the street.

BELLE CLUTCHED DAX'S SHOULDERS AND HUNG ON WITH HER feet. They rushed through the streets of Draakland to the northern wall. People rushed out of the way or peeked out their windows to see a woman riding a giant white bear, flanked by a large black wolf and a pale vampire. She could only imagine the tales that would be told about them.

Dax headed straight for the gate and the guards jumped out of the way as he bounded through it. In front of them loomed three large mountains. Alabrax flew straight for them.

They had to find Chloe, they just had to. Belle would die before she let Klaus or that bitch Morgana have her.

The sound of hoofbeats caught Belle's attention as they headed up a path to the mountains. She looked over her shoulder and spotted the Gwyns, Cinder, Aurora and Stil moving fast upon their steeds.

She looked forward again just as they hit the trees and Snow raced past them, joining Sage. The scent of the forest filled Belle's nostrils. She tried to keep her eyes on Alabrax as he flew low inside the canopy, but in the darkness she couldn't make out his form. She realized for the first time that she was completely helpless. She had to rely on Dax and Alabrax to get her where she needed to go. She only hoped they got her there in time.

CHAPTER TWENTY FOUR

Klaus blinked several times trying to clear his watery vision and follow the directions Morgana had given him as to where to meet her. He sucked in a ragged breath, causing his ribs to scream in pain. He wondered if he'd killed Belle back in the castle. Had they found her? Did they realize Chloe was gone yet? Part of him prayed that they had realized it and that they would already be on their way to stop him.

In the hour since he'd grabbed Chloe, he'd begun to regain a small amount of control of his thoughts, even though he had yet to gain full control of his mind or his body. It was like he was in a twilight state; neither fully awake nor completely asleep. He wanted to take control. Wanted to force himself to stop moving, but the magick running through him could not to be resisted.

"Stop," said Chloe, groggily. "Take me back."

Klaus blinked and continued up the mountain, trying to

get Morgana's command out of his head. He tried to close his swollen fingers around Chloe tighter, but the bones ground together at odd angles, shooting with pain.

"Chloe. I have to get Chloe," he said, his throat cracking from having said the words so many times.

"Don't take me to her."

Klaus wanted to stop himself. He'd told his feet to stop moving and his legs to stop walking over and over, but his body wouldn't obey. His body ached beyond exhaustion. The blisters he'd accumulated on his feet had long since rubbed raw. His arms burned and shook from carrying Chloe. And his legs wobbled as he continued moving forward. Even so, whatever the potion Morgana had forced down his throat wouldn't allow him to stop.

"She's going to kill you."

Klaus looked down at Chloe. He wanted to apologize. To tell her he loved her. To tell her he didn't want to be doing it. He didn't want to give her to Morgana. But all that came out of his mouth was, "Chloe. I have to get Chloe."

Klaus had lasted over twelve hours with Morgana taking him to the edge of death and then bringing him back. When the collar had failed to produce any effect, she'd broken every finger one by one. Then she'd taken to breaking his ribs. And after those too had failed, she'd given him the potion with the words. "Get Chloe."

He had no memory of getting up off the floor. No memory of getting to the castle. His first real memory was of standing in the dark bathing room and wondering what had happened. Then he'd heard Belle's voice along with another woman.

When Belle had entered the bathing room he'd attacked. Hands screaming out at him, ribs crackling and making it difficult to breath, he'd taken her to the ground with one thought; the only thought that Morgana would let him have.

"Chloe. I have to get Chloe."

After Belle had stopped struggling he'd gone into the bedroom where he'd found Chloe. He'd fought his body as he picked her up. Fought his body as he covered her mouth as she tried to scream. Fought his body as he wrapped her in a blanket and carried her to the bedroom door. Outside he'd pulled a pouch of dust from his pocket and had blown the dust at the guards as he recited the words Morgana had taught him. They'd petrified instantly. Then he'd walked down the hallway, out onto a balcony and jumped to the roof below.

And now, climbing the mountainside, he wanted nothing more than to take it all back. He wished he'd just let Chloe and Belle go. He wished he'd married Belle when he had the chance. He wished he'd been a better man.

Klaus slipped and hit the ground with a thud. He groaned and rolled on his side, cradling his ribs. His grip loosened on Chloe and she rolled out of the blanket and got to her feet.

Klaus fought to regain control of his body as it reached for her.

Chloe backed up several steps and Klaus struggled to get the words out of his mouth.

"Cccccccchloe. Rrrrrrrrrun!"

Chloe looked at him, turned and looked over her shoulder, and then back at Klaus again.

"Klaus..." Her voice sounded far too adult for her small frame. Tears dripped from her eyes.

Klaus's body began to get up, not of his accord. "Chloe. Run... Run... now!"

She looked at him for one second more and then turned and scampered down the way they'd come.

Klaus pulled himself to his feet and lumbered after her. "Chloe. I have to get Chloe."

CHAPTER TWENTY FIVE

D ax breathed deep. "*I smell her.*"

"*Me too*," said Adrian.

Belle hopped from his back and walked by his head. Behind them the horses came to a stop.

"It's getting steep for the horses, we should go on foot from here," said Erik.

Belle started up the hill. Dax wanted to slow her, but there was no slowing.

He walked with her as she climbed the steep terrain. The sound of something rushing down to meet them hit his ears and he stopped. Belle stopped as well and looked back.

"What is it?"

Sage listened and then started up the hill. "The footsteps are light and quick. I think it's Chloe."

"Chloe!" Belle called, rushing up the hill. "Chloe!"

"Mama!"

Dax growled and followed Belle up. Belle called for

Chloe again and Chloe's voice sounded closer.

Her small form rushed toward them, followed by a tall dark shadow. Belle and Dax hurried forward and Belle scooped Chloe up in her arms. Dax stepped in front of them waiting for the figure to emerge.

Klaus stumbled through the trees. He fell to the ground and rolled several feet before stopping by a tree and groaned. Dax sprinted to him and pushed him on his back with the swipe of his massive paw. He reared back up to pound Klaus into the dirt, but the look on Klaus's face had him halt mid-air.

Even his bear was disconcerted. Klaus's face was a mass of bruises. His eyes were completely bloodshot and pooled with black ooze. Deep black veins snaked from his eye sockets and slithered down his cheeks. His lips pulled back in a skeletal grin. His entire face looked more like a thing of nightmares rather than the man he'd seen several times before.

Klaus reached for Dax with twisted and mangled fingers. "Kkkkkill mmmmmeee," he hissed.

Dax backed up a step and his bear returned to all fours. Adrian and Sage met at Dax's shoulder, both of them staring down at Klaus.

Klaus coughed and grabbed his side as blood trickled out of the corner of his mouth. Suddenly Belle appeared around the tree and looked down at Klaus.

"Bbbbbelle..." He reached for her and Belle stepped forward. Dax's bear stepped in the way, but Belle put her hand on his shoulder and rounded him.

She walked to Klaus and knelt beside him. He grabbed

her hand and flinched.

"Look what you've done now," she whispered. "Why couldn't you just..." She shook her head.

"Chloe. I have to get Chloe."

"You'll never touch that child again," said Sage.

Klaus looked to Dax and his eyes went wide. "She's... cccccoming." As the words left his mouth the collar at his throat lit up. Klaus got to his feet and everyone backed up as his eyes went blank again. "Chloe. I have to get Chloe." He shook his head. "No!"

Klaus looked at Belle and a black tear oozed from his eye. "Tell... hhhher... I'm... sorry."

The collar went off again and Klaus' body jolted where he stood as if attached to a bolt of lightning. Blood spewed from his mouth as every inch of him writhed in agony.

"We have to do something," Belle cried.

Dax looked at Sage, unsure of what to do. Sage took a step forward as Klaus bent at the waist and vomited black ooze on the ground. Snot dripped from his nose and he got to his feet again shakily. He looked at Belle so pitifully even Dax felt sorry for him.

"She... will never lllllet me... stop ccccoming for Ccccc-chloe." He sucked in a deep breath one more time, and then without warning Klaus ran straight into a tree and bashed his head against it.

Belle screamed, and Dax's bear got between her and Klaus.

Klaus backed up, his head bleeding. "Ccchhhlllloe. I haaaave to get Ccccchloe." Again he ran at the tree.

"Klaus, stop!" Belle screamed. "Stop him!"

He backed up a third time, head gushing. "Cccchhhhhll-llllooooeeee—"

Before he could run at the tree again Sage grabbed the knife from his boot and rushed Klaus, slicing his throat. Belle let out a cry as Klaus gurgled and blood poured from his throat. He stared at Belle, his mouth opening and closing, and then fell to the ground in a heap.

Belle grabbed onto Dax's fur for support as they stood in stunned silence.

BELLE COULDN'T MAKE HER BODY MOVE. SHE HAD NO IDEA what to do. Klaus... wasn't Klaus. She didn't know who was in there or what had been done to him, but he was gone. She thought she'd feel relief, possibly happiness, at knowing he could never hurt them again, but a pang of sadness pierced her at his awful demise.

She looked over her shoulder to see Aurora holding Chloe's face away from the awful scene.

Belle stepped toward Klaus when an arc of red light shot through the trees and hit Dax in the shoulder. His bear roared and reared up on his hind legs as red light coursed down the side of his body.

Everyone gathered together in a huddle with Chloe in the center. Belle scanned the woods and her heart dropped. Dozens of males marched toward them, surrounding them, weapons at the ready, their collars glowing bright green.

"The dragon riders," breathed Aurora. She stepped away from Chloe. "Fader! Fader where are you?"

Morgana chuckled. "How sweet. The little princess wants to know if Fader is all right. Touching. But Fader, like all the others, is mine."

Alabrax swooped down to a branch just above the group's heads and shot a spray of blue lightning fire in an arc around them, splitting trees and setting branches alight, pinning the dragon riders on the outside of the circle and the rest of them on the inside.

Morgana took no notice as she marched closer, her long white hair cascading around her body like flames. She walked closer to Klaus and glanced down at him. "You know, when I began sleeping with Klaus two years ago I had no idea he'd be more than an infrequent bed fellow. If I could have imagined then that he would bring me both Prince Thaddeus as well as little Chloe, I would never have let him out of my sight."

Zelle stepped forward with Flint at her side, his hand on her shoulder. "You cannot have them, mother."

Morgana smiled. "Rapunzelle, you naïve child. Do you really think you have the magick enough to stop me?"

"Maybe not alone, but combined with the others I do."

Morgana clucked her tongue. "You've become weak here Rapunzelle. Like your brother and sisters. And for what? That impaired human?"

"Come over here witch and let me show you how impaired I am," Flint shot back.

Morgana chuckled. "Ooohhh I like his spirit. I bet he's a dragon in bed."

Cinder and Stil stepped up to Zelle's side.

"Why don't you crawl back to the cave you slithered out

of," said Stil.

She spoke in a low voice and fanned her hand out around her, dashing the blue flames.

"I'm not leaving until I get what I came for." Morgana pushed the stone on her ring. "Kill them all. Except the child and the bear."

Belle grabbed onto Chloe.

The dragon's collars lit up, but they didn't move. Morgana pushed the stone again and several of the men fell to their knees.

"Hunter, if you don't want the rest of your men to suffer the same fate as Malius, get them moving."

A tall man with shaggy blond hair stepped forward and stopped.

Morgana pushed the stone in her ring. "Kill them!" she demanded

"Enough." Cinder threw a bolt of light at Morgana. "Alabrax defend!"

Alabrax roared and spit lighting at Morgana as Zelle formed a bright ball of magick and thrust it toward Morgana. Several dragon guards raced forward as Stil drew a stone from his pocket and threw it in the air saying words Belle couldn't understand. An invisible shield covered Belle, Dax and Chloe. Morgana shot magick at Cinder, who whirled out of the way and shot back. Zelle hit a dragon rider in the chest as another ran at her. Flint shoved his red glasses in his pocket as Erik sped to his side. The brothers stood back to back, swords at the ready. Adrian, Sage and Snow fought as a group, slashing at the dragon riders as they attacked.

Morgana threw a bolt of magick at the shield surrounding Dax and Belle and it bounced off, making her scream in fury.

"Get the mage!" she yelled.

Belle stood helpless, wanting to aid those that fought to protect them but knowing she was useless without her blunderbuss. Two dragon riders ran at Stil. Belle yelled at him to look out but he didn't hear her. One of the riders knocked Stil to the ground from behind and raised his sword to strike as Adrian tackled him to the ground and ripped out his throat. Stil cast a spell and the other rider flew through the air and slammed into a tree twenty feet away, falling in a heap.

Dax lumbered from foot to foot and growled. Belle knew he wanted out. He pushed against the barrier Stil had made, but it held fast.

Zelle shot magick at Morgana and Morgana deflected it into the chest of a dragon rider who dropped to the ground. Flint and Erik fought like Belle had never seen before. Even with Flint's blindness, he fought like a sighted man.

"Stop," said Chloe. "Make her stop. She's killing them."

Belle picked Chloe up and pressed her face into her chest. "Don't look, baby."

"Make her stop! She's killing the dragons."

Belle wanted more than anything to make Morgana stop.

Aurora fought with two small curved blades. She twirled and slashed and took down men faster than Belle had ever seen.

Above them Alabrax circled, unsure of who to fight,

instead he shot blue fire at anyone who got within five feet of their shield.

Finally, Morgana focused on Stil's stone that hung in the air above the shield. She fired magick at it making the stone flicker. Belle clung to Chloe.

"Get ready," she said to Dax.

Belle's heart beat so fast she was afraid it might stop altogether. She poised, ready to run and hide as Cinder shot magick at Morgana, but Morgana took the hit undeterred. She shot her own magick again at the protective stone and this time, the stone flickered and dropped to the ground.

"The barrier's down!" Stil yelled.

Cinder and Zelle both volleyed magick at Morgana at the same time and Morgana caught it, pushing it back. Zelle and Cinder ducked just in time for the magick to fly straight at Belle and Chloe. Belle turned, shielding Chloe from the blast knowing she couldn't out run it. *Not my baby girl. Please not my baby girl.*

There was an ear-splitting roar and then everything went silent. Belle stood for a minute, eyes closed waiting for the pain, but it didn't come. A large thud sounded behind her and she turned to see Dax on the ground, an enormous black hole where his shoulder should have been.

Morgana screamed.

"Dax!" Belle set Chloe on her feet and they dropped to his side. "Dax! Oh my... Dax. No." She ripped at her shirt trying to fill the hole that spurted blood all over the ground. "Dax. You're going to be all right. You're going to be fine."

He looked at her with his wide hazel eyes. He was going to be fine. He had to be.

"Zelle! Stil!"

There was a rush of feet and Zelle dropped to the ground next to them along with Cinder.

"I can stop the bleeding," said Cinder. She thrust her hands onto Dax's wound and tendrils of magick flowed out of her fingertips, but the blood didn't slow.

"What's wrong?" Belle demanded.

"I... I..."

"Let me try." Zelle touched Dax's shoulder and her mist flowed toward the wound.

"You can't heal him," Morgana yelled. "None of you can. Mixing magicks created something no one can heal."

"No," said Belle. "I don't believe that. He has to be healed. Stil, do something."

Stil knelt beside her. "Morgana is right. This kind of magick from Cinder and Zelle..."

"So you're just going to let him die?" she screamed.

Everyone looked on as Dax's bear whimpered and his breathing became shallow.

"Please Dax. Please. You can't go. You can't leave me. I just got you. Please." She kissed his muzzle and pressed her forehead into his. "I need you, Dax. I need you... I love you."

Dax whimpered again and nudged her with his head.

"I love you," she whispered. "I love you."

He chuffed once more and then his body went limp.

Belle's body wracked with a sob but then filled with fiery rage. Her gaze went to Morgana.

"You did this." Belle got to her feet.

"Me? No. If you want the person responsible you need

look no further than your own bedroom mirror Belle. You did this. If you'd just let him come back to me, none of this would have happened. If you'd just given me the child—"

"*My* child. And I'd rather be dead then hand her to you. Even her own father killed himself to be rid of you and save her."

"Yes, well now it won't matter because with Dax, Klaus and you out of the way, the child is mine."

Morgana threw a bolt of bright red light at Belle. Everything slowed as the bolt arched toward her. A scream pierced the silence and everything came to a stop. The magick hung in the air like a hummingbird. Someone gasped and Belle turned to find Chloe standing behind her, hand outstretched, a silent scream on her lips. Her hair fanned out around her face like a giant mane and her eyes shown with a bright white light.

"Your magick is broken, unclean one," Chloe said in a voice too old and too deep for a child her age. The shot of red magick burst into a shower of sparks and disappeared. "Be gone."

Morgana took a step forward. "Don't toy with me, child."

"BE GONE!" Chloe thrust her hands wide and a huge sucking sound surrounded them. The air around them shimmered and then Chloe clapped her hands together. A giant a hole opened behind Morgana. The surface shimmered and swirled with light, sucking her backward. Morgana screeched and thrust her hands out in front of her right as she sucked backward into the portal. She said three short words that Belle couldn't hear over the sound of rushing wind, and then a beam of magick shot out of the portal headed straight for Chloe. At the last second Aurora stepped in front of Chloe, shielding her. The blast hit Aurora straight in the chest and then the entire area went black.

Belle rushed to Chloe. "Are you all right?"

Chloe looked at her with a gentle smile and then she looked to Dax. Stil rushed to Aurora's side.

"Where does it hurt?"

Aurora took a deep breath and straightened. "Uh... it doesn't."

Stil looked her over and felt her stomach. "Maybe you're in shock."

"No." Aurora touched her body and stretched her arms. "I'm not. I feel fine."

"Maybe whatever she was trying to do didn't work," said Cinder.

Stil continued to inspect Aurora, a concerned look on his face. "I'm pretty sure Morgana wouldn't waste her magick on something that wouldn't work."

Chloe dropped to the ground next to Dax, petting his fur and touching his chest.

"It is not your time, Prince Thaddeus of the Draaklands. You have work yet to do." Chloe pressed her hand to Dax's wound and white light ebbed from her palm into the wound, which sealed itself shut. Then Chloe pressed both hands into Dax's chest. The air around him shimmered and his entire body shook as it broke and twisted back into human form.

The light dimmed, and Chloe removed her hands. She

blinked several times and when Chloe looked at Belle again, her eyes were their normal bright blue.

"We fixed him, Mama." She smiled.

Belle moved to Dax and Chloe tentatively as everyone else backed away. Stil removed his robe and covered Dax with it and Belle knelt at his side, brushing his hair from his face. Minutes passed and finally Dax opened his eyes.

He blinked several times and then focused on her face. "So, you love me, huh?"

Belle let out a cry and kissed Dax. He fought to sit up and she helped him lean against the tree. "I do. I love you. And you can't ever scare me like that again."

"I promise to try not to take a kill shot again." Dax looked around as a myriad of footsteps came closer.

Belle looked around to find the dragon riders heading toward them. They all stood in a tense silence for a long time.

Finally, Dax said, "Thank you Hunter. If it hadn't been for you, we wouldn't be here."

The leader walked to Dax and dropped to his knee. "My Captain."

The other dragon riders followed suit. Bowing and pledging their allegiance to Dax.

"Can you ever forgive us," asked Hunter. "We were forced to do those things. We never—"

"Stop." Dax held up his hand. "I know more than anyone what magick can do to a person. We witnessed it with our own eyes just before you arrived. What happened to all of us was my fault. I'm the one who went searching for

Morgana. I was the one naïve enough to think we could take her down by ourselves. And we all paid the price."

"Now that her magick is broken is the best time to go after her," said Aurora. "Right now. Tonight."

"No," said Stil. "We've had enough bloodshed for one night. We need to get Dax home. And bury our fallen dragon riders."

Aurora clenched her jaw. "But if we let her go—"

"Aurora." A dark-haired dragon rider with crystal blue eyes stepped out of the darkness. Aurora looked at him and a smile played across her face.

"Fader." She ran to him and threw her arms around his neck. The man hugged her back, but his eyes stayed fixed on Hunter.

Everyone watched the scene for a moment as the two parted and began to speak.

Belle turned back to Dax. He breathed heavily and his face had grown beyond pale.

"We need to get you home," said Belle.

"And I should look over your wounds," said Cinder.

Dax sat for a moment gathering his thoughts. Then he looked up at Belle. "It's gone."

Her chest squeezed tight and she looked over at where his left arm should be. "It doesn't matter." Belle stroked his cheek. "You're here. An arm is a little thing to lose compared to your life. I can live with you having one arm. I couldn't live without you."

Dax looked at her and shook his head. "Not my arm. My bear. He's gone."

CHAPTER TWENTY SIX

The next week passed by agonizingly for Dax. The loss of his arm had been tough, but the loss of his constant companion of five years hit him harder than he thought possible. Though he was overjoyed that Belle and Chloe were both safe, it was weird having his mind and body back to himself. He no longer felt the presence that had driven him to eat, sleep, fight. No longer had to fight urges that threatened to consume him. No longer had to worry about anger or fear forcing him to shift. No longer had to fear shifting one too many times and not being able to come back to human form. All of the worries and stresses of his life for the past five years... were gone. But with them, so was the feeling of being completely connected to another being.

He lay in bed staring at the ceiling with his good arm around Belle, and Chloe snuggled in on the other side of her. Belle had refused to let anyone near Chloe since her episode in the woods. But Chloe wasn't far from anyone's thoughts. Dax and Stil had spoken at length about the little girl, and even Cinder and Zelle had talked to him about her, but Belle had refused to leave his room with her. He'd even had to have Cinder come up and create a door between Belle's room and his, connecting them because she refused to let the royal architect come near them to cut the door out.

But it had been a week and it was time. Dax's arm itched, and he reached to scratch it before realizing that the limb was no longer there. He touched the wound that had been covered in bandages, even though there was no need. The wound had been closed seamlessly. He looked over at the small sleeping form of Chloe and still couldn't believe what they said she'd done for him.

Belle rubbed his chest and looked up at him, her eyes still full of sleep.

"Did you rest at all?"

He nodded and kissed her head. "A bit."

She looked over her shoulder at Chloe, pulled the covers up around the little girl, and then snuggled next to Dax and kissed his chest. He pulled her in.

"Maybe Chloe and I should sleep in our room. You need sleep," she said.

"*This* is our room."

Belle looked up at him. "You know what I mean. Chloe's room."

"I want you right here with me."

Belle bit her lip. "Well... maybe tonight Chloe can sleep in her room, then."

Dax swallowed. He knew what Belle wasn't saying. And he wanted her too. To feel her body joined with his. To kiss her skin and make love to her but... He looked over at his missing arm and shoulder. He'd not let her see it or touch it. His father had taken to helping Dax dress in the mornings. As much as Dax thought the idea of his father helping him would bring him shame, but it had been a great comfort and had begun to help mend their relationship. His father had even stopped inviting Violet to the castle, and had been more accepting of Belle.

Though his relationship with his father grew stronger, his relationship with Belle remained tentative. He loved her. And she loved him. But when it came to making love to Belle... Dax had not been able to bring himself to allow her to see him like this. As if the scars on his back hadn't been bad enough, now he was missing an arm as well.

Belle pulled his mouth to hers and she kissed him. She tried to deepen their kiss, but he held back. Finally, she sighed and pressed her forehead to his.

"Why won't you let me in? You know I don't care about your arm."

"I know."

"Mama?"

Belle rolled over as Chloe awoke. "Morning sweetie."

Chloe yawned, and Belle kissed Chloe's hair and hugged her tight. Chloe reached across Belle and took Dax's hand. Their eyes connected and he got the overwhelming feeling of peace.

"Morning Dax," she said.

Dax kissed her hand. "Morning baby girl."

Chloe popped up and jumped from the bed. "Bathing room." She raced from the room as Belle laughed.

"So what are you going to do today?" he asked.

Belle shrugged. "Eat. Maybe read to Chloe a bit."

"Why don't we take her down to the library?"

Belle's brow creased. "I don't know."

"You can't stay locked up in here with her forever."

"I know that, I just... She's not ready."

"She's not ready, or you're not ready?" He didn't want to push her, but he could see the conflict in her eyes. "How about we have breakfast and then go down to the library. Just for an hour. She needs to get out of these rooms."

"Why? They are ten times as big as the cabin we lived in just a few months ago."

"I understand that, but it's not good for either of you. You need to see that you are safe here. No one is going to take her. No one is going to point or stare or say anything."

"Dax —"

"It's just down one flight of stairs, Belle."

"What's downstairs?" asked Chloe.

"The library." Dax turned as Chloe walked back in.

She jumped up and down and clapped her hands. "Please, Mama. Please can we go down and see the books?"

Belle looked between them and then nodded. "Just for an hour."

Chloe laughed and climbed up on the bed, hugging them both at the same time. "I love you."

Belle and Dax both hugged Chloe tight. "We love you too, baby girl." He kissed Chloe's hair and she looked over at him and smiled, her eyes glowing with white light.

. . .

Dax walked down the stairs with Belle and Chloe. Maids curtsied as they passed and Chloe hopped down the stairs holding her stuffed dragon.

"Can I see Alabrax today?"

"Not today," said Belle.

"Tomorrow?"

They walked to the doors of the library and Dax opened the door.

"We'll see," said Belle.

They walked inside and the smell of paper and ink hit Dax's nose.

Chloe spun in a circle wide-eyed. "Can I read all of them?"

"Maybe someday." Stil walked out from behind one of the stacks of books and smiled. "Hello Belle, Chloe."

Belle turned to Dax, an icy glare planted on her face. "Chloe come here."

Dax closed the door to the library and Belle grabbed Chloe's hand.

"Let us out," Belle demanded.

Dax saw the wrath written all over her face. "Just hear him out."

"You had no right to do this without my permission."

"Which is why I'm here." Erik appeared out of a different row. "I'm here to make sure you feel safe."

Dax knew Erik's words were meant to soothe and comfort Belle, but they still stung.

"Belle, I've respected your decision for a week. Stil

helped Cinder with the door between our rooms and he didn't come near you or Chloe. He's been here every day hoping to speak with you and I've not once pushed the issue. But it's enough now. You need to listen to him. He can help."

"Chloe doesn't need help."

"She does if you want her to survive," said Stil.

Belle whipped around. Stil set down the book he'd been reading and held up his hands.

"I'm not trying to alarm you or trick you, but Chloe does need help. You saw the kind of magick she possesses. If she doesn't learn to control it, it will consume her."

"And you know how to help her?" shot Belle.

Stil shook his head. "No. Honestly, we've not seen magick like this in a thousand years."

"We? So you told the other mages?"

"No. Cinder, Zelle and myself. All three of us have been working. Searching for answers, and we've all come to the same conclusion."

"And what is that?"

"That's she's a prophetess called an Oracle. Like the seers who spoke the original prophecies."

Belle scoffed. "That's not possible. She's just a little girl."

Stil looked at Dax and Dax laid his hand on Belle's shoulder.

"Why don't we go to the reading area and let Chloe pick out a book and we can talk a bit more."

He could see in her eyes that she wanted to protest, but also that her curiosity had been piqued. They walked in silence to the back of the library to the place where Dax and Belle had lain and napped when they first arrived. She set Chloe down and Chloe ran to the nearest bookshelf and began pulling the books off one by one and looking at them.

Erik, Stil, Dax and Belle sat a little ways off on the pillows.

"WHAT CAN YOU TELL US ABOUT YOUR PARENTS?" ASKED Stil.

Belle looked to Erik and then back at Stil. She bit the inside of her cheek. She'd never told anyone before. Not even Klaus.

"I... I don't know who they were," she said.

"But you lived with your father in Westfall," said Erik.

Belle shook her head. "That man wasn't my father. His wife had been a midwife. She helped my mother give birth to me and then she went to bathe me. When she returned, my parents were gone. So she took me home."

"I had no idea," said Erik.

"I never told anyone. Though he was kind enough to remind me every day that I wasn't his kid. He reminded me with his words. With his fists. With..." She stopped. After all the years of being away from him, she still couldn't say what he'd tried to do to her the night she'd fled from his house and straight to Klaus. She remembered the man showing up on Klaus's doorstep hours later, drunk and screaming for Belle to come back. Klaus had beaten him almost to death. She'd never seen him after that. Klaus had never asked her what happened. He'd never needed to.

"So it's possible you could come from magickal blood," said Stil.

"Well she's got a way with making things," said Dax. "I've never seen some of the stuff she makes before."

"It's not all that difficult," replied Belle. "Clockmakers make stuff all the time too."

"Not like yours, Belle," replied Erik.

Stil studied at her for a moment. "May I try something?"

Belle wasn't all that sure that she wanted Stil to try anything. But she couldn't deny the fact that his ideas were sparking questions within herself that she hadn't voiced in a long time.

She nodded.

Stil moved forward and pulled three vials from his pocket. He set them on the floor in front of Belle. "Can you tell me what each of these are? Or better yet, what they used to be?"

Belle looked at the vials and then picked up the first one filled with pure white dust. She held the vial in her hand and then took the lid off and tipped a little into her palm. She swirled it around and a picture formed in her mind.

"It was a phoenix feather." She looked to Stil. His face remained impassive.

She picked up the second vial with black dust and poured some into her hand. Again, a picture came to her mind. "Rock and ash from the Wastelands."

She picked up the third and repeated the process. A picture came into her mind but she wasn't sure if she was seeing it correctly.

"What do you see?" asked Stil.

She concentrated. "I... I'm not sure. It's a man, but... not a man. He has a tail like a fish."

"A nereids," said Stil. "An oceanic type of fae."

"So she was right?" asked Dax.

Stil nodded. "Yes. You have the gift, Belle. If we'd found you when you were young, you would have been brought to train in the towers immediately."

"I don't have any interest in becoming a mage."

Stil chuckled. "I understand. But this could explain where Chloe's powers come from, at least in a small part. I doubt the Oracle would have come by someone who had no magickal abilities at all."

"You keep saying that Chloe is an Oracle, but she isn't. She's just my little girl. She's Chloe."

"Yes," said Stil. "She is Chloe, but she also has the spirit of the ancient prophetesses inside her. She possesses the knowledge and magick of every prophetess who ever lived. Making her not just an Oracle, but the Oracle of our time."

"But why? Why now?"

"Probably because the prophesies have begun to be fulfilled. But the important part is that the kind of magick she possesses is volatile and dangerous, but also life changing. For all of Fairelle."

Belle went numb. She couldn't wrap her mind around the words. She'd seen what Chloe had done. Break the dragon collars and forcing Morgana to leave with two little words. It was beyond powerful.

Belle squeezed Dax's hand. "So what do we do? I won't let Chloe be taken away."

"No one wants to take her away," said Erik.

"Then what?"

"I want to work with her. And I want Cinder to work with her."

"Here, at the castle," said Dax.

Stil nodded. "Wherever you are comfortable."

"And you won't do anything that would hurt her," said Belle.

"Of course not. We aren't stupid, we saw what she did when she was upset the other night."

Everyone laughed, and Belle looked over at Chloe. She was so little to have something so powerful inside her.

Belle glanced up at Dax. She didn't want to make the decision alone.

"I trust Stil and Cinder with my life," he said. "They've each saved it more than once. I trust them with Chloe and you know I don't say that lightly."

She leaned into him and he gave her a one-armed hug. He'd been shying away from her due to the loss of his other arm, but she intended on showing him that his missing limb didn't matter one bit.

"Fine," she said. "I'll let you work with her. But either Dax or myself must be present at all times."

Everyone nodded.

Chloe skipped over and plopped into Dax's lap. "Read."

Dax smiled and kissed her head. "Of course, your highness."

Chloe looked up at him and her head cocked sideways. "Am I a princess now?"

"Absolutely," said Dax.

She pondered for a moment. "But I thought you had to marry Mama first."

Dax and Belle looked at each other. Dax opened his mouth and then closed it again.

"Maybe we should make sure that happens then." Erik walked to Chloe and held out his hand. "How about I read you a book and we let your mommy and Dax have a little time to themselves?"

Chloe nodded and hopped up, taking Erik's hand. "I hope I can sleep in my own bed again soon. They take up too much room."

Belle chuckled and looked at Dax. He watched Stil follow Erik and Chloe out of the area and then looked down at Belle.

"So," she said. "What do we do now?"

CHAPTER TWENTY SEVEN

Belle led Dax into his room. His stomach twisted knowing what she wanted. The problem was, he wasn't sure he could give it to her. She closed the door and locked it. He walked to the fireplace and stared into it. He wanted her. He wanted her more than he'd ever wanted a woman before, but...

"Dax."

He turned to find her already naked. Her dress on the floor, her chemise and pantaloons on top of it. His body heated at the sight of her naked. He took in every inch of her beautiful curviness and his body responded.

She walked to him and tugged at the hem of his shirt. She untucked it and ran her hands underneath, pushing her hands up his chest. When they reached his shoulders, Dax closed his eyes and fought the urge to back away from her.

"Dax, look at me."

He opened his eyes.

"Why are you ashamed?"

"I'm not ashamed," he said.

"Then what? Is it me? Do you not want me anymore?"

He slid his arm around her waist and pulled her body against his. "Never."

"Then what is it that is keeping you so far away?"

"I..." How did he explain when he didn't know himself. "I want to hold you. Touch you. Carry you. Caress you."

"Well, I'm right here." She moved his hand down to her rear.

He cupped her creamy flesh and his excitement spiked.

"One arm is plenty for what we want to do. Two is a luxury." She reached between his legs and stroked him, which made him grip her rear tighter. "See what I can do with just one hand?"

His arousal grew and he fought against the doubts in his head.

"And this." She moved her hand and pulled his lips to hers. "I can do this with just one hand."

His tongue dipped into her mouth.

"And this. I can do this with one hand." She reached for his breeches and untied them before dropping them to the floor.

"There are many things you can do with just one hand." She kissed him again. "And other things that require no hands at all."

Belle lifted his shirt off of him and then swirled her tongue around his left nipple. She kissed and licked her way down his torso to his hip. Kneeling before him, she took him in her mouth. Dax groaned and grasped the fireplace for support. Her tongue flicked delicately over his length and he fought to keep his wits about him as she enveloped him. Up and down she stroked him; kissing, licking, teasing him with her mouth. Pulling him closer and closer to the edge of release.

Dax grabbed her by the hair and pulled her to her feet. His lips attacked hers and he stumbled to the floor. It wasn't graceful and he hit his elbow on the stone beside the animal skin rug but Belle remained unharmed.

"Ouch."

She snickered. "Are you hurt?"

He smiled as she pulled his mouth to hers again. Wanting her. Needing to feel her.

He tried to figure out how to get inside her while propping himself up until she broke their kiss and pushed on his chest, rolling him onto his back. He bumped into the table and she grabbed the glass vase of flowers as it tipped sideways.

"We're going to get the hang of this, I promise," she said.

Leaning in, she kissed him again and then swirled her tongue down his throat to his collarbone. She licked over it and then kissed toward his shoulder. Dax stiffened as she kissed his skin over where his arm should be and then back across his chest. He fisted his hand in her hair and pulled her mouth to his as she slid down on him. His entire body shook with the need to hold back. Belle kissed him once more and then sat up.

"I'm in charge this time. We do this the way I want."

Belle rocked on Dax's hips, arching her back as he grabbed her breast. She squeezed her body tighter around his as she thrust down on him again. Every part of her sizzled with desire. Soon his hand dug into her hip and he pulled her down on him harder.

Belle gripped Dax's shoulders and allowed everything else to float away. Her body responded to his every touch as she spiraled closer to the edge.

"Dax," she whispered.

He pulled her hips to his. "Belle?"

"Dax. I love you." She looked at him again and then bent down and kissed him. Their tongues entwined as he pushed and pulled their bodies together. Their rhythm built until she cried out, and her body pulled tight around his.

"Dax. Dax. Dax," she panted his name as she climaxed and every nerve in her body flooded with pleasure.

"Belle," he roared her name as he came and then kissed her again.

Their breathing and heartbeats mimicked each other in speed as she fell atop him sated.

Dax rubbed her back and she peppered his chest with light kisses.

"Marry me, Belle."

She stopped kissing him.

"I know this isn't the life you expected. And I know I'm not—"

"Yes." She kissed him. "Yes. Yes. Yes."

A wide smile broke across his face and he kissed her again, and then rolled on top of her and kissed her until she couldn't breathe.

CHAPTER TWENTY EIGHT

ONE MONTH LATER

Belle stood in the back parlor and stared at herself in the mirror. Her heart beat like a stampede of horses as the queen fluffed her veil. Belle had told Dax she didn't want anything formal. Nothing fancy. Not too many people. But in the end, she found herself letting go of her frugal ways for the first time and allowing herself to say what she wanted.

So instead of a plain cream dress with no adornment, she wore a beautiful beaded and lace dress with a train long enough for four people to help carry. The veil trailed down to her feet and underneath it she wore the necklace and earrings Dax had given her the night of his homecoming ball.

"Mama, you look like a princess," said Chloe.

Belle smiled down at Chloe dressed in a beautiful pink dress adorned with flowers.

A knock sounded on the door and the queen turned Belle to face her. "You look beautiful, my dear."

"Thank you."

"I know this is early and I know we have many, many years ahead of us to get to know each other, but I would love it if you would call me mother. In the months that you and Chloe have been here I have come to love you both so much."

Tears welled in Belle's eyes. "Thank you... mother."

The queen hugged her tight and Belle fought to keep from ruining her face.

"Can I call you Mimi?" asked Chloe. "I read in a book where a girl called her grandma Mimi."

The queen knelt to Chloe and hugged her. "I would love for you to call me Mimi."

Chloe beamed. "I'm gonna call PawPaw, PawPaw."

Belle laughed and wiped her eyes.

"Are you ready?" the queen asked.

Chloe nodded and took her hand. The queen opened the door and Jamen stepped in.

"We'll see you out there." She left the two alone.

Jamen hugged her.

"Thank you for coming," she whispered.

"Thank you for asking."

They looked at each other, and for several minutes, shared a silence for all they'd been through. The years together as friends. And for the loss that they also shared at Klaus's demise. Though Belle felt no love for Klaus, and hadn't for a long time she realized, she still hadn't wished that kind of horrible death on him. No matter what he had done.

Jamen offered his arm and Belle linked her arm in his. "I couldn't imagine Dax marrying a more wonderful woman."

Belle blushed and wasn't sure how to respond. The outpouring of love and support by his family and all of their friends had been more than she had ever hoped for.

"I couldn't imagine a better man to be marrying," she replied.

She blew out a breath and Jamen led her out to the small corridor behind the great hall. "You know there was a time I was sure one of my brothers would step up and give Klaus a run for his money, but things happened and then..."

"I love you all dearly. You've been more of a family to me than anyone else in my life. I can never repay you for all you've done."

Jamen looked at her seriously for a moment. "Just love him. And let him love you in return. Be happy. That's how you repay us."

Belle nodded. "I can do that."

Jamen bent her head down and kissed it. Flutes began to play and they stepped up to the door leading to the great hall.

"Do I go now?" asked Chloe.

Belle smiled and nodded, and Chloe stepped through the door with her tiny basket of flowers.

Belle blew out a long slow breath, she could do this.

Dax tugged at his collar and fidgeted with his tunic.

"Stop," said Flint. "You look like you're going to run for the hills."

Sage snorted. "Don't worry. He's not fast enough anymore."

"I could magick his feet to the floor," whispered Stil.

Adrian laughed and then coughed.

"You lot are hysterical," said Dax.

He looked out at the great hall. More than five hundred people packed into the area so tight that he thought some might be sitting on each other's laps. All around, beautiful white and pink flowers adorned the hall. Down the center lay a long golden carpet.

In the front row, Redlynn and her and Adrian's five children sat with Angus. A little red headed girl sat on his lap, tugging on Angus's beard. Snow held Jamen's oldest son and Scarlet held their youngest. Zelle sat with the twins and Cinder sat next to Rome. Gerall, Hass, Ian and Erik sat proudly next to their family and friends. Aurora sat with their mother in a surprising pale pink dress on the opposite side of the hall. The dragon riders took up the front two rows next to them, back in their official uniforms.

It'd been a tense reintroduction to city life for them, and not everyone was ready to forgive and forget, but Dax knew that with time everyone would come to heal from what had been done to them.

The flutes began to play, and Flint squeezed Dax's shoulder.

"Straighten up, your wife is about to walk down the aisle and see you."

Dax couldn't help but grin at the thought.

Out of the back Chloe appeared in a pretty little dress with a basket of rose petals. She dropped them along the way as she walked toward him. All around, people sighed and smiled at Chloe as she passed. She headed right for Dax and stopped in front of Flint. She tugged on his tunic and Flint looked down at her.

"You have the rings, right?" she whispered loud enough for others to hear.

The audience chuckled and Flint pushed his red glasses up his nose and patted his pocket.

Chloe nodded her approval and headed back to sit with Dax's mother and Aurora.

The trumpets sounded and Dax straightened himself as butterflies settled in his stomach.

Jamen rounded the doorway and then Belle appeared. Dax's heart almost stopped at the sight of her. Though he couldn't see her face, he knew every line of her body. She stepped forward on Jamen's arm and he could feel her gaze upon him. He fought the urge to straighten his tunic again. He wanted nothing more than to look presentable for her.

Over the last month as they'd prepared for the wedding, he'd tried to show her he was still a man and worthy of her, but what he'd found is that *she'd* shown *him* that instead.

She walked down the aisle and as she approached, Dax reached out and took her hand from Jamen. Jamen held onto her for a moment and leaned in to Dax.

"Make her happy, brother."

Dax nodded. That was his plan.

Belle took his hand and stepped up next to him.

Dax's fingers shook as he tried to lift her veil. It didn't work so well with only one hand and she had to help him. He fought his embarrassment as he looked out at the huge gathered group of onlookers. She took his hand again and squeezed it.

"Hey, handsome."

Dax stared into Belle's large, beautiful blue eyes. "You look amazing." He wanted to kiss her right then, but refrained.

"Are we ready?" asked the king.

Belle and Dax nodded and turned to him.

DAX TRIED TO CONCENTRATE ON THE WORDS HIS FATHER spoke, but all he heard was the blood pounding in his ears. He wondered what his bear would have thought of the whole affair. If he would have been contented or if he would have paced and wanted to run away. The fact that he didn't have the answer saddened him.

"Thaddeus Mitchum Kensington the Third, do you take Isabelle Chloe Morgan to be your wife. For now and forever. To love and to cherish until you both die and return to the ground from whence you came?"

A grin spread across his face. "I do."

His father smiled and turned to Belle.

"And do you, Isabelle Chloe Morgan take Thaddeus Mitchum Kensington the Third to be your husband. For now and forever. To love and to cherish until you both die and return to the ground from whence you came?"

Belle gazed at Dax. "I do."

"Do you have the rings?"

Dax turned to Flint, who pulled two rings from his pocket. He handed them to Dax who handed one to Belle.

"Belle. With this ring I promise for now and until my dying breath to love you, honor you and cherish you."

He shook as he slid the large ruby ring onto Belle's hand.

Belle lifted his right hand in hers. "Dax. With this ring I promise to give you all that I am. My heart, my body and my soul. From now until my dying breath."

"Then, as King of the Draaklands, and happy father of the groom, I now pronounce you husband and wife. To be written in the books of our fathers and recorded for all time," the king concluded. "You may kiss your bride."

Dax hesitated but Belle pulled him to her and kissed him. The crowd erupted into cheers. Dax wrapped Belle in his arm and dipped her as he kissed her. She was his. His bride. His wife. His everything.

A small set of arms wrapped around his legs and Dax laughed. He and Belle looked down to Chloe hugging them both. Belle picked her up and hugged her tight. Dax kissed Chloe's head and Chloe touched his face.

"I'm glad you guys got married before my brother came," said Chloe.

Dax looked to Belle whose eyes widened and she opened her mouth, but then closed it, and then opened it again.

Before she could speak, Flint clapped Dax on the shoulder and then hugged him. Their friends crowded around for hugs and kisses all around, and no time for Dax and Belle to speak about what Chloe had just said. Their daughter had yet to be wrong about something, which meant one thing was for sure. Belle was going to have a baby.

BELLE CLOSED THE DOOR TO CHLOE'S ROOM AND WALKED TO the bed where Dax waited for her. She hopped up onto the bed and he stroked her leg.

"Hello, Princess Belle."

She smiled. "Hello Prince Thaddeus."

Dax chuckled. "That sounds really strange."

"What? Me calling you Thaddeus?"

"Yes."

"The name suits you, but I still prefer Dax."

"Me too."

A thread of nervousness trickled through her. "I, uh... wanted to give you your wedding present."

Dax raised an eyebrow. "You mean more than a son?"

Belle laughed and pushed her hair behind her ear. "Yeah, about that..."

"Is it true? Are you having a baby?"

"Until she said something, I hadn't thought about it. But I did my calculations and my woman's time is over a month late."

He smiled but his eyes held conflict. "And you're sure it's..."

"I told you Klaus and I hadn't had sex in a long time before I left."

He squeezed her calf. "I wouldn't care. You know I

wouldn't. If the baby wasn't mine, I would still love him the way I love Chloe."

"Well, you don't have to worry about that because it can only be yours."

Dax grinned. "A son. I'm going to have a son."

"We're going to have a son."

"Are you ready for that?"

"With you, I'm ready for anything," Belle assured him.

His hand skimmed up her calf to her thigh as he climbed on top of her and kissed her. "I love you Belle. I love you and I will love our daughter and our son and any other children you give us."

She loved the feel of his body on hers. The touch of his hands on her body. The taste of his mouth.

He kissed down her chest to her stomach and laid his head on it as if trying to hear something.

"Dax, it's too soon to hear anything." She ran her fingers through his hair. "I want to give you your gift."

"You are gift enough."

"And yet, I have a gift for you nonetheless." She slid out from underneath him and off the bed. She pulled a large wooden box out from under the bed and took a deep breath as she set it on the bed next to him.

"That is quite the box," he said.

Belle climbed back on the bed next to him. "Open it. I made it. With some help from Stil and Cinder."

His brows furrowed. "You needed magick to make something for me?"

She shrugged and bit the inside of her lip, hoping he would like it.

Dax opened the lid. She watched his face as he stared at his gift for a long time.

"You don't like it? It's too soon. I'm sorry. I should have—"

"Will you help me put it on?" he asked.

Belled smiled and nodded. She reached into the box and pulled out the mechanical arm she had made him. Fashioned from brass, copper and silver, she'd designed and then made every inch of the arm. From the joints to the veins to the pistons. She took the shoulder piece and pulled it next to him as Dax stripped off his tunic. She lifted the arm and pulled back the switch, pressing it into his socket and then pushing the switch again to engaging the clamps that dug into his skin.

She adjusted the straps on it and checked to make sure the clamps held fast to his skin. "Does that hurt?"

"No."

She fiddled with it. "It's not pinching you anywhere?"

"Nope."

"If the straps start to chafe, you need to let me know." She sat back and chewed her lip, waiting for him to say somcthing.

"What do I do?" he whispered.

"Well, if what we did worked right, then all you should have to do is think what you want the arm to do, and it will do it."

Dax looked at her and then looked at his new arm. He sat staring at it for a long minute, but it didn't move.

"Hey." Belle linked her fingers with his new, cooler metal

ones and squeezed his hand. "It's all right if you don't like it."

He stared at their joined fingers and then a slight smile broke over his face. "I... I can feel your hand in mine."

She nodded. "That's the magick."

He traced his new metal hand up her arm and over her shoulder. Then he ran it over her chest and he squeezed her breast.

"I can feel you," he whispered. "Every beautiful inch of you."

"That's the idea."

Dax pulled her into his arms and crushed her body against his as he kissed her. "Well," he said. "I have another idea."

Dax kissed down her throat to her stomach. Lifting her nightdress, he kissed down her thighs making her tangle her fingers in his hair.

She grabbed the sheets as Dax's mouth planted deep against her core. She arched her back and looked up at the canopy of his bed.

"I love you Prince Thaddeus," she moaned.

"And I you, Princess Isabelle."

EPILOGUE

Morgana spit black blood onto the floor and clutched her stomach. She dropped to her knees knocking over several bottles on her table and sending them crashing to the floor.

Rasmuss rushed to her side and sat her up.

"Where were you?" she croaked, ripping her arm from his grasp. "I needed you and you did nothing."

"I couldn't show myself, you know that. I would have been recognized."

"So instead you let me be beaten by a child. A child!"

"An Oracle. The Oracle of our time mother. How was I to compete with that?"

Morgana sucked in a ragged breath, anger and fear coursed through her. She'd never actually feared before. As she'd watched prophecy after prophecy be fulfilled she'd never feared. Never wavered from her task. But now the game had changed. Chloe's magick was something not to be ignored. More than that, the fact that she hadn't felt it or recognized it meant her powers were waining more than she could possibly have imagined.

She'd thrown her last bit of magick at Chloe in an effort to bind the child to her, but it hadn't worked. Thaddeus's insipid younger sister had stepped in the way. The one who'd asked for Fader. *Her* Fader.

Rasmuss helped Morgana to her feet and then ushered her to her bed.

"You need rest."

"I need my magick back."

"Yes..." Rasmuss mused.

Morgana turned her gaze upon him, gripping his arm with her talons. "You know a way?"

His face scrunched up deep in thought. "There's... a possibility."

"Tell me." Morgana sat on the bed and laid back on the velvet pillows.

Rasmuss covered her with a silk shawl and poured her a glass of mead. "Sabine's daughter... Olivia."

Morgana sipped the mead. "The daemon fae girl."

"Her magick is untapped as far as I know. If we could find her, it's possible that her magick could be syphoned enough to bring you back to your full strength."

Morgana grabbed his hand. "Find her."

Rasmuss nodded. "It may take some time. She disappeared almost a year ago."

"Then you must hurry. Every day my arms grow heavier and my legs barely hold me up."

Rasmuss headed for the door, took his cloak from the

hook and wrapped it around his shoulders. "You'd have to drain her completely. Everything she has."

Morgana nodded. "Whatever it takes. Find the girl. Bring her to me. We've come too far to be stopped now."

Rasmuss strode back to her and knelt at her side. "I will, Mother."

Morgana squeezed his hand, allowing her talons to dig into his skin. "Do not betray me again."

Rasmuss gave her a solemn smile. "Never."

Rasmuss rose and walked back to the door. He opened it and pulled a girl inside the room. Her vacant eyes stared blankly at the far wall.

"Come here," Morgana commanded.

The girl walked to Morgana's side and sat next to her. Morgana stroked the girl's cheek.

"So pretty this one is. So young. Are you sure she has enough power?"

"She should last you until I am able to return with another. I pick only the best."

Morgana stared at the girl's passive face as she pulled the girl toward her. "I hope you are right," she said.

She leaned in close and pressed her mouth to the girl's. She breathed in and the girl choked and gasped. The girl's life force whooshed into Morgana's body making her tingle like fireflies danced under her skin.

More. She needed more.

THE END

GERALL'S FESTIVUS BRIDE

FAIRELLE BOOK SEVEN

By Rebekah R. Ganiere

CHAPTER ONE

Gerall smiled and ran his blade through the vampire's neck. Its eyes widened before he turned to ash. Breathing a contented sigh, Gerall coughed. *Damn.* It had been so long since he'd fought vampires that he'd forgotten to take a step back, so as not to get corpse dust in his mouth. The taste of charred wood coated his tongue, sucking all moisture from it. He tried to spit, but couldn't produce any saliva.

"Is that all of them?" Jamen called, crunching through the thick leaves toward them.

"I think so," replied Erik.

Gerall glanced around, and even in the dark, he could make out the bright yellow, orange, and burgundy leaves on the autumn trees. He wiped his mouth on the back of his sleeve and shook ash from his unruly hair. It had been almost a year since he and his brothers had gone out on the hunt, and if truth be told, he missed it.

Ever since Sage and Snow had taken over ruling Tanah Darah, there'd been little for the brothers to do. While going out and hunting vampires had once been a nightly ritual for them, they now did little more than engage in occasional sport with the dissenters.

The tracking late at night, racing on his steed while the world slept, being with his brothers. Forgetting their fractured family. It soothed his lonely heart.

He didn't miss the broken fingers or the gashes that needed stitches, having to replace his glasses every month, or living a double life. He missed the camaraderie of his brothers. He missed being together. He missed... His family.

Though life and happiness finally filled the house again, Snow had been gone for well over a year, and no one could replace her. Jamen's and Flint's marriages and babies they produced blessed all of them, but things were not the same without Snow and Kellan. Even Dax, Belle, and little Chloe's absences left a hole.

"I do not understand why they bother trying to come down here and hunt. They know we'll come after them." Jamen mounted his horse.

"Guess it's in their nature. To hunt for food as opposed to have it sitting willingly at the table waiting to be eaten." Gerall took off his glasses and wiped them on his tunic.

"Did you see the girl?" Erik sheathed his sword and grabbed the reins of his horse.

"No," replied Jamen. "If she was among them, she fled."

"She wasn't." Gerall wiped his blade on his pants. "There were only five."

Erik shook his head. "Damn. All right. Let's head back to the manor house. I'll clean up and go to Tanah Darah to inform Snow."

"That vampire girl has been gone for long enough—"

"She's most likely dead." Hass and Ian strode to their horses and hopped into the saddle.

"I promised Snow and Sage I would locate the girl. I, at least, need to find out what happened to her." A hard edge crept into Erik's voice.

"What does one girl matter?" asked Jamen.

Erik's expression darkened. "I made a vow."

"And what about your vow as Lord?" asked Jamen. "Tomorrow is Westfall day. The first day in the week-long Autumn Festivus. You need to meet with the magistrate. With enemies all around meaning to undermine our position, we need to be present more than ever."

"I'll go." Gerall slid his sword into its holster. "I need to go into town anyway to pick up a few things. Jamen, Scarlet, Flint, Zelle, and the children can accompany me. It would be good for Westfall to see how our family has grown. Let them know that we aren't going anywhere."

"What?" said Ian.

"We're not invited?" asked Hass.

Erik nodded. "Gerall's right. He can go in my place, and the rest of you can enjoy Festivus. I'll head back out to find the girl and will return within the week."

Jamen shook his head. "You and your damned honor."

"I call the bath when we get back," said Hass.

"Not if I get there first," replied Ian.

The two kicked their steeds and sped off.

Gerall smiled to himself. He missed this.

The group piled through the solar door to the manor house and the smell of beef stew and warm rolls struck Gerall. He gave thanks for Zelle and Scarlet and the way they cared for all of them, though they didn't have to.

"How did it go?" Flint entered the solar, carrying his daughter Lucia. Without his glasses on, his sight was all but nonexistent. But over the passing months, Gerall had seen Flint become more and more comfortable without it. Flint knew every inch of the manor house and rarely bumped into anything anymore. Especially with Loca always hovering around or perched on his shoulder.

Gerall's gut clenched, and he studied Flint's face, but there appeared to be no resentment at Erik telling him to stay home instead of joining them on the hunt.

"We got rid of them," said Jamen.

"Did you find that girl?"

"No," replied Erik. "I need to see Snow and find out what we do next."

Flint nodded. "Before you do, there's someone you need to see."

The brothers looked at each other.

"He's waiting in the dining hall."

They walked with Flint through the front hallway.

Erik pushed open the door and Gerall's brow furrowed.

"King Adrian." Jamen advanced and offered Adrian his hand.

The wolves never left Wolvenglen to go anywhere but

Volkzene. For Adrian to visit, meant the news couldn't be good.

"Is something wrong?" asked Erik.

Adrian stood, towering over all of them except Flint. "One of my wolves went missing. We are still looking for him"

"Missing?" asked Gerall.

"His name is Fendrick. He went out with his children to play in the woods, and the children came back, but he did not."

"Is it possible he ran off?" asked Flint.

"No. Fendrick isn't like my other wolves. He's... unstable. His only pleasure is being with his wife and children. He would never leave them."

"I remember him," said Jamen. "Hanna's husband. Tall, thin man. Eyes like a cornered rabbit."

"Yes. And if you remember, I couldn't send Hanna with you to help Scarlet's aunt because of his instability. He would never leave of his own accord. And especially never leave his young. It's not possible."

"What can we do?" asked Erik.

"I tracked his scent to the edge of Westfall, but then I lost it."

"He came here?" asked Flint.

"Not of his own accord." Adrian ran his hands through his hair. "I don't want to cause any problems, but I would like your permission to search Westfall. Not intrusively, just look about the town and see if I can pick up a scent."

"Of course," said Erik. "Anything you need."

"Would it be all right if I spent the night with you?"

"Our home is your home," said Jamen.

Adrian nodded. "I thank you."

"Why don't we get you something to eat? Tomorrow is Westfall Day, and there is going to be a festival. All of the town folk will be out. It will help you blend in better."

Adrian nodded. "Again. I thank you."

"I'll be heading to Tanah Darah within the hour," said Erik. "I'll let Sage and Snow know of the missing wolf in case they've seen or heard anything."

"Come on." Jamen clapped Adrian on the back. "Let's get you fed and find you a bed."

Adrian strode out with Jamen.

"First a vampire missing, now a werewolf," said Erik.

"Whatever is going on, it can't be good," replied Flint.

"It's got to be connected to the murder of the doctor and his wife and Scarlet's aunt. And the conspiracy against us being the ruling family of Westfall," said Gerall.

"Sir Malcolm and his sons aren't back, are they?" asked Flint.

Gerall shook his head. "No. Someone would have notified us if they'd returned. And Jamen would have mentioned it."

"Let's not jump to conclusions quite yet," said Erik. "I'll go to Snow's. You lot go with Adrian to town tomorrow. Feel things out. See what you hear. Hass and Ian can even ride by Malcolm's to make sure he, Edward and Lyden haven't returned. But if this is connected to the death of the doctor, and Scarlet's aunt, it can't be good for any of us."

"Agreed," said Flint.

Erik gave Gerall a tight smile and then headed out of

the dining hall. A flutter of anxiety lodged in Gerall's gut. What would someone want with a vampire girl and an unstable werewolf? Hell, why did someone want to hurt his family?

"There will be blood," said Flint, breaking the silence. "I can guarantee you that."

"Let's hope not," replied Hass.

"Because there's a good chance if that's true, it's going to be innocent blood," finished Ian.

To read more go to your nearest retailer!

Dear Reader,

Thank you for taking the time to read *Belle and the Beast*. This book has been a long time coming. I thank you all for waiting so patiently for it. It had a lot of unexpected twists and turns, even for me, but I am really happy with how it turned out for Belle and Dax.

If you enjoyed the book, please take a moment to leave a review on your favorite retailer. Your reviews make all the difference to an author and the success of books.

If you'd like, email me and let me know what you liked about the book or who your favorite character is. I love hearing from readers. It makes writing so much more fun when I hear from my readers.

VampWereZombie@Gmail.com

To find out more about me and my Upcoming Releases, Join my Street Team for Swag and Freebies.

I also love connecting with readers! Stalk me everywhere! I look forward to hearing from you!

Rebekah R. Ganiere - BOOKS WITH A BITE

Award Winning–*USA Today* Bestselling Author

Rebekah R. Ganiere

Fairelle Series

Red the Were Hunter - Book One

Yanti's Choice - Fairelle Short Story

Snow the Vampire Slayer - Book Two

Jamen's Yuletide Bride - Book Three

Zelle and the Tower - Book Four

Cinder the Fae - Book Five

Belle and the Beast - Book Six

Gerall's Festivus Bride - Book Seven

Jak the Giant Healer - Book Eight

Wolf River

PROMISED at the Moon

CURSED by the Moon

RECLAIMED from the Moon

TAMED under the Moon

UNLEASHED with the Moon

FATED despite the Moon

NEWSLETTER

To claim your Two **FREE** Books and find out more about
Rebekah R. Ganiere and her other Upcoming Releases
You can Go Here:
www.RebekahGaniere.com/Newsletter